Shadow's Oath

The Sojourner Saga

By
Moira Katson

Acknowledgments

Shadow's Oath would not have been possible without the encouragement of a great many people. I would like to thank the readers who asked for another story in the Light & Shadow universe—your love of Catwin and Miriel inspired this return to Heddred and Priteni! A special thank you to Christine, Courtney, Holly, Jamie, Jillian, Matt, Monta, Sam, and Shari, my wonderful beta readers, and to my husband, Bryce, who has very patiently listened to me ramble on about plot points and characters. Thank you also to my parents, who gave me a childhood filled with stories and travel, and who have encouraged me every step of the way in my writing. Last but certainly not least, a big thank you to my readers!

-M

Chapter 1

They did not bargain on me, the armies of the Cornovii. Nor did they bargain on the changeable whims of fate and the old, dark magics of Priteni, where mists may sweep across the land and leave the world utterly changed in their wake, and a traveler might stumble into the ebb and flow of time and never emerge. No, the Cornovii did not know what it was they did when they rode on Dun Druim—and their first mistake was not knowing about me.

It was winter when they came, sweeping out of the west with the thunder of hooves on frozen earth, and I was the one who saw them first and rode to warn the court at. Had I stayed in the halls that day, had I failed to climb Cathair Reul so that I might see for leagues....

But it is no use thinking on chance. Miriel would call it fate, later, and I would bite my tongue in public but call it luck in private, for I have never liked to be thought of as a tool of fate, which Temar liked to say blows mortals where it will, whatever our preferences in the matter. Countless lives are measured quietly, around the seasons and the crops, around wars that change the world and bury thousands, forgotten. In another life, I might have been one of them. I was born to the Winter Castle, in the furthest reaches of Heddred, to live and die in the snows of the mountains or by the pikes of the Ismiri. It was prophecy and chance that led me away, to play my part in stopping the ambitions of others.

When the storm of war and rebellion was over, fate led me here, and left me on the shores of Priteni, a land known in Heddred as the Shifting Isles and thought to be no more than legend. And while it is a land of earth and stone like any other, a land where people fight and love and scheme as anywhere else, it is also a land where they still speak of old magics, where they claim that the veil between worlds is thin, and the very fabric of reality is interwoven with myth. A land of mists and shadows, where it is easy to remember those who walked here before me: Temar, the man I loved; and the Duke, the man I hated above all.

It is a land of deep memory, and in memory, it calls on old wounds and old scores. It was not difficult for me, treading the hills and watching the clouds, to think that this was a land with blood-soaked earth. Quick to love and quick to battle, are the tribes of Priteni, not changeable as are the great noble houses of Heddred, but loyal to memory. Every tribe had stood side by side with every other to face down invaders, and turned on each other as well when another claim of loyalty emerged. Back and further back, so intertwined that the battles never stopped.

From such old scores did this war begin, for when I say that the armies came in winter, well—the war had started long ago, and only now come to open battle. Moving armies in winter is no easy task. Much better when the ground is softer, the food ripe on the vine. Still, for men who live in cold huts, who know their enemies will be feasting in their halls, a march in winter is not such a bad strategy.

They just did not bargain on me.

In any case, it was not so great a chance that I saw them. I rode out often in those days, for the winters of Priteni are not as harsh as in the land of my birth, where breath turns to ice in the air and to be stranded is to die. Winter in Priteni was a time of singing and dancing and good-natured bickering in the close, smoky halls, and I often slipped away before dawn to be alone in clean air and silence, even if I paid the price in frozen ears and fingers.

Being alone suited me that winter, for it is a lonely business, learning to live again. Especially so when you have never learned to live once—only watched others make the decisions that will shape lives, and made your peace with it, or not. Even in defiance, Miriel and I were only ever choosing between sides of a line that had been drawn long ago. Even when we rebelled, it was against the roll of the die. And when we left, taking a path few others would think to choose, it was the only path open to us.

Two years since we had arrived as guests of dubious good honor. There was no doubt that we had freed Priteni of its

—

greatest enemy—but it was indisputable, as well, that we were outsiders, members of the Duke's family, and with no trade to support ourselves. Miriel could entertain endlessly with songs and dancing, and converse on any topic from poetry to economics, but I was little more than a foot soldier, a relic of a time when she had needed a bodyguard. I had no purpose any longer, and it disquieted me to be purposeless within the clamor of the halls.

Cathair Reul, the highest peak for miles around, lay an hour's leisurely ride from Dun Druim. It had taken the better part of the morning for me to make my way to the top, for I took a harder path up the rock faces and through the trees. My fingers were stiff with cold and somewhat the worse for wear after the rock and ice of the hillside, but I was still flushed and pleased with myself when I reached the summit.

I was humming a tune Miriel and I had learned, one of the great epics and much-repeated in the long, dark winters: of the Gwyddu, kings who had walked the earth with wisdom and grace until magic came to their line. It was an intricately told tale, and it had taken Miriel and myself many nights of puzzling over the Pictish until we could figure it out. Mage kings, the Gwyddu were, and abominations—for no man or woman can resist the siren call of absolute power. I was half-singing about the desperate, ragtag alliance that had opposed the Gwyddu when I caught the shadow on the horizon.

There was only a split-second of curiosity before fear gripped me. Not everyone has seen an army on the march, but it is a sight that stops the breath. Like a forest, it seems, or a hill, only a shadowed blur—until there is the hint of movement, a great wave surging forward. I had seen such a thing before, advancing on me while I was half-hostage in Penekket's tower fortress, and then I had wanted more than anything to run. Now, I did: I was flying down the hillside in a moment with the cold air burning in my lungs, pushing my legs to go faster, faster, take obstacles at a bound. Running, running, for now I had somewhere to run and something to protect once more.

The horse heard my whistle from halfway down the hillside and she was stamping and snorting when I reached her.

It took all my restraint to urge her only to a trot, then to a canter, letting her muscles warm slowly again in the winter air. When at last she began to toss her head and pull against the reins, I closed my eyes in relief, then bent low over her neck and prayed for her to run like the wind.

Was this exhilaration I felt in my blood? Fear, yes, and urgency, the scent of danger on the wind—but just for a few minutes, did this not give me purpose in the slow drift of my new life? The mare's hooves struck the ground in a rhythm to match the pound of blood in my ears, and I wrapped the reins in one hand, laid the other on her neck. Had I looked behind me, I would have seen nothing at all—the army was still a day's march, perhaps two. It did not matter. I was riding as if the god of death himself was at my heels.

It was on the plains outside Dun Druim that I came across Fidach, the queen's son. At first I took him for an enemy rider, and my hand was at my dagger as I spurred my horse on. His horse was thirty paces from him, perhaps more. I pulled up hard when I saw whom it was, so hard that the queen's horse whinnied at me in distress; she liked to leap and gallop. I stared at Fidach, breathing hard, thanking all the gods that I had not thrown my dagger.

"Catwin." He had been kneeling, drawing his bare fingers over the earth. His fair hair was held back in a braid, and a gold torc lay at his neck. It was the only concession to his heritage, for he wore nothing else to mark him as a prince. They dressed simply, here in Priteni, but even by their own standards, Fidach was careful not to stand out. He wore leather armor over his tall frame, and well-worn boots, and a brown cloak over his tunic of deep green. Even the clasps holding the cloak in place were of brass, and simply made.

He looked as if he had been caught out at something, but I had no time to care about that now—and his blue eyes narrowed when he saw the fear in my face.

"Riders," I managed. "It's an army. Your highness."

He was running for his horse in the next instant.

"From the northwest?"

"Aye." I held my horse to a trot as he swung into the

saddle and joined me. "How did you know?"

"The tribes are split now. Only the Cornovii would have an army you could see from Cathair Reul."

"You knew where I was?" Mistrust. Had he been tracking me? I looked around us, and to the rich earth still clinging to his fingers. As if sensing my gaze, he brushed them clean against his pants; his jaw twitched. I narrowed my eyes, and he swallowed, but recovered quickly enough.

"You ride past me often in the mornings. If not Cathair Reul, you ride to nothing and back. It was a guess, Catwin, nothing more." He had seen my instinctive worry, and his smile was gentle. For all that I avoided the prince, I knew that Fidach did not like to fight. Now he cast a look behind him, and took the reins more firmly in his hands. "Shall we?"

A nod, and we both bent low to spur the horses to a gallop. Dun Druim was close enough for us to push our horses to the limit—and with an army behind us, I was only too eager to do so.

Chapter 2

The guards on the walls had never seen me in such urgency. The wind tore the words from my mouth, but they did not need to hear me. I had only to point, and my face—and Fidach's urgency—said the rest. A clamor went up even as we passed through the gates: a bell clanging, shouts rising along the walls as runners took off for the Great Hall. We thundered down the dirt path, outstripping them all and barely coming to a halt to slide from the horse's back and pull open the doors.

The members of the court turned to watch us. Warriors, the Morini liked to call themselves, but in truth there was little war. They might talk of their days as farmers and herdsmen out on the land, fighting off raiding parties and mounting their own, but those days were long past. In Dun Druim, the court was soft, reduced to sparring and feasting in place of warring or working. Miriel and I had hardly noticed at the start, accustomed to such excess within the Heddrian court that we found life in Priteni harsh by comparison. And yet, over the years, we had come to wonder. These were a people without direction, without conflict or purpose.

Yes, hardened warriors they might think themselves, but Miriel was the first one on her feet, running for me. There was a moment when it was only the two of us, relief in her dark blue eyes to see me safe and well, for who could say what the alarm bells meant? There was relief in my eyes as well—the army would not be here yet, no, but Miriel was my charge, and there was danger once more. Miriel took my hand as we walked to the throne. I could feel her shaking, and knew she was watching me.

"How bad?" A low murmur in Heddrian.

"I don't know." I looked up as the queen held up her hands for silence; the whispers were beginning already.

"Catwin." Aoife's eyes flicked from between me and her son as she rose calmly. Her hand rested on the hilt of her dagger.

I squeezed Miriel's fingers and released her as I knelt before the queen. I could see retreat, to stand at the edge of the dais. Half-royalty, she was: advisor, confidant, an object of interest in the court. At my side, Fidach took no such pride of place yet, but instead knelt with me.

"Tell us your news," the queen commanded, her voice pitched to fill the hall. When I looked up, I saw no fear in her eyes. Once, Aoife had been afraid to rule, had sought comfort in the arms of the Duke—but no more. Her greying dark hair fell free over her shoulders, and a torc of gold lay heavy at her throat.

"My Queen, there is an army on the horizon, moving from the northwest." I did not match my voice to hers, but enough heard for the whispers to kindle. Aoife's jaw clenched.

"How many?" Connor, Aoife's nephew by her younger sister. I felt a stab of pain when I looked at him. I always did—his eyes were Temar's, slanting and dark, and the sight never grew easier to bear. Temar should be here, I thought. He should be advising his sister. I could almost see him, lounging in the chair by her side, trading jokes and offering wisdom. But the vision faded, and it was only Connor, knowing that he must show himself as a war leader now.

"I do not know, your highness," I said politely. It was not Connor's fault that he resembled his uncle and in any case, it does not pay to be rude to the royal heir. "I saw them from the peak of Cathair Reul, and I rode at once to warn you."

"You have our thanks." Aoife gestured to one of the servants lining the hall. "Bring ale and bread for the rider."

"My Queen." One of her lords, named Nuall. "My Queen, it is the Cornovii. I know it in my blood."

"My lord Nuall." Aoife was skilled in the game of leadership. Her voice was at once warm, and warning. She gestured to a chair at her side. "Come, give us counsel."

"I tell you, they come to use magic against us!" Now alarm sounded in the whispers, and the faint tightening of Aoife's fingers said that this was what she had hoped to avoid. But Nuall would not let them wallow in fear. Even as Aoife beckoned him forward, he turned with his arms out, seeking the approval of the crowd. "Well, let them come, I say! We still have the finest archers the land has seen!"

A roar went up from the crowd. He stood tall and well-made, a man the ladies whispered over. A skilled warrior, as I knew from matching blades with him in sparring. A quick study, as well. But he and I had never warmed to one another, for his dislike of Miriel was palpable and I, well—I could not forgive that. He smiled now as he strode to join Aoife at her throne, and I caught Miriel's eye to see her grimace.

I staggered to one of the benches nearby and a man shifted over to give me room. Another reached out to clap me on the back, and one of the warriors slid his mug of ale into my hands. Bread was offered by a servant. A cut of meat followed, and wine redolent with spices—it seemed I was to be served from the Queen's food as thanks for bringing the news. In a moment of humor, I remembered the feasts of the Heddrian court, where even the servants might taste the leavings from a dozen meat dishes. We had been richer there, Miriel in her silks and me in my uniform of black, but for all my uselessness, it was nice not to be looking over my shoulder every day.

I wolfed down a few mouthfuls, answering the warriors' questions around bites of food. They were all leaning close, and all had their own version of the questions: where on the horizon? What direction did they move? Were there riders, or did they come on foot? It did not matter that I had no answers—they kept shouting for my attention, and the babble of Pictish threatened to overwhelm me.

The turmoil on the dais stopped us all. A glance at the throne showed the highest lords and ladies clustered around Aoife. Although Fidach, having taken his place on the dais at last, stooped to whisper in Miriel's ear, perhaps telling her of the tribe's enemies or the plans for defense, I saw that the rest of the warriors had gathered with their backs to her, cutting her away from the Queen.

I was not the only one who had seen it. Miriel's shoulders had stiffened slightly, though she smiled up at Fidach just as radiantly as she might otherwise. Indeed, those at the throne might think Miriel entirely ignorant of what they were doing—

but they had not seen Miriel play a long game for acceptance in the Heddrian court. I had; I knew when Miriel was putting on a show to appear just as happy out of the seat of power as in it.

The soldiers clamored when I stood to leave them.

"I'll tell you more when I know it, I promise." My Pictish was still rough, but they never minded. I snagged another hunk of bread and clapped a soldier on the back, smiling at their chorus of goodbyes before making my way to Miriel's side.

I saw in an instant that it was different between us now, but I could put no name to it. How long since I had stood at her shoulder like this? Months, at least. More than a year. It was safe in this court, and over time I had drifted from a silent presence at her side to the tables with the warriors. She cast a glance up at me, and I saw the same mix of hesitation and gratefulness in her eyes. Danger brought us together, light and shadow once more, but was that truly what we were any longer?

And there was something deeper in her gaze, as well: resentment. I had not been there for months, and Miriel had felt abandoned, I saw now. While I had spoken with the common folk, and she with Aoife and Fidach, she had felt alone. Discontent simmered there, and my own anger, always an answer to hers, spiked quickly. Miriel could always call that out in me.

"I was telling my cousin that Lord Nuall is correct: these warriors are most likely of the Cornovii Alliance," Fidach said courteously. He spoke as if it were idle conversation, as if they others had simply neglected to tell us by chance, and I marked his choice of words. *The Lady Miriel*, the others often said, with a twist to their mouths. They had no trust for our counts and dukes and earls. Miriel's title, as everything else about her, marked her 'other.'

I thought back now, and remembered the times he had stressed her loyalty. Miriel was family to the Queen, he reminded the others; it was the only protection he could give her. It was at times like this that I remembered just how intelligent the man was. More comfortable taking orders than giving them, always seeking harmony, Fidach was easy to overlook—until one noticed the skill with which he turned tense conversations. How he was always there when the conversation grew heated, and how his companions were the first to laugh.

Even Aoife, I thought, could not always see it. Fidach was too different from the Duke for her to understand. Intelligent, yes, but where the Duke had used his uncanny skills in observation to find weakness, Fidach used his to bring peace. Where the Duke was content to send hundreds to their deaths in the bloodiest battles of the war, Fidach would lead the charge. A better man, for all that the sight of his father's looks gave me chills. Now, as the lords and ladies jockeyed for position by Aoife's throne, her son stood with us to give us credence.

When Aoife stood, the talk died.

"I will withdraw to discuss this with my generals." Her eyes swept the room. She had a way of speaking, as if every person in the room was the only one she saw. "Look to your weapons," she told them now. "We will ride in the morning."

A cheer went up and she smiled out at them, men and women hoisting cups and shouting clan names. Aoife indulged them, raising her own dagger high over her head to catch the light while they roared their approval. Then her gaze turned on those clustered around the throne.

"Come with me, all of you."

"Perhaps...it should be only your war leaders." It was a man named Nuall who spoke, tall and fair. They had seen her nod to Miriel. "Others do not know the way of our battles."

No one here was ignorant of what was happening. Fidach shook his head at us to urge silence, and I put a hand on Miriel's arm for caution, but she would not have it. Her chin came up and she stood.

"My Queen." Her voice was sweet and clear. "I have faced invasions and watched the strategy of troop movements. I should remain with you to offer counsel." She sank into her most perfect curtsy, her head bowed.

It was a rare moment of miscalculation; an indication, perhaps, of how long we had been gone from a court in which lies and manipulation were our only armor. Miriel's curtsy was designed to impress, for no one in this court had such elegant manners. And impress it did—it could hardly be otherwise, to have such a beautiful woman curtsy before them—but it reminded them once again why they did not trust her. Miriel, with her unreadable face and her polished manners, had been subtle in Heddred's over-elegant court; here, her gestures and stillness were a mark of extravagance.

Aoife's eyes had pity in them, and regret. *Understand that I would have you here*, her glance said. But she had read the mistrust in her generals. Her voice was steady as she said,

"We will call upon you if you are needed."

"Your Majesty—"

"Fidach will accompany you to your rooms." Her eyes found his. "Join me when you have done so."

I needed to loop my hand through Miriel's to move her. I pulled her from the hall, near forcibly, and felt her trembling with resentment. As we left the hall, the crowd parting to let their prince through, I looked back, and saw triumph in Nuall's eyes.

Chapter 3

"How dare they?" Miriel demanded. Fidach had brought us and left at once, his face set with worry, and now Miriel was pacing the floor of our rooms, whirling when she reached the walls so that her green skirts snapped behind her. Away from the eyes of the court, she was dragging her fingers through her curls to free them of pins and ribbons. Her hair tumbled down over her shoulders as each section was freed, a wealth of shining black. Miriel had never worn her hair as the ladies of Dun Druim, falling over her shoulders, and it occurred to me now that this was one of the first times I could remember that she had not been a leader in court fashions. "Sending us away. I know the machinations of war better than any of them."

"We're outsiders," I reminded her from my place at the door. "Of course they won't trust us now."

"You're the one who told them about the threat!" She was as perfectly beautiful in fury as she was when playing the courtier. And that, I realized, was exactly what she was doing. All it had taken was the narrowed eyes and the sly suggestion of her inferiority, and Miriel was primed for combat with words and laughter and sweet poison.

"I did," I agreed. "Still. And if they hear us arguing like this in Heddrian..."

"Oh, what does it matter?" Her eyes were narrowed. "*We're* Heddrian. Of course we speak it together."

"Yes. We are Heddrian. And that's why we're not at the council meeting now."

"That, and the fact that you tried to hold me back," she accused.

"What was the point of fighting Nuall? You know Aoife will ask for your counsel before riding out. Perhaps not with her lords there, but she'll come to you."

There had been many nights that Aoife came to our

14

chambers, alone or with Fidach, to take spiced wine and speak of politics, warfare, justice, even Heddrian history. For all that we sometimes disagreed heartily on matters of governance, the Queen was wise enough to seek the opinions of an outsider, and I had seen it in the measures she enacted. Miriel took pride in the queen's trust, though she knew better than to show it before the court, or suggest that such measures had been inspired by her words. Now, however, she could not be content. She shook her head emphatically.

"No. It must be there. It must be in front of them." She had paused, and her eyes were faraway. "As long as she is sneaking around behind their backs to consult me, even she will never trust me entirely. She'll hesitate to take my advice, because they'll know where it came from."

"Why is this bothering you now?" I demanded.

"I don't...something's gathering, Catwin. It's been building for weeks. In my dreams, in my..." Miriel waved her hands. Ever inclined to see the mystical, was Miriel—and she knew it was not my way. "It's nothing. I'm needed now. That's all."

"But Miriel...How do you know?" I asked finally. "Why does she have to take your advice at all?"

"How can you even ask that?" She rounded at me, her blue eyes shining in the candlelight.

"They've fought these wars for generations. Her war leaders *will* know what to do." I clenched my fingers. I should have known better than to pick this fight, and pick it now.

"Yes, to keep the war raging for generations more. I would end it for her, forever."

"Maybe that's not what they want. Her allies now were not always on the same side. Any war to end all wars would destroy kin, even if they're on the other side of the battlefield."

"You're content just to live here in fear of invasion, always waiting?" Her eyes narrowed at me. "That's no way to live, Catwin. And I didn't say I would destroy them. There are other ways of ending wars."

"Oh, can't we just leave this one to them?" My voice broke on the words, bursting out of me with more force than I had anticipated. Miriel stopped pacing, skirts swirling around her.

"What? Why?"

"Because it's the same thing all over again! Even when we made our own choices in Heddred, it was always someone else's war. We were always cleaning up someone else's mess. And when does it stop? When do *we* get to choose what we're embroiled in?" Tears pricked at my eyes and I turned away to press my hands against the door. Did I hear footsteps retreating? Had someone been listening at the door, or was I going crazy, falling back through time into the constant paranoia of Heddred? I did not want to wonder these things any longer. "I'm sorry."

"Catwin." Miriel was at my side in a moment, her hand on my arm, her voice soft. Her dark eyes were full of pity. "I know."

"Do you?" My anger flared up at that. "Because this is your court, your family. You're the reason they keep me here. I don't belong." *And until now, I've been no use even to you.* I did not speak the words.

"*You* don't?" She stepped back, and her voice rose. "Who rides out into the kingdom on the queen's own horse? Isn't it you? Who knows the land like a native? Who spars with their warriors and jokes with the men? Who dresses like them, is known as the savior of Priteni and the lost prince's love? You, you, it's always you!"

I pressed my lips together, hard. We never spoke of Temar, she and I. In her heart of hearts, Miriel could never forgive me for loving him—and I could never forgive her for hating him. Oh, she might be glad that he had saved my life, but I knew Miriel was glad he was dead, and I could not bear to ask her why, for fear of what she might say. What I might learn. I did not ask her of Temar, and she did not ask me of her mother. This was our bargain.

"What do you mean, savior of Priteni?" I asked her, when my voice was steady.

You killed my uncle, didn't you?" Her voice was bitter, her beautiful mouth twisted. "Me, they suffer only because *she* says they must—but I've spent my life being tolerated. I know what it looks like. Not a one of them trusts me. And they would have trusted you if you'd come alone." She whirled away, fists clenched, but in a moment the fight went out of her. "Catwin, what are we doing here? This isn't our home."

"Heddred wasn't really our home, either, though—was it?" I took a seat in a chair by the fire and sank back, my eyes on the flames.

"We knew the rules there." Miriel perched on the other chair and bit her lip. "Even when everyone hated me, I was a part of the court. I could move up, I could play the game. Here, I don't know what I'm doing. I'm still trying to *win*, but win what? I don't want Aoife's crown. I can barely see Fidach without thinking: that's the heir, my uncle will want me to smile at him."

"He's your cousin," I said, aghast. "And the Duke's son, not to mention."

"Like my uncle would have cared. He would only have minded if it got found out." She was right, and I crossed my arms with a grimace.

"Anyway, Fidach's not the heir."

"I wouldn't be so sure." Miriel was staring into the flames, twisting a ring on one of her slim, pale fingers. "She says it's Connor, but...she watches Fidach. She watches how people watch *him*."

"He *is* her son," I pointed out.

"And she's not tried to marry him to any of the ladies of the court, nor sent him with any of the raiding parties, nor allowed him to take command of the warriors as royalty should. There's something there, Catwin, I'm telling you."

"But what? You think she wants to replace Connor?"

"She'd be a fool to." Miriel's voice was flat. "Fidach doesn't have the head to rule. No, it isn't that." Her fingers toyed with a rough ring of silver. "Sometimes I think she worries that *he* wants that, but I don't think that's it, either. And no matter how much I think, I can't guess."

A knock at the door startled us both, and I reached out to touch Miriel's arm when she began to rise. Spite had woken the courtier in her, and danger had woken the Shadow in me. She sank back into the chair, the hint of a smile on her lips, and I cracked the door open to see Fidach. His hood was pulled up over his telltale fair hair, a rarity in Priteni, and he beckoned at us both.

"Come with me. We do not have much time."

He led us at half a run, pausing at cross-corridors to check for the lords. But no one was there—we could hear the roar from the halls that said a feast was in progress. The normal dirges and haunting melodies of winter were replaced by marching songs, with hundreds of voices joining on the chorus. Miriel, who had seen war, looked down at the floor with her pale face still and set, and her caution made me shiver. All well and good to sing of glory in a warm hall, but it was quite another thing to face the grim certainty of a battlefield.

Fidach ushered us into the Queen's chambers and, with a last look down the hallways, slipped in the door behind us. The door shut behind us with a dull click, and all of a sudden I was dizzy, breathing slowly, trying to calm my racing heart. Something was wrong. Something was very wrong; all at once I knew what Miriel meant when she said something was building.

"Catwin?" Miriel asked softly, and I felt her fingers slip around mine. I looked down at her, and it took me a moment to focus on her face. It was as if I had never seen her before.

"Be careful," I said, and she did not laugh. She only nodded. Hands clasped, we turned to the throne where Aoife waited.

Chapter 4

"Catwin, you may leave us." Aoife's voice was eerie in the silence. She sat still as death on her throne, the shadows from the fire swallowing her until all I could see was the glitter of her eyes.

"Catwin stays," Miriel said flatly.

"These are matters that only family may share." Aoife stood, and nodded to me. "Catwin, I beg you to forgive me this. You have done us a great service by warning us of the invasion, but I must speak of this in confidence with my cousin."

"Catwin *stays*," Miriel said again. Her voice was dangerous.

"I can trust only my bloodline with this."

Miriel flared up, and I put my hand on her arm to still her. A furious glance showed me that she had no intention of heeding me, but I stepped in front of her and knelt at Aoife's feet. My heart was still racing, and I could feel sweat at my temples.

"Your grace, you know me as Catwin, and you know that I protected your cousin in the court of Heddred." Aoife nodded. "But you do not know the whole of the oath I took. When I was bound to Miriel, I swore that I should be her shadow, as your brother was Eral's—with no fate of my own, will of my own, soul of my own. Miriel and I were made as one, she the light, and I the dark, and I vowed to go where she would go, to listen and watch and protect her from harm in all ways. What loyalties she has, my queen, so have I."

Aoife had swallowed at the mention of Temar. Her face was white as she watched me. Out of the corner of my eye, I saw Miriel standing as if frozen, the two of us sharing the memory of her uncle's voice—the words we had not accepted until years later, until we realized how closely we were bound to each other. At last, Aoife nodded.

"A blood oath. Very well." She sank back onto the throne

and raised her eyes to Miriel's. "Then tell me, cousin. What would you do in my place?"

No formalities, then, and no apologies for having dismissed us earlier. No witnesses. Miriel looked around the room and then back to the queen. There was nothing at all behind her eyes. Her face was a mask. I, who had watched her deceive her uncle a hundred times, knew the expression. I wondered what Aoife made of it now.

"And where are your war leaders?"

"Preparing." Aoife did not rise to the bait.

"Then why seek my counsel at all?" Miriel was still angry on my behalf, and I would have smiled at it, had I not remembered why we were here: the shadow on the horizon, and the fear in my heart.

"Because wars are not won and lost by a single stratagem." The queen's voice was sharp. "As I think you know. So I ask again: what would you do in my place?"

"Tell me first whose army this is, and why they send it."

"It can only be the Cornovii. As to why..." Now she did stand, and her hands twisted in the fabric of her shawl.

"Our alliance was made three generations ago." Fidach spoke from the corner of the room. "This much you know, yes? The land had fallen into violence, each tribe for itself. Our clan and its allies joined with five others, enemies and friends, to create a new age of peace."

"My father's father freed our people from the shackles of magic," Aoife said, and I thought I saw Fidach grimace. "The Cornovii would not accept this. They hold their mages as advisors to their kings and queens. They would tempt themselves to destruction."

Miriel bit her lip at the absurdity of this. *We are not children,* her look said to me, and even I struggled to hold my face impassive, listening to a queen speak of magic. But this was not our court, these were not our ways—and did not our courtiers speak of the machinations of the gods? We held our peace and nodded.

"There is more," Fidach said, and his mother looked at him sharply. "Their pride would not let them join with enemies and make vows of peace, and their honor would not let them cast aside the gifts of the gods. They told us that we would one day face retribution, that our alliance would fall from within and without at once."

"For seeking peace?"

"Old grudges are not easily laid aside." Humor, but dark. "We offered three times, but they would not accept our bargain. When it came to battle, the Cornovii—so they called themselves, after their ruling line—were defeated, horribly so. They were driven back beyond the midlands, to the sea's edge in the west. It is the most desolate land in Priteni. Poor land, not fit for crops or beasts. They knew they would not live well, and they made promises that they would return for us one day—though the treaty forbade them to do so. So we have been waiting, all this time."

"To condemn them to poverty was to push them to retribution," Miriel said simply. "What reason would they have to embrace peace?"

"The decision was made long ago," Aoife said wearily. "None alive today created that treaty. It has hindered us, as well. There are times when we have thought that its strictures were...unnecessary."

Miriel looked at me, and I knew she was thinking of the hall, warm and filled with warriors gone soft. No farmer could claim an easy life, but the business of the court had shown us that the crops were plentiful, the silos well stocked. Those who came from the outer holdings at festivals were not wealthy, but not hungry. I had long wondered how the land was so profitable, farmed by so few. Now we knew, and I could see from her expression that Miriel agreed with me: Aoife and her people had little to complain of.

"Perhaps," Miriel said diplomatically, biting her tongue on questions. She had always been better at that than I. "But neither have you amended it, or called them back. And now an army rides for all of us."

"Yes," Aoife said simply, and Miriel began to pace again, her fingers interlaced behind her back, her eyes half-closed.

"So you ask what I would do."

———

No one spoke for a time. Miriel's feet beat slow and rhythmic against the wooden panels. Aoife sank back onto her throne to watch, and Fidach leaned against the wall, his arms crossed. Firelight glinted in his pale hair, and I watched him with new interest. Secrets, Miriel said. What was Fidach hiding behind his still face? What did Fidach want in this?

"You have three choices," Miriel said at last. "First: you destroy them completely, army and citizens."

"We fight only those who can meet us in battle," Aoife said sharply. Miriel, who had not even blinked at the brutality of her own suggestion, raised her eyebrow in a way that suggested that she did not quite believe this, but she held her tongue. She raised three fingers, and tapped on the second.

"Second: you fight as you always have, and leave the field of battle when they have been driven back."

"They will come again," Fidach said from his place at the wall, and in Aoife bent her head in assent.

"My son is correct. They will come again if we drive them back."

Miriel's smile was thin, but triumphant—a ghostly echo of the Duke.

"Third: you sue for peace and forge a new alliance, neither Cornovii nor Morini."

The words dropped into the silence of the room, and I saw the queen nod, slowly. Miriel's words were no surprise to her.

"And how would I do that?" she asked softly. "It is something I have pondered, cousin, I tell you truly. I tell you also that I my court has grown fond of its hatred for the Cornovii. The war that divided was bitter, indeed. There are those who were left with no clan at all—Nuall is one, lest think you has no cause for his anger. His clan was cut down by Cornovii mages, and he and his children are the only three left of what was once a powerful family."

"And the Cornovii?" Miriel asked. She did not respond to Aoife's bleak outlook on peace. "What do you know of them?"

"Very little. Every once in a while there is a farmer or a fisherman who will bring us some piece of knowledge. Their queen is Branwen, or was several years ago. Her horsemen have made incursions into the midlands, and there are reports that trees were felled for lumber. We drove them back."

Miriel sighed and rubbed her temples.

"If Fidach has told the truth, then this is not revenge so much as desperation. They are starving. They need good land for crops and livestock."

"Land that is already owned by others," Aoife said sharply. "It was not cruelty that drove them from the midlands, it was safety for our outer farms. You wish to make peace, and it is not the Cornovii I fear—not so much. But my own war leaders would never stomach it."

"You are their queen. They should do as you say."

"Were you not the one who had your own king sign a treaty with rebels?" Aoife looked at her bitterly. "You can hardly deny my clansmen a say in their lives now. And what would you say if I gave your land to the ones who killed your grandfathers?"

"It is your duty to make them face the facts of that war," Miriel said sharply.

"Then tell me how," Aoife snapped. "That is what I need from you. That is why I called you here. I accept your words. I would undo the spite of this division, I swear it. And I have reason to know that we cannot win this war. I *must* force my lords to accept peace, but I know of no way..."

"There is a way," Fidach said softly. "If it comes to it."

"It cannot. Be at peace." Aoife did not look at her son. To Miriel, she said simply. "You know of courts and queens and lords. Tell me what to do."

"Ride out to meet them," Miriel said. "A small party. Secure peace. Tell your war leaders that you wish to regain the strength of the Cornovii, not drive it to destruction as you must otherwise."

"A small party." Aoife made her way to the edge of her room, where a window showed her the hall below. She stood in shadow, where the light would not catch her, and she looked down at the clan, gathered below.

"Riders have gone already, to summon the clansmen to war." She did not look at us as she spoke. "Nuall rides at dawn with the first wave. Say what you will, my lady, I could do no less. There are children here as well, and the Cornovii would cut them down." Miriel only waited. Her eyes were narrowed in speculation. "I tell you, cousin, we must have peace. All will be lost if it comes to battle." In the corner, I saw Fidach close his eyes in anger, and I watched him speculatively. *If it comes to it,* he had said. *There is a way,* he had said.

"Why does Fidach not lead the war parties?" Miriel asked bluntly. She lifted her chin and watched, her eyes flicking between Aoife and the prince. Both had frozen at once when she asked, and Fidach recovered first.

"My lineage makes me unsuitable."

"Why?"

"This is not the time." Aoife's voice was like a whip crack. "What you must know is that battle will bring us ruin."

"How can you *know*?" Miriel demanded.

"I know." Aoife watched us with a face like stone. "That is all. I know."

"Is it only me you do not intend to tell, or them also? Because you are correct, your grace, it will be difficult, indeed, to hold them from battle without reason."

"Leave that to me." Aoife twisted her gold ring from her finger and held it out. "I give you a different charge—both of you. By the debt you bear us."

I thought I heard Fidach give a strangled exclamation, but when I looked over he was staring down at the floor, his arms crossed over his chest. When I looked back, I saw Miriel bridle at the rudeness. For certain, we had drunk their ale and eaten their bread, sought shelter in their halls. But it been shelter freely offered, for services given to the people of Priteni. I would have guessed Miriel might spit curses on a woman who would claim this for her bargain, but she went very still. Watching.

"Yes?" she asked simply. Nothing more. Aoife swallowed, and her voice grew deeper, melodic.

"By this debt, I call my right to your service. Go to the Cornovii. Ride out to meet them, and do what you must to ensure that the Morini do not fall, that I may pass my crown to Connor, and he to his heirs."

Beyond her, I saw Fidach standing still as a statue. Try as I might, I could not say what he was thinking—whether he was raging not to be chosen, whether he was relieved, whether he simply feared to appear power-hungry.

"You wish us to stop the army," Miriel said slowly, almost to herself. She was gazing into the middle distance. She did not reach for the ring.

"I would prefer it if you stopped them before they reached us, yes." Aoife allowed the shadow of a smile to touch her lips. A poor joke. A blatant attempt to lighten the mood. "I do not know if Queen Branwen rides with them. If not, you must persuade them to take you to Dun Beal, their stronghold. Do what you must to put your case before their council. The battle must be avoided."

"And you?"

"I will do what I can to make my leaders accept peace in lieu of victory." Her mouth twisted. "Which I tell you now will be easier if our armies do not meet in battle. I tell you also, and truly, that there is no one else I can trust with this. The others are too eager for war."

"Even you?" Miriel asked Fidach, and he smiled tightly, shook his head. He was watching us now as if we were something alien to him, as if he had never seen us before in his life.

"I—"

"Fidach will accompany you," Aoife said. She was looking away as she said it, and she did not see Fidach's look of alarm.

I frowned. Everything about this meeting was wrong, just slightly outside the boundaries. I knew it. I thought that Miriel knew it, for she was watching all of this with her eyes narrowed.

"Will you do this for me?" Aoife asked.

She held the ring out still, the seal of a dragon winking on its face, and Miriel only looked at it for a moment. Then she turned and came to me, drawing me away from the royalty who waited.

"Do we have a choice?" I asked her, before she could open her mouth. "Don't offer me what we can't have."

"There are always choices." Her voice was fierce. "We

---

could ride at dawn, take a boat and go for Heddred. Or we could strike out to the east, find a place to make our home."

"And leave, knowing what they'll do?"

"It might be better." Miriel was expressionless, watching me. "She's hiding something from us."

"You saw?"

"Anyone could see. I don't trust her, Catwin. But I think..."

"What?"

"Well, you said before that that this isn't our fight. And you were right. You were. It wasn't our ancestors who made this mess." She was looking away from me, and it took me a moment to understand why. When I did, I could have laughed or cried. Miriel might play the ruthless courtier, but she never had been so in her heart. Not really.

"You're staying, aren't you?"

"I'll go with you if you say we should leave."

"You'd never forgive yourself." Gods help me, her sense of justice was going to kill us both. Miriel would never walk away, knowing that she might have averted a slaughter.

"You don't have to stay." She was twisting her hands. "I'll go with Fidach. I'll be safe."

"Like I could let you face down an army without me!" My voice was a hiss. "How can you even ask that of me?"

"How could I ask you to go? Catwin, it's as likely suicide as anything."

"And you think I would *ever* let you face that alone?"

"You aren't my Shadow anymore." When she saw my face pale, she shook her head. "I didn't mean it like that. I'm sorry. Catwin." Her hand twisted in my tunic to pull me back. "Catwin, please. I'm sorry. I only meant..."

"What?"

"That was a promise you made to my uncle. That was when I was for the king. I only meant, you don't have to stay now."

"I do," I said, and I felt it down to my bones. "It can't be undone. Wherever you go, as long as you'll have me..." I couldn't finish the sentence.

"I'll try not to get us both killed, then," Miriel said, and I couldn't help myself. I laughed. In a moment, she was laughing, too, but there were tears trembling in her eyes. She did not say thank you, but it was like she had shouted it. She had not wanted to do this alone. She turned, in a swirl of green skirts, and I saw her chin lift. The courtier was back.

"So?" Aoife looked between us, her eyes wary at our laughter.

"We will go," Miriel said. Her hand squeezed around mine. "When do we leave?"

"Dusk." Aoife rose to place the gold ring in Miriel's hand. "Ride hard, for you will have Nuall at your back. I cannot guarantee that you will obtain peace—but if you want it, my lady, this is your only chance."

Chapter 5

Dusk came slowly. Miriel would have stayed in the great hall, seeking to learn more about the war between the Morini and the Gwyddu but neither I nor Fidach would take the chance of someone seeing all three of us leave together. Fidach promised to tell Miriel anything she wished to know, and I, in return, secured her promise that she would remain in our rooms. I left her staring into the flames, deep in thought, and went to the stables to see to the horses while Fidach dealt with supplies.

As the shadows began to slant, I wondered if I should have taken Miriel's bargain: run to the hills, or perhaps to the southern shore, leaving Priteni behind entirely. This was not our fight, not ours to put our lives on the line. Alone in the stables, I had been able to think on the sight of the Cornovii army. I knew my own fear, and knew also that it was well justified. A good bodyguard, I thought, would have taken the chance to get Miriel away, to safety. No one who sent an army was ready for peace, and most especially not when they sent an army to avenge generations'-old wrongs. And what Aoife thought, what Aoife would agree to, was a mystery as well.

I did not like that.

"Could she be sending us as a ploy?" In the privacy of our room after the negotiations, we had tested one another's resolve. The words were bitter in my mouth, and the angry press of Miriel's mouth told me that she wondered the same.

"Why send her son if so?"

I only looked at her. The question might have been comforting, if we could think of any other reason Fidach should be there at all. Anyone might have done to tell us how negotiations should proceed. Any lord might have lent weight to the proceedings. It did not need a prince, and Aoife's only child at that.

And that left us Aoife's mysterious assertion that this could be trusted only to family, an assertion that had been followed by secrets, yes...but nothing that would warrant such worry. Either Aoife was a fool, with little grasp of how dire the situation was, or she had a secret she had not yet shared—how, for instance, she knew beyond doubt that a battle could not be won.

"You notice she didn't tell you what you could and couldn't bargain for," I said after a time, and she smiled thinly.

"I did. I wonder if that's why she's sending Fidach."

But neither of us believed that. We were becoming aware of how much we did not know, and neither of us liked the fact. Was this as dangerous a dance as it had been in the last court, only now with no one to guide us? The Duke, abhorrent as he was, had seen to it that we knew our enemies—and if that was everyone, well, at least we knew their histories as well. Here, we knew nothing. I had told myself that it did not matter any longer, that we were not seeking power and had no enemies to make.

I was beginning to think that I had been wrong.

My companions appeared quietly, walking together in the dim light. Long ago, they had been prickly with one another, both a memory of the Duke: Fidach in his easy good looks, Miriel in her training. They did not speak, afraid to let the lords of Aoife's court think there was some new plot afoot, the Duke's revenge come at last. But in time, when they had spun no plots and made no moves, the court had ceased to watch so closely, and they had come to move in quiet understanding. Both, in this court, were tied by blood to a man who had nearly destroyed Priteni; both knew the danger of power. *They practice old magics here,* Miriel said once. *They say blood calls to blood—debts and destiny passed down the line. They say that Temar turned my uncle's fate, and now it walks the earth of this land, searching for someone to claim.* The lords of Aoife's court still remembered. Oh, yes—they remembered. Miriel and Fidach might not be thought to be conspirators any longer, but they were watched, and they knew it.

I had never seen Fidach dressed as he was now: not in the armor of a warrior, but the pants and shirt of a laborer, and a cloak of deep green. The hood, I could see, was embroidered heavily in blue and gold, the edge picked out in seed pearls.

Miriel saw me looking at the finery and lifted her shoulders by the slightest fraction, and I pondered whether or not to advise Fidach to hide his heritage. I would not be keen to stand down an army, marked as the queen's heir.

Perhaps Fidach thought the same, for he seemed nervous. It was the first time I had seen him so, and my worry grew. If even Fidach was afraid... Whatever he was, Fidach had never been foolish.

But there was no time to think. We secured the saddlebags in place—me smiling to see Miriel poking at the buckles, for she rarely rode far enough to need a pack—and Fidach swung Miriel into the saddle. She straightened her skirt and raised her eyebrows at me.

"What?"

"I don't know how you stand to wear gowns."

"It's not so bad. Don't fuss over me, Catwin, you know I hate that." Even as I sighed and looked away, I smiled. Miriel, prickly as she was, knew my worry when she saw it. After a moment she took pity on me and leaned over to place her hand over mine. "We'll be safe enough, Catwin. They do not kill emissaries. If we can bargain, we will be safe."

That this mission reeked of secrets and impossible odds, she did not say. She did not have to. We only guided our horses silently out of the stables and, at Fidach's signal, across the dark paths near the walls.

We took a side gate, so conveniently devoid of guards on the eve of attack that I looked sharply at Fidach. He held up a flask, and then cocked his head to tell me to listen: the song of singing filtered from the little guard tower on nearby.

"Only the best for our soldiers," he said slyly. My grin was answered by a flash of his teeth in the dim light, and a low chuckle. He urged the horses forward and we followed with our hoods drawn up, skirting the shadows.

I did not doubt that the guards were well occupied, but the back of my neck prickled as we rode away. Anyone might see us—a lord, come up to the walls to gaze towards the army; a guard stumbling to another tower. They would ask questions we could not answer, and it disturbed me to see a prince mislead his own army.

More so, Fidach's silence disturbed me. To see him in the darkness of the stables, or holding up his flask, I might think him giddy. There was repressed excitement in the set of his shoulders, freedom in the way he drew air and looked up at the night sky. And yet, looking over once to mark the small landmarks I knew so well by daylight, I saw the prince sitting in silence, his eyes one the ground, looking for all the world as if he were grieving. When he saw me looking, he turned his head away and I made a point not to watch him after that.

As soon as we were out of sight of the castle, and the wind had shifted so as not to carry our voices back, Fidach reined in his horse and looked over at us.

"You are kin, and not," he said abruptly. We said nothing to this ambiguous statement. Clouds scudded across the moon and I could make out the gleam of his eyes as he watched us. "My mother has sent you to bargain for peace, but do you know all of your charge?"

A tiny motion of Miriel's fingers stopped me from reaching for my knives.

"Tell us," she said.

"You are bound to bargain peace, yes, but for your queen. You bear her ring, and you are bound to her twice over now: through kinship, and through your debt, freely acknowledged. You swear to be loyal."

It was uncharacteristic of him, this fierceness. He was agitated, and his horse was stamping and tossing its head. I could see the muscles of his legs rigid, his hands white-knuckled at the reins.

"I have sworn to bargain for peace," Miriel said. "And you know peace is my wish. You heard me speak of it. I would not condone murder."

"I do not doubt your devotion to peace. But will you carry out the queen's wishes, to keep the armies from her and her on the throne? If you must choose between the Cornovii and the Morini, if you must choose between peace and my mother's queenship, what would you choose?"

"Don't answer." My voice came out abruptly when Miriel

—

opened her mouth, and I swung down from my horse. I jerked my head at Fidach to do the same and Miriel, with practiced grace, kicked herself free of the saddle. I spent a moment wondering where she had learned that before turning back to him.

"What game are you playing?" I demanded of him. "What is your mother asking of us? Truly, Fidach. No games."

"Everything I have told you is true," he said carefully.

"But always slanted! Never whole!"

"We cannot win this war," he said bluntly. "Not win it, and keep the throne. Don't ask me how I know, Catwin. But the lords will not understand. So when I ask you to bargain for peace, it is to keep my mother in power...and Connor after her." He looked down rather than meet my eyes, and I put my hand on his arm.

"You know the oath I swore to your cousin."

"I do."

"Her oaths are mine, her loyalties are mine. She agreed to help, and I will protect her to the death. But Fidach, I cannot bring her blindly into danger. What aren't you telling me?" This would appeal to him, I thought. Loyalty and protection. I prayed Miriel would have the good sense to stay quiet.

"I would tell you if I could," he said finally.

"Not good enough."

He turned away and ran his hands through his hair, and I watched him. Silence, Temar taught me, was a valuable weapon, and Miriel played along. I saw her out of the corner of my eye, gleaming pale in the moonlight, a little ghost. We watched Fidach until he turned back to us.

"If they meet us at Glen Tuam, and we bargain for peace, you will know the truth then."

"I don't like secrets." I cut off Miriel's words with a jerk of my hand. My eyes met Fidach's, and he shook his head.

"Neither do I. But we do not always choose what we can tell the world. I ask you to remember that, when you know the whole truth. Come. We must ride quickly to be there by dawn." He lifted Miriel back into the saddle, and swung himself into his own. I followed, watching him closely.

"How will they know to meet us?" I asked, and Fidach

smiled.

"They may not. It is a gamble. But I think...I think they will know."

We rode quietly, with the moon slipping over our heads and the stars glittering cold. Miriel and I tried not to look at one another, and Fidach looked ahead as if he would will the future into being.

"Have we been to Glen Tuam before?" Miriel asked, when the silence had become too much to bear. Fidach's mistrust still weighed heavy on our minds, and I knew she was trying to draw him out, earn his trust slowly.

"Once," he said, after a moment's thought. "We go there to pay homage to the dead. It was there that the Gwyddu were defeated. Every family of the Morini lost someone to that war."

"They were real?" I had heard songs of them, but had never realized this fact. To my surprise, Fidach—that serious, logical warrior—nodded seriously.

"Oh, yes. The war that toppled them was when my line first came to power." He tilted his head. "Truly, you do not know the story?"

"I, er..." I would never have thought him one to accept tales of magic. I looked over to Miriel for help, but she was studiously looking away, having honed the art of not talking herself into corners. I resolved to give her a piece of my mind later for not helping me. "I suppose not."

"I see." Fidach looked ahead, as if trying to decide where to start. He was silent for so long that I glanced over at Miriel, and she only shrugged, swaying slightly in the saddle as the horse moved. "Well, you know the songs, I think. That's the story: the Gwyddu, the old royal line, they were rich in mages. It was no more than chance to produce so many in their last generation, but they embraced it. The kingdom wasn't...perhaps, something you would recognize. The halls were scattered. Dun Beal was my family's home, but it was nothing like now—just a few huts, some stables. Fealty to the kings was paramount, of course, but the Gwyddu only presided over squabbling clans. They kept the peace. And then...they decided they wanted more.

"It started with summoning the leaders for an oath of

fealty. Well enough, but soon it was more even than that: lumber and stone for great halls, gold so the Gwyddu could wear rich clothes. They began to take a say in marriage between clans. They kept asking for more, every year. And when we began to deny them...they used their magic."

"It was the first time the clans fought united, you know. They came to fight the Gwyddu, and the battle was decided at Glen Tuam—though then it was Glen Veagh, Valley of Birch. You'll have heard the song that talks of the ghosts in the trees?"

I had, and I shivered. It was one thing to sing fairy stories in a dark hall, and quite another to hear that the place had been the site of a true battle, and that we would rest there tonight. Relentlessly practical I might be, but there was something in this land that suggested there might indeed be spirits roaming for mortals to claim, that there might be mage kings turning magic against their subjects.

"And so your clan rose to power." Here we were again, ferreting out information. I, who had never truly learned to trust again, who had kept a network of kitchen boys and the queen's maids well fed and well bribed, had nonetheless never learned the full history of Priteni. It was difficult, I told myself, when one could hardly tell fact from fiction. Still, I had been remiss.

"Not directly. The factions splintered as soon as the battle was done. The three mages were taken and bound in iron, and the rest of the family put to the sword. My clan spoke for mercy. It turned into war again, for there were no more mages after that, for three generations. Then my great grandfather asked for peace, for the unity of the clans once more. He said magic had forsaken us because we would not swear to keep it from the throne."

"And the Cornovii could not accept it."

"No," he agreed. "They could not. There have been whispers, always—it was no true vision of the gods that led him. Many families had lost all in the war, and he wanted lands the Cornova family had. Some say it was to strike at them, nothing more, that there was no reason to fear—" His voice had risen, passionately and he broke off, cleared his throat. "In any case, the Morini have had no mages since. Perhaps they hid themselves away, seeing what happened to the Gwyddu, seeing the mood of the Morini court. They knew their talents would not be welcome."

"What talents?" Miriel asked delicately, and I, who knew her moods, heard disbelief in her voice. Fidach did not seem to notice.

"There are three branches of magic: the call of time, the call of earth, and the call of storm. A strong mage will have one, and master it. A rare mage will have two. The rarest have three."

"And the Gwyddu?" We were drawn in despite ourselves.

"Had three mages, two with the whole of the magic, one with only the call of time—they said he was a truthseer to rival all others, and dreamed his enemies' secrets, to destroy them. The others went with the army. I told you Glen Tuam was once Glen Veagh—but legend says it was *Sragh* Veagh, a floodplain, and the Gwyddu sank the very earth to try to swallow their enemies."

"How were they stopped?"

"Bowmen." He smiled. "The only thing that can stop a mage is the wind itself, and the darts it carries. The alliance brought rows upon rows of archers, and all it needed was a few arrows to find their way through the storm the Gwyddu raised." He smiled, trying to break his ill humor of the story, and gave a flourish and a bow from the saddle. "And so now you know the story of Glen Tuam."

"Why meet there?" Miriel asked, and Fidach looked away.

"It is the only place we can trust one another."

The moon arced overhead as we rode for Glen Tuam. We spoke little, letting the mist swirl around our horses' hooves. I rarely saw this land by night, but Fidach seemed to know the way. He led us over the gentle swell of hills and around outcroppings where the stone seemed to have punched up through the greenery to show its grey face to the world. As our eyes grew accustomed to the dark, Cathair Reul rose in our vision. We curved north of it, following a road only Fidach could seem to see, and our horses picked their way delicately over the waving grasses.

I rubbed my hand along the mare's neck, but it was more

to comfort me than her. When Fidach had spoken, the three of us flushed from our flight, the words had sent a thrill down my spine. Mage kings and great battles, like the stories Roine told me when I was young—tales to catch the fancy. But now that the night was dark and quiet, I admitted to myself that it was unsettling, to hear a hardened warrior speak of magic as if he believed it.

Unsettling, as well, to know that we would face an army by dawn, if all went according to plan. I looked over at Miriel, and saw her swaying slightly with exhaustion. In the court of Heddred, she had been last to bed and first to rise, driven to perfection by fear of her uncle. Here, however, we had no pretenses to keep and no tricks to master. Our lives were our own; we were now unused to the strictures of court life, of intrigue.

She felt my eyes on her and looked up.

Are you well?

A faint nod. Strange, indeed, how this felt familiar and alien all at once. Danger had brought back what we once shared, the bond forged in fear and pain—and honed in the long silences of our time here. I had not realized we still share this; I had not realized that I missed it. It was jarring. I had told myself that I never began to trust, but was that true? Had I not, perhaps, relaxed into the belief that no one would come for us here?

Worst, I began to wonder if this might have been prevented. What if I had asked more questions, followed the members of the court to learn their secrets as I would have done in Heddred? Could I have seen the seeds of this war beginning, and warned the queen?

And then I remembered her cold eyes when she looked at me, the look of an animal that believes an unknown is an enemy. Temar had taught me that...and who had he learned it from, truly? The Duke, or his sister?

What I could not understand, above all, was why she might trust Miriel, but not me. Had I ever put myself forward? Surely not. I sparred with the warriors but never kept my skills hidden, and her soldiers were better trained for my help. I did not court the patronage of any lord. It was Miriel who drew eyes from Aoife, with her quick wit and her sharp insight. I was a nobody. I should be a nobody.

And now we rode with her son, who, Miriel claimed, harbored a secret—and at the instruction of a queen who did not trust us. There was no one else she could trust, she had said, but I rather thought that we were simply the best of a set of bad options, to her. And there was something about this that even Fidach did not like, though another piece of him seemed to be rejoicing. I saw Miriel watching him out of the corner of her eye, but if she could make anything of his silence, I did not see it in her face.

We reached Glen Tuam near dawn, with the sky pale at our backs. It was hardly a valley at all, such as you might find sheltered between mountain crags. No, Glen Tuam was a long dip in the earth, as if a giant had reached down to scoop away a handful. The barest scraping of rocks showed at the edge of the dip, and the valley seemed new, somehow—or perhaps that was only Fidach's tale of the Gwyddu catching my fancy in the last moments of the night.

The birch swayed and rustled, leading down the gentle slope to a cairn of stones topped in black metal, and something flashed in my vision: bodies, piled one atop another. Three figures knelt at the stones, their hands dripping with blood, collars of black at their throats. The warriors behind them raised swords, flashing in sunlight—

"Catwin?" Miriel's voice called me back to reality. I leaned over the horse's neck and shuddered, and she leaned to take my hand. "What is it?"

"Nothing." I did not want to tell her. The vision was too fresh. I blinked and shook my head. "It's nothing."

We rode to the center of the valley in silence, descending into shadow, and tied our horses nearby at Fidach's instruction. I looked around myself fretfully. There was nowhere here to hide Miriel, for the leaves were tamped down with autumn rains. A perfect place for an ambush. Fidach saw me looking, and smiled a little; it only served to show how grim he looked.

"There is a reason we come here to bargain," he said.

"Can you trust them?" I asked him urgently, and he

thought for a long moment.

"If we can convince them that they can trust us."

"How do we do that?"

"Do not worry. You need do nothing save watch. And it will not be long now, I think," he added, watching us shiver. Miriel gathered the heavy fabric of her cloak around herself and nodded. She was watching Fidach out of the corner of her eye, as if she might divine his secrets in the early dawn light.

Some minutes later, I saw Fidach stiffen, look around himself at the hills. I cocked my head to listen, and heard it: a chirp and a whistle. I inched my fingers towards my knives and Fidach shook his head.

"What is it?" Miriel kept her voice low.

"That wasn't a bird," I explained.

"How do you know?"

"Not now."

We waited, hearts pounding, and it was not a few moments later that the horses began to shy and whinny. We, who could hear nothing, looked on warily, but it was not long before we felt it too: the very lowest tremble in the earth. An army, I had told Fidach. Riding from the northwest. And while they should make for the gap between Glen Tuam and Cathair Reul, I was suddenly as sure as Fidach that they would stop here.

"Stay back," he told us. "Stand tall, but with your weapons at your feet. Do not hide your hands." He paused. "And now, I suppose...you will know."

From his pack, he pulled a length of green fabric. A heavy iron ring went on his left index finger, and it seemed to me that he shuddered to wear it. His golden torc, he slipped from his neck, and placed one of iron on instead, not finely wrought but heavy. I bit back an exclamation—the torc reminded me of my vision, of the kneeling captives with their collars—and Fidach looked at me sadly, then turned his face away.

He did not look at us again as he slipped the ornate hood up over his head, and then he walked forward alone to stand at the cairn, his right hand stretched out to rest on the iron headstone.

I frowned at Miriel, and she shook her head at me. If this

was Fidach's great secret, we could make nothing of it—and with the thunder of hooves bearing down on us, we could not spare much thought to it. So we stood, and waited, and as dawn broke over the hill and flooded the valley, the warriors of the Cornovii rode down to meet us at Glen Tuam.

Chapter 6

In truth, this was no army—it did not come with heavy wagons full of supplies. There were no catapults, no foot soldiers, no siege engines. The Cornovii came with horsemen alone. They took shelter only in scant tents and ate what they could carry. Still, this was no little raiding party that could arrive by stealth and be gone with grain or gold and no one the wiser. These were three hundred warriors, and where they went, the ground shook.

Fidach hardly moved as the first riders arrived at the crest of the hill, but it took all of my courage not to flinch. Miriel, who had never known me to falter, looked at me curiously.

"You planned to sneak into the heart of the Ismiri camp," she reminded me, and I nodded my head at her insistence.

"Yes. Sneak. Facing down an army is different." *And suicidal.* I had scouted the valley as soon as we came to it, and despaired. There was nowhere to hide save the stands of birch, and how long could shelter there last? I should have hidden Miriel, I realized, and claimed the horse was for one of their emissaries.

How they had known what they would find, I could not say—but the Cornovii did not seem to fear an army. Their riders came up along the edges of the valley, and in a moment we were facing a hundred bows.

"All this," Miriel said softly, "for three of us."

"They wouldn't have known we were three."

"They can see it now. And anyone with sense would hide their numbers."

We were interrupted by the appearance of their party: a man wearing armor and a golden torc, a woman wearing the same array, and another woman in white robes and with a hood—and iron collar—to match Fidach's.

"Is it some mark of kinship, do you think?" I asked softly, and Miriel frowned.

"We've never seen him like this. Even when the outer clans came for the feasts."

The woman in white came first. With her hood, it was difficult to see anything about her beyond her strong stride. She walked to where Fidach stood, and he waited as if he were carved in stone until she had placed her hand, as well, on the iron lump of the cairn. She raised her left hand to show a ring, as his.

"Miriel?" I asked.

"Yes?"

"We're supposed to be negotiating."

"Yes."

"And we can't explain what's going on."

"Yes."

"Doesn't that bother you?"

"What do you think?" Frustration sounded in her voice. "I thought about it, you know. Maybe Aoife doesn't mean for us to get peace, but I don't think she would mean for us to die so quickly, either. She must have thought we would figure this out. We *have* to—or Nuall will get what he wants, and these people will die. For now, we'll just do what *they* do." A nod of her head indicated the other emissaries, who were now making their way down the hill, and shedding their weapons as they went. Miriel stepped delicately over her own little dagger and strode forward, and after a brief, glum moment of deciding that my knives would do nothing against a hundred archers, I followed. I did not like being weaponless. It made me feel vulnerable, and I couldn't help but feel that casting aside one's weapons but keeping the archers was a trifle disingenuous.

Still, as we walked, both of the Cornovii emissaries raised their hands in a signal. Arrows were placed back in quivers, bows were unstrung, and archers folded their hands in front of them. A formality—they could be ready to shoot us before we reached our horses—but an oddly comforting one.

"Greetings," one of the emissaries called to us. "You treat with Lugh—" a deep nod "—and Seiysell." His gesture took in his companion, who nodded. Her eyes were fixed on Fidach, speculatively.

"I am Miriel, and this is Catwin."

"And Gwydion?" Lugh gestured to Fidach, and Miriel hesitated, unsure of the name, unsure what to say. Fidach had told us no lies to tell.

"This is Fidach, son of Aoife."

"Queen Aoife?" Seiysell asked.

"The same."

"So we heard truly. Has the line of Morin turned from its grand oaths, then?" There was a spark of cold humor in the man's eyes. It was a bold question, but even I, who had known Miriel for a decade, could not see hesitation in her eyes. She inclined her head gravely.

"The Morini offer you good wishes, and the continued offer of peace. My cousin the queen bids me tell you that it is past time for us to heal old wounds and atone for old wrongs." Her words rang clear with sincerity, and the emissaries paused. Clearly, they did not know what to make of this young woman with a strange accent and dark eyes, bright with intelligence.

It was the woman in white who was not charmed. Her head came up slowly, and she stared at Miriel with open dislike.

"You use half-truths to deceive us."

It was Miriel's turn to look startled. In the world of our birth, such bold words would be unthinkable. Veiled spite, clever insults, derision—all to be expected, and any who bargained knew that the truth would be twisted. The words, however, would be presented with smiles, made as delicate suggestions. Such was the nature of peace negotiations.

"I speak the truth when I say that my cousin sought my counsel and accepted my advice—she has no wish for the devastation that would come with war. She has accepted, as well, that many injustices of the war should be righted."

The dark-haired woman crowed with laughter.

"Injustices! So now that she has what her grandfather shunned, she now thinks it is of worth?"

Fidach lifted his head at last.

"No." The word was quiet, but it dropped between us all with force. I heard anger. I heard grief. Even the emissaries stilled, their faces softening. "I will never take the throne. I am forbidden to be what I might be. I wear this iron always."

The woman in white, who had looked down at the ground once more, raised her head sharply. Her eyes bored into Fidach's, and she seemed entirely beyond words. Fidach met her eyes only for a moment before looking away; his shoulders were rigid, and his face was twisting with misery. I tried to keep myself calm, shoulders down, and yet it was all I could do not to go to him and ask what was wrong—what these words meant, that they caused him so much pain. He had never seemed to care about the throne before.

"Aoife casts aside a gift of the gods?" Lugh's brow furrowed. "No true leader would deprive their people so."

"She and her court would say it is no true gift, but instead a temptation to madness."

At my side, Miriel stood, wound like a spring, holding herself to inaction. A lesser woman would have fidgeted or demanded answers, but Miriel was accustomed to stillness. She was watching them all, her eyes darting everywhere.

"A gift is a gift," the emissary named Lugh said at last. "It was this that led us to reject the Morini alliance. It fills us with sadness to see them mistreat you, brother."

A swift glance at me showed Miriel's confusion, but still we did not speak. What could we say, when we did not understand the first part of what was happening?

"And yet..." Seiysell murmured. "Perhaps Aoife is not so faithless as we thought. You tell us she truly desires peace?" A sharp, quick question for Miriel, who only smiled.

"Yes," she said simply. The woman in white frowned, first at Seiysell and then at us.

"Then why does an army also ride to meet us?" How they would have heard that, I could not have said, but Miriel hardly flickered.

"Why do you ride on Dun Druim? Old grudges, and old scores—and so it is with my cousin's court. She has sent us in secret, ahead of the army, to go to your court and make peace. "

The emissaries looked at Miriel, contemplating, and the woman in white leaned forward, her hand still on the stone, to murmur something in Lugh's ear.

"We will not be taken in by false offers of peace," Lugh said sharply, to her and to us. "We have known Morini *peace* for too long. Tell me why we should not simply ride onwards."

"War is in no one's interest," Miriel said sharply.

"No? What of the families who starve on the western shores?"

"Yes, let us speak of them, who will lose their sons and daughters in battle no matter the victor. Are those lives worth so little to you that you would refuse even to bargain?"

This was not the Miriel I had known in Heddred. There, she was a woman of habitual caution and soft words—in negotiations, regretful instead of fiery. This was a strange place to try a new ploy.

But I had forgotten her skill, the skill I had never had even in part: to match her opponent perfectly. In Heddred, with known players in the game, she had formed herself into the perfect adversary, anticipating their moves. Here, though she had no such knowledge, Miriel could at least match the Cornovii in tone. She stepped into the fray, her words more direct than I ever would have dared, and she did not flinch. Indeed, it did not seem to have offended them: Seiysell looked contemplative, and the woman in white was watching us closely.

"Those are lives Aoife would take herself if the cold and hunger did not do it for her," Lugh said.

"Father," Seiysell said softly, and Lugh shook her hand away from his arm.

"No. They will give us nothing more."

"Do not be so hasty."

"Child..."

"Your presence here tells me that you were asked to bargain for peace," Miriel interrupted. "I am here for the same: peace. An end to bloodshed."

"You lie, emissary."

"This one, at least, desires peace." The woman in white looked evenly at Miriel. "That much I can vouch for."

"Miriel speaks the truth," Fidach said. "I swear it on all that I am. My mother does not wish for battle."

The man looked at him curiously.

———

"Even you? You bargain for Aoife, after what she has done? The secrets she has kept?"

"She is my mother," Fidach said passionately. "She is my blood, and a woman of honor, for she has cast aside all chances to make use of what I am. If she seeks peace I will see it done."

The woman in white pressed her lips together, and anger flared in her eyes, but Lugh and Seiysell were nodding.

"Well enough." Lugh flicked a glance over to Miriel and myself. "And these two?"

"Miriel was my father's heir by his sister," Fidach said formally. "Catwin is oath-sworn to her—and beloved of Necthan, my mother's brother."

"The lost prince," the woman in white said, and Fidach nodded.

"Just so."

"He went as cloak and shield, and he did not return in this life. But his soul was at rest when he died." I looked at her, transfixed by the words. I wanted beyond anything to believe them, and know that Temar had found peace before his death. Tears were trembling in my eyes. The woman nodded to me. "You did him a service, and us—although I have never been able to see what. Your land is far from my eyes."

Miriel looked down at her feet and I tried to keep my face still. Talk of Temar, and impossible knowledge. Caution told me that this woman was trying to unsettle us, but I could not keep myself from hoping that she did know, that she was right—that Temar had died at peace.

"And yet something orphaned walks with you..." The woman in white tilted her head. "The fate of a man who might have remade Priteni." Lugh and Seiysell looked at her sharply, but the woman's eyes were fixed on Fidach. "A single shade, or two? I cannot say. I see two princes, and I see a man with pale eyes like yours. Your father?"

"Yes," Fidach said shortly.

"You do not wish me to speak of this? Perhaps you do not wish to carry his fate?" Her eyes were narrowed in speculation.

"My wishes are irrelevant." The Cornovii looked at one another. Seiysell's eyes locked with Lugh's, and a wealth of meaning passing between them. I lifted one eyebrow. It had been an evasion, surely enough, and misdirection besides—clear to me, but not to them, and a faint settling of Fidach's shoulders told me that the Cornovii had taken the bait. I was not pleased that I could not say what the bait was, or the truth—and I was not pleased, either, to see his eyes drift to Miriel for a moment. His face was a mask, and yet his gaze roiled with pity and jealousy both.

"Come with us," Seiysell said. She tried to keep her voice low, but there was urgency in it. She smiled, sweetly, a jarring expression against her warrior's garb. "It seems you bargain in earnest, and a call for peace will always be heeded by our kin. We offer you safe passage to our court, safe lodging, and our own protection back to your borders." Her words were a lie, but Fidach nodded, and Miriel curtsied.

"We would be glad of it."

With a sigh, Fidach removed his hand from the stone and bowed. A gesture took in the torc at his neck, the ring on his finger.

"A gesture of goodwill," he said, as if it explained anything, but the woman in white laughed.

"Wear it or not, young one. Our queen does not fear you."

"She should," Fidach said slyly. A hint of tension in his eyes showed that this was a gamble, but the three Cornovii emissaries laughed as if this was a tremendous joke, and he smiled and ducked his head. "We will gather our horses."

There was ease in his movements that I had never seen before, and he sang softly to his horse as he unwrapped the tether from a nearby tree. The heavy iron jewelry was wrapped away again, and his golden torc was placed back at his neck.

"So now you know," he said to us. He did not look over.

"No." Our words, spoken in unison, stopped him in his tracks.

"No?"

"What happened back there?" I asked in a furious whisper.

"What do you mean?"

"You put your hand on a rock and told them you weren't

your mother's heir. What did any of that mean?"

"You truly don't know?" Fidach gestured to the bundle of green cloth in his hand. "I bound myself in iron. I thought certainly...Catwin, I've *heard* you sing the songs. Surely Miriel— well, I half-thought you might know already. You watch me closely enough. Their emissary even *said* it, at the stone."

Miriel shook her head.

"Said what?"

"Gwydion." Fidach looked at us, and his brow creased when he saw that we still did not understand. He looked back to the east, as if seeking guidance from his queen, and then back to us. And something in him broke: he stood a little taller, and raised his eyes to ours.

"I'm a mage," he said at last.

Chapter 7

We rode in silence. There was only so much idle conversation one could make while galloping, and even less one could plausibly make with people who had been planning a vengeful invasion. Miriel rode with her eyes forward, so focused that it seemed she was moving her mount by force of will alone. Fidach rode with the woman in white, and though they did not talk, I saw a kinship there. Lugh watched Fidach with a strange intensity, and at his side, Seiysell's eyes were also fixed on the prince. What she was looking for, I could not say.

I, for my part, tried to think of anything except what Fidach had told us.

It was hours before we stopped to rest the horses, and then we walked and sat in awkward silence. Though I wanted nothing more than to speak with Miriel, we had spent enough time in courts to learn patience. We kept our silence as the soldiers milled around us, men and women with sun-darkened skin and worn clothes. Only their weapons looked well taken care of, and every one of them was wiry, strenuously lean. The Cornovii emissaries walked among them, making a show of kinship with the riders. Their laughter was harsh, their dark eyes searching us for weakness.

When the crowd cleared slightly, Miriel took out her water flask to shield her mouth.

"He did not want to bargain," she said in Heddrian, her lips hardly moving, and I nodded.

"But what persuaded him?" I spoke just as quietly, leaning over to check the fastenings on my boots. It would not do to let them hear us speaking secrets in Heddrian; just as surely, this was something we must understand. Miriel stared out at the army, stretching and rubbing down their horses. Her brow was furrowed, and it was some time before she said:

"His daughter. Talk of our prince's fate."

"There's something they want with him," I agreed. I could

see Lugh approaching behind her, and I twitched my fingers for silence, the old habits of Heddred returning to us. We smiled at him and mounted up. Whatever words we wished to say to one another, it would have to wait—this was complicated enough without earning more mistrust than Lugh already carried.

I did not believe for a moment that they had forgiven Aoife's clan for driving them back. If they agreed to peace, it would be no more than necessity that drove them. Even then, I was sure that Aoife could expect poison in her drink, an assassin's blade between the ribs. *To condemn them to poverty was to push them to retribution.* Miriel's words echoed in my head, and the worn saddles, old boots, sunken cheeks, bore testament to her words.

No matter how I tried to focus on what I could see of the Cornovii, knowing that it would be precious beyond belief in negotiation to have secrets, it was Fidach's words that held my mind. It took me until midday even to accept the possibility of his words. I had spent a great deal of time raging in my head that entire wars could be started for something so useless as myth and legend. It was not until we mounted up again after lunch and my muscles cramped painfully that I began to look for distraction.

Suppose it was true... It was a trick Temar taught me, more a thought puzzle than anything else: suppose one impossible fact, and follow the consequences. For his first puzzle, he asked me what might happen if all horses were blue. For the second, what would happen if fabric dissolved in rain. In the grim necessity of my training, it was a rare moment of levity— and it dissolved entirely when I asked him why.

Isn't life ridiculous, Catwin? I looked up at his dark eyes and was startled by the sadness I saw there. *That a king might accept the help of a merchant's son. That a noble family would cut down the royalty in their beds, as they slept—but leave just one, and ensure their enemies would survive another day. Learn the art of supposing impossible things, and you will learn to see the world as it is.*

Very well, then. Suppose Fidach really, truly believed he was a mage and so did the rest of them. Suppose one fact—

———

49

which seemed to be, I thought sourly, that we were surrounded by children—and watch the rest fall into place. They thought Fidach could use magic. What, then?

Find where the fact touches the world. The grief and pain and muted anger when Fidach said he was not his mother's heir. An act? Certainly it would not be above Aoife to tell her son to play a part. That she desired peace, I was certain, but I was also certain that her desire was more self-preservation than benevolence. The woman had already hedged her bets and bought herself time by summoning an army and consulting us in secret—I did not think she would make much of a fuss about a little theater.

Still, the tension between Fidach and his mother had not, I thought, been staged. This would be why Aoife had tried to send me from the room: she did not want anyone beyond her blood kin to know what Fidach was—what she thought he was. And why? Why?

Think carefully. Leave out no detail. It was important, as a spy in a court of professional liars, not to assume much of anything. It was equally important to trust the instinct that said the answer was close. This was that moment. I tried to calm the whirl of my thoughts. Aoife had hidden what Fidach was—thought he was, I reminded myself. Were all mages bad, then? I did not think so. I could remember songs about great seers and one heroic mage that had ended a drought by calling the rains, sacrificing his life in the process.

And then I remembered her words: *the Cornovii hold their mages as advisors to their queens and kings. My mother's father freed us from the shackles of magic.* Fidach's story, so difficult to remember when it was not dark and eerie, filtered back into my mind. Mage kings. It was not that mages were evil, necessarily, though Aoife did not seem to trust her son's abilities. It was that mages and monarchs should not be close. Should not have the same goals. That Aoife's rule would be suspect if it were known that Fidach was a...

This was ridiculous. I looked over at Miriel as we drew up our horses to make camp, and was pleased to see my own feelings reflected in her face. She swung down from the saddle, graciously accepting Lugh's hand, and set to work on the buckles herself. It made me smile that she did not want to seem ill-taught, and ill-equipped. I maneuvered my own horse so that she could copy the steps, and saw the flash of her smile.

As if continuing a conversation, she said:

"But it doesn't matter if it's true, does it? It matters that *they* think it's true." I nodded, and hoisted the saddle off my mare, who shook herself gratefully.

"Do you want me to get yours?"

"Yes, please." Pragmatism won out over pride and she stepped back to let me loosen the straps.

"Do you know how to rub a horse down?"

"Not really." She dug around in the saddlebags until she found a brush to match mine. "I should just do what you do?"

"Yes." We worked quickly, by the fading light of the sun. Miriel was, if anything, too exacting. Her strokes followed precisely, and she missed nothing at all. Her horse lowered its head to sniff the cold ground, and snorted in frustration when it found nothing to eat.

"Shall I take your horses?" Fidach's voice startled us both, and I swore. He laughed under his breath, and I looked into his blue eyes and wondered what on earth I was feeling right now: comfort for a familiar face, or comfort that he still seemed to be the same Fidach I knew—or unease, that he still seemed to be the same Fidach and he'd been hiding something so monumental? All hidden behind eyes that looked so kind.

"Yes, please. Will you come back after?" Miriel's voice was sweet as honey, but there was no mistaking that this was an order. Fidach nodded. Perhaps, I reflected, he had been expecting this.

"I will."

He returned to us not long after. I was crouched on the ground, trying to make the kindling catch, and Miriel was pacing. I had a feeling she was going to pace an awful lot more before this was over; it made me tired just thinking about it.

"Magic?" Miriel asked abruptly when he returned, and Fidach lifted his shoulders in a helpless shrug.

"At least we are evenly matched," he said, as if that helped anything. "The Cornovii have Morwen, the Morini have me. But I fear I am more harm than help."

We said nothing, I because I had nothing to say, and Miriel from anger. She only crossed her arms, and Fidach rubbed a hand across his brow.

"You know why I could not tell you. You've heard the songs. Think of the one they were singing when we left, that speaks of the spirits in the birch—the second verse."

"*Never again shall the mage kings rule,*" Miriel said, after a moment thinking, and Fidach nodded. He had knelt on the ground and was digging around with his fingers, carving out a fire pit.

"After what happened before, any royal family that produces a mage is bound to step aside. The Cornovii rejected it, and you saw my mother's court—Nuall would have ridden to kill them all a dozen times if my mother had not spoken against it. If my mother were to try to make me her advisor...I do not wish to think what would happen."

"That is what your mother wishes us to negotiate," Miriel said flatly. "Keep her on the throne through all of this."

"Yes." Fidach shrugged his shoulders helplessly and Miriel clenched her teeth. *It only matters that they think it's true.*

"Is that why they rode on us?"

"Yes." He bowed his head, all humor gone, and I could not keep myself from speaking.

"But how could they really—"

"If you do not mind," he said, somewhat desperately, "I wish to be alone."

We watched him walk into the mists, and then Miriel looked over at me silently.

"Oh, good," I said. My head felt a little light. "He's crazy."

"He doesn't *look* crazy." Miriel looked to where his shape had disappeared entirely, and shook her head. Her hands were clenched around one another, twisting.

"Miriel, you heard him."

"I did. I still think he isn't crazy." She looked over at me, her eyes like pools of pure night; I could not see the blue at all. "And that means he's lying to us, doesn't it?"

"But why?" I asked her. I was shaking my head. "Why would he—"

"I don't know," she said fiercely. "But I do know I don't like this at all. We'll have to be very, very careful."

Chapter 8

I woke with her words ringing in my ears and the clamor of the camp rising around me. Another day of hard riding—it would be a full week before we were back at the Cornovii stronghold of Dun Beal. A normal journey, we had been informed, would take two weeks or more, but the Cornovii rode hard and carried little. Miriel and I, knowing a test when we saw one, only smiled and tried to keep our weariness and our pain to ourselves.

"Good, you're awake." Fidach's voice startled me, and I winced as I sat up quickly and shook Miriel's shoulder. The prince handed me a dense cake of oats and fruit, and set to packing his bedroll. His sadness of the past night seemed to have been put aside, for he looked over at me with a grin. "Feeling it, are you?"

"A bit." I sat rubbed at the muscles of my calves. I was avoiding his eyes, my shoulders hunched. I did not want to look up at him and realize that he was lying. He had to hold the little jar of balm right under my nose before I saw it, and then I jumped to see him so close. I couldn't decide if I wanted him to be a liar, or mad.

"This will help a bit tonight," he said kindly. "Tomorrow will be worse. Are you feeling all right? You don't look well at all."

"Mmf." I smelled the spicy scent of the balm and handed it back, and he gave a sympathetic smile.

"It's not so bad, you know. They know you'll be in pain, so you don't have to try to hide it entirely. It's how you deal with it that they'll judge. So—"

"No complaints and no asking for special treatment," Miriel finished for him, sitting up at last. Her eyes might be luminous and her hair shining, but even she looked a little the worse for wear after a night under the cold sky, bleary-eyed and red-skinned. She took the oatcake Fidach offered and stared at it for a moment. She, too, looked out of her element. She did not seem to know what to say.

"Exactly," Fidach said, as if he had not noticed that both of us were acting oddly. "They think you're soft. You want to show them that you can survive the way they do."

"I see."

Miriel bit her lip in concentration, and then she began to transform. She sat a little straighter. Her face became a little more alive, as if she was simply waiting for a reason to smile. Her eyes grew a little wider. Her chin came up slightly. If I could not feel the cold air myself, I would think she was at a picnic on a summer's day, and if I had not tasted the oatcake, I would think she was eating the most delicious food she had ever tasted. A single raised eyebrow in my direction asked whether she had been successful, and in response I only jerked my head at Fidach, who was staring at her as if he had seen a ghost. Miriel gave him her most brilliant smile, and he looked over at me. I shrugged.

"You said they'd be watching."

"Yes, that should work," Fidach said. He looked away and swallowed, his face pale. "You used to do that all the time when you came to our court, I remember now."

"Habit," Miriel said, after swallowing a delicate mouthful of oatcake. Her smile was warm, her body leaned towards the two of us, her face alight. Anyone not close enough to hear would think this was the most fascinating conversation she had ever had. "At least it may come in useful now."

"Doesn't it *hurt*?" Fidach asked abruptly. I stared at him, taken aback by his tone, but Miriel hadn't noticed. She waved a hand.

"I *have* ridden all day before, you know."

"No, I mean—" He broke off and looked away.

"Fidach? What is it?" I pushed myself to my feet and went to him, kneeling awkwardly at his side on the hard ground. His hand closed over mine where I touched his arm, but he looked right past me.

"When you do that," he said to Miriel, "it's like you're shouting your memories."

"Of the court?" Miriel's brow was furrowed, her pretense

55

forgotten.

"Of what my father did to you." His voice came out harsh, and Miriel recoiled as if she had been slapped. I looked between the two of them anxiously, unsure who to comfort. Miriel looked as if she wanted to turn and run, and Fidach's pain was practically shining in the air.

"I didn't know you knew," Miriel said finally. Her voice was shaking.

"I didn't, until you showed me."

Miriel shot me a furious glare and I tried not to shrink away. She clamped her mouth shut, and I knew well why she was doing so. There was no one quite so eloquent as Miriel in a rage. When angry, Miriel could twist a knife as precisely as a surgeon. Now, reminded of magic and with Fidach dragging her past out into the open, she was furious. If she spoke freely, she would find Fidach's every weakness and exploit it.

And, mad or not, lying or not, Fidach was our only ally.

"What do you mean," she said softly, icily, "that I showed you?"

Her fear was apparent to me in her bloodless lips and the flare of her nose. We might have become safer and softer in Aoife's court, but that did not dull our instinct now. Where we had come from, for someone to see truth and secrets was for them to have the power to kill. She cast me a look, questioning, and I shook my head. I had not told Fidach what befell us in Heddred. I was not her undoing.

"Your memories are written all over you," Fidach said. He said it gently, apologetically, as if perhaps we should have known and he did not want to be the one to point it out to us.

"Then do not look at me." I had never heard Miriel's voice so cold. "For I would prefer you did not watch me and pity me."

"It is not pity. You are my blood, and so is he—it is pain."

"I said do not look! Do not watch. Do not think you have the slightest idea of what was done to me or what it means. I have done you a service by never telling you what I knew of your father."

He flinched, and my hand clenched, reflexively. He did not seem to be lying, not to my eyes—and I had seen a lot of lying.

"It is I who am doing you a service," he said, teeth gritted. "I am not the one exposing your secrets, my lady, and I am not the only one who can see them! What will you think if Morwen sees it all as well?"

Miriel's hand slammed down onto the ground. A few of the Cornovii looked over, but she did not notice. Her face was twisted, she was near to baring her teeth in her rage. Her voice was a furious whisper.

"Magic? No. Don't *speak* to me of magic! No more! I won't have it."

"It's the reason we're all *here*," Fidach hissed back.

"Yes, and you think about that! You think about what you've gotten us into." He reared back as if she had slapped him.

"Thank you for your reminder." His face was white. His eyes were icy now, and he did not move when Miriel leaned forward.

"And do not *ever* speak to me of your father," she said precisely. I heard her emphasis on the word *father* and knew it for deliberate cruelty; indeed, Fidach's jaw tightened. "You don't have the right. My memories are none of your concern."

Fidach opened his mouth to speak, his eyes narrowed, and a slight cough alerted us all to the emissaries' presence.

"Will it suit you to ride out?" Seiysell's voice was warm, her face neutral, but Lugh's eyes were dark and grim. Behind him was Morwen, watching Fidach closely. Miriel pasted a smile on her face before she turned back to them; her curtsy was elegant, her head tilted almost flirtatiously..

"Of course," she said. "Let us make haste to Dun Beal."

Fidach looked away as Miriel smiled brilliantly up at Lugh. She was, once more, the perfect courtier, and even the dour emissary was taken aback. Something flickered deep in his eyes—distrust or dislike, I did not know. But after a moment he bowed, elegantly, and held his hand out to help her up from the frozen ground. They stared at one another for a moment, the hardened warrior and the hardened courtier, and I could not guess who might win in the confrontation—for I had not lived in Penekket without learning to scent battle in the air.

—

Chapter 9

We thundered into the Cornovii stronghold at noon on the eighth day, rear scouts trailing us and one hard-riding group leading the journey. When they rejoined us after every mountain and overview, they exchanged a slight nod with Lugh. When Miriel questioned the custom on the third day of our journey, Lugh gave a small laugh.

"I think, my lady, that given our memories of the Morini, you will forgive me if I do not trust your peaceful intentions."

Not overly concerned with courting our favor, was Lugh. That would have been easy to say, and even true, at times—but not always. Try as I might, I could not get the measure of Lugh. By turns he was watchful, courteous, and contemptuous. He might change moods in an instant, and I spent whole mornings with my eyes trained on him through my lashes, trying and failing to find the trigger point. What pleased him in the morning might infuriate him in the afternoon, and when Miriel glanced at me to see if I could make sense of his changing moods, I could only signal to her that it was a mystery to me.

For a time I wondered if he might fear his power as emissary, and I spent some time wondering who he might be. I could have asked him, or perhaps Fidach, but it pleased me to puzzle over it myself on the long ride. In Heddred, I could have scrutinized his clothing for the minutiae that betrayed rank: the careful simplicity of nobles' clothes, the opulence of merchants, the signet ring of a head of household, the small gold cloak pin that conferred a claim, however distant, on the throne.

What I had was Lugh's air of easy assurance, the deference of the warriors and a torc of bronze with the symbol of horns at the ends. He seemed accustomed to leadership, and the soldiers followed him without a moment's hesitation; it was not command, then, that troubled him. I briefly considered that Lugh might be the true leader of the Cornovii, but I was certain that Fidach would sense such trickery and warn us of it. That left

Lugh as a high-placed lord, or as a member of the royal family: a brother, perhaps, or a cousin, or a consort. I hoped for cousin, or brother—for the loyalty of love and family might then be tempered by childhood slights and resentments, something Miriel could exploit.

For even my memory of Miriel's skill could not give me faith that she would succeed now. She was playing, I thought, impossible odds. What could she say to reconcile the Cornovii to peace after such mistreatment? For all that Lugh's anger was no help to us, I thought I might understand it better than his courtesy. For certain, the Cornovii had borne the brunt of the war. They had participated in it, had led massacres, had used magic against troops still fresh to the memory of the Gwyddu—but their children, and their children's children, still suffered for it. Who could say that was right? Who could say they should forgive and forget, when the queen of the Morini hid her son's talent to keep the throne?

Morwen and Seiysell were kind, the older woman watching us to ensure we had our needs tended to, Seiysell asking what seemed like a thousand questions about the Morini. Lugh was the one who worried me. As the days wore on, he sank into quiet dislike while in Miriel's presence—and Miriel, in turn, became almost entirely silent, shedding the charm she had so cultivated. I asked her about it in a murmur of Heddrian one night, when I knew the guards Lugh had assigned us would be upwind, and our voices drowned by the crackle of the campfire.

"He dislikes charm," she said softly. "He was warm to me in the first days, but something has changed. He does not like pretty smiles or flirting anymore. It is like when we were with the rebels. When I try to charm, he retreats. I must be as close to nothing as possible—and then when he finds nothing objectionable, he will tip his hand." Her voice was low and dreamy. She gave a small sigh. "It feels so good to lie still."

"It does." It had been a long time since we rode so many hours in a day, and never had we done so at such a punishing pace.

"Where's Fidach?" Miriel asked suddenly. Her voice, though quiet, was sharp.

"With Morwen," I said softly, naming the Cornovii seer. I turned towards her in the darkness and grimaced at the feel of hard earth under my shoulder. I was constantly turning in the nights, keeping all parts of myself frozen and burning by turns.

"He's with her every night," Miriel said, and her mistrust was clear. "He shouldn't be. I wish I knew what they were talking about."

"Miriel..." I sat up suddenly. Things were coming into focus, and I did not like the shape of them.

"What?"

"He's what started this war," I said, and Miriel propped herself up on her arm, wincing at the movement. "Right? They all think so."

"Well, they'd say Aoife started it by not ceding the throne. They thought she was breaking the covenant that they'd been driven out for refusing. And to them, she is, there's really no denying it. Oh, don't look like that, they can't understand us even if they can hear."

"But they all think Fidach's the reason she should, don't they?"

"Yes, and?"

"Who's the only person who would actually *know* he's lying?" I looked over at her and I saw her eyes widen.

"Do you think they're in this together? She seems to like him well enough, and she's the one talking to him—not Lugh. You know he'd make much of it if she told *him*."

"She can't, can she? That would give away her secret as well."

"Maybe." Miriel lay back and chewed her lip. A sigh said what she would not say out loud, that this was only getting worse as time went on. And then, as if she had said it: "Still...our only choice is to keep going forward."

"You'll still bargain for them? After she lied, even knowing he's making this into a trap?"

"Of course I will." Miriel's voice was indignant. "Well, not for her. Fine. For peace. Look at these people, Catwin. They're all hungry, they're young. Look at Seiysell—she has a good mind to her, and what will she inherit if this falls to war? They're just like the people in the way of the Ismiri. Why should they have to die because kings and queens are fighting? I'll save them from her, from Lugh. From my cousin, if I have to. That's why Wilhelm—that's why the treaty was so important."

And we lay awake in the darkness for a long time after that, silent and pretending that Miriel's voice had not broken on Wilhelm's name. Pretending that we were not both homesick and wondering what we had gotten ourselves into. Pretending that we did not want to go back, because no matter how bad it had gotten in Heddred, we had known the rules there.

And so the days passed. Fidach spent time with Morwen, and Miriel and I watched. It was impossible to miss the lightening of his mood. The prince shone with a new confidence. He hummed to himself as he rode, and though he was all smiles, he hardly talked to the two of us. Once his hasty dinners were over, he would make for Morwen's campfire and they would withdraw to the edge of the camp—to practice, they said.

Miriel watched Fidach, and he stared back coldly. Even I was frightened, beyond knowing what he might do next. He was playing a game of extraordinary skill, and I could not see how he might have honed himself with only the court of Dun Druim for practice.

"He's going to turn on us," Miriel said.

"He's not," I tried to assure her, but I could not say that she was not correct. How could I believe he would turn on us when there was no hint of a lie in his eyes? And yet, how could I look at the facts he told us and not face the truth? Miriel heard the waver in my voice and bent her head. When she brushed her fingertips under her eyes, I was shocked to see them come away wet with tears.

"He already has, hasn't he?" She gave a little hiccup of a sob. "We never should have come. What was I thinking? I'm not one of them and they know it. I have nothing to work with."

"You have me," I said softly, and she shot me a look that was half-furious, half-despairing.

"Don't tease me."

"I wasn't," I said, stung.

"How could you possibly help now?"

61

"How did I ever help? By noticing the things you can't while you draw their attention. By running messages and knowing how to get servants how to tell the truth about their masters. By saving your damned life when some reckless fool tries to stop the negotiations!"

My vehemence took her aback.

"I didn't mean—"

"I don't want to hear it." I wrapped my arms around my knees and stared into the fire.

"Catwin, why..." Her voice trailed off at my expression. She waited for me to speak, and I did not. I did not think I could possibly explain it to her, child of a noble house as she was. She had been taught that nothing was impossible, so long as she played the game correctly: that anyone could take power, secure it, hold it. Now, even when she bitterly told me that it was no use, I knew that she did not think so in her heart.

It was easier for me to believe that danger had returned to us. In my life, I had learned to trust only three people: Roine, who betrayed me; Temar, who gave his life for me; and Miriel, who had journeyed with me to the ends of the known world. What was left for me in Heddred? Nothing. Temar was gone, Roine destroyed. I had neither lover nor enemy, and Priteni, for all its feeling of timelessness and permanence, was not my home.

I could not even call myself a shadow any longer, could I? I was no longer a bodyguard to follow Miriel through predictable dangers. There was no game for us to win. I had freed us when I killed the Duke, and Miriel had found us a way to leave the court we hated so, but now I was nothing. I had no purpose. What use was there for a retired Shadow?

I had, as it happened, only a single friend, and even though she had resented it when I left my post at her side, she did not seem to remember why I had ever been there. *I took a vow*, I had told Fidach, and I wondered now if Miriel had ever considered me her other half. If she had ever wondered if she was a whole person on her own.

Finally I curled up in my bedroll with the fire to my back, my face turned from Miriel, and she went to bed with a whispered goodnight that I did not return. Fidach returned late, and paused when he saw my open eyes gleaming in the darkness, but when I did not speak, he curled into his own bedroll and fell asleep quickly, easily. A man with not only one place in the world, but two. I remembered his face as he laughed with Morwen, and I could feel only a terrible storm of envy.

We rode the next day in a stony silence, Miriel and Fidach and I, until we came to Dun Beal. Then, all three of us exchanged a glance that was sheer awe. Fidach had not lied when he said the land was poor, for we passed stunted trees and expanses of rock instead of soil, and the soil itself was sandy, providing little for even wild plants.

Out of this uninspiring landscape rose one of the most menacing forts I had ever seen. I, who had ridden into the shadow of Penekket Tower, felt an unlikely shiver at this place. The walls were rough-hewn stone, piled with precision but no grace. It was a town built for defense, different indeed from Dun Druim's wooden walls and open feel. If the Cornovii had come with the means to attack a place like this, I thought, Dun Druim would have fallen in a day.

As we trotted through unpaved streets, and Cornovii peasants came out of mean little huts to stare at us. The smell of the sea was very sharp, lying close as it did beyond the fort. I saw dried fish hanging in the interiors of the houses and smelled the rot of seaweed. Gulls circled overhead and were shooed angrily away from stores of food.

In her gown of bright green, her eyes shining blue and her hair released to tumble down her back in a mass of curls, Miriel looked like a figure from a myth. I could only hope that she would catch the fancy of these people, that they might speak to their queen and beg her to accept Miriel's peace. For certain, Lugh would do no such thing. Miriel was right, he looked on her now with contempt. It was Fidach Lugh courted, murmuring how very sad it was that the Morini did not accept his gift. When Lugh was done with him, the Morini court would fall into chaos.

Watching Fidach's careful evasions, I wondered all the more at his game. If he accepted Morwen's friendship so readily, why did our prince not court Lugh as well? What benefit to him in remaining neutral? What game did he play that left him

---

neither our ally, nor Lugh's? I would have to wait for clues. Wait, while cut off from allies and at the mercy of an army. It made me ill-tempered, for an ill temper was easier to bear than the fear that we were utterly helpless.

Branwen waited for us herself at the gates to the palace. A tall woman, she wore her red-gold hair in two thick plaits, draped forward over her shoulders, and in her right hand she held a spear. Her left hand held out a single thistle.

"Cousins," she said. Her grey-green eyes held a storm, anger and hope roiling together as she looked at us. "You are welcome in our halls, and under our protection. We weary of war. Come, let us make peace."

It was a warm invitation, and promising—but at our side, I caught sight of Lugh's grim face, and nearer, Fidach's calm, secretive countenance. I knew there would be no ease found in the Cornovii court.

Chapter 10

The great hall of the Cornovii stronghold was dark and smoky, smelling of peat and the ocean. The salt wind had bleached the wood of the buildings to grey, and even the great trestle tables of the hall were weathered and rough. The people who sat there, taking shelter from the cold winds of a sea winter, looked on us with open dislike.

I could see why: hollowed cheeks and sharp chins spoke to the poverty Fidach had mentioned. Next to them, Fidach's broad-shouldered height and our well-fed frames were a luxury. We were the ones complicit in the exile of the Cornovii now.

Branwen led our procession through the silent ranks of her citizens, Lugh at one shoulder and Miriel at the other. Fidach walked with Morwen, both wearing their ornate hoods to shade their eyes. Whispers trailed them—*Gwydion*—*the usurper's line*—and I could see tension in Fidach's shoulders. Fear? Anger? I could not say. Behind them, I walked with Seiysell, as uneasy as she was at home in this hall. I saw her smiling to those she walked with, and saw their answering smiles die when they met my eyes.

Never had I felt at once so out of my element and yet so accustomed. Surrounded by the horde of angry faces, the accusing eyes, I could have been in the court of Heddred, with our eyes to the throne and the dislike hanging in the air like mist. We were outsiders here, as we had ever been—being in the retinue of a merchant-made-noble.

Familiar, yes. And yet here, we did not understand the laws that bound us. There was a bargain to be made, and we would have been at a loss even if one of our allies were not playing his own game. I felt the skin on the back of my neck prickle, and wanted nothing more than to take Miriel's hand and run. Fidach had always been so kind, hadn't he? And now he was lying to us, and not—it seemed—for the benefit of the Cornovii. Instinct told me to flee, and instinct told me to trust him, and I did not know what to do. I stared ahead at the backs of my fellow emissaries, and knew what Temar would say: *play only those games you must. If this is a loss, then run from it.*

"So." Branwen took her throne and stared down at us. "I sent my army to the Morini, and they returned with emissaries— emissaries, I am told, who ask for peace. Is this so?"

"It is, your grace." Miriel's voice was perfectly accented.

"Morwen told us that Aoife might ask for peace." Branwen's grey eyes found the woman in white, who nodded silently. "Does she fear battle, then?"

"Your grace, my uncle once told me that any wise ruler fears to unleash war on their people, for war is as a fire that will escape its hearth and burn all in its path." I had seen Miriel bridle at the suggestion of magic, but she held her tongue and spoke clearly.

"A wise ruler should then bring the battle to their enemy's home, then, and leave their own untouched," Lugh said, and Branwen shot him a look. There was much in that look, love and frustration all tumbled together. I began to fear that I had been correct—that Lugh was the consort. The gods help us all if he had Branwen's heart, this changeable man.

"My uncle," Miriel said, breaking the moment, "would have told you that a ruler who begins war lights fires also in his own court."

"Your uncle seems a wise man," Branwen said, with a quelling glance at Lugh when he opened his mouth.

"Perhaps. But he showed me as well," Miriel said delicately, "that ambition is another flame that may burn out of control."

"Indeed." At last, a flash of humor. "So, emissary, place before us the case of Aoife of the Morini, that we may decide if we find her plea worthy."

A slight nod from Fidach, and Miriel moved forward gracefully. She might have been preparing to step into the whirl of a pavane, for she was as light on her feet as a dancer.

"Queen Branwen of the Cornovii," Miriel said formally. She had practiced the words of the address with Fidach on our ride, and I had often looked over in the evenings to see her

———

staring fixedly at the fire. There was no private room on the ride, for her to test the tilt of her head and the set of her shoulders, the expression on her face—but she had whispered the words, over and over again. We could afford no mistakes, Fidach said, and it was sensible advice for peace negotiations. Enough, barely, for us to trust him on what to say at this audience.

"I am Miriel, of clans DeVere and Celys, and of a land long since lost beyond the mists of Priteni. I am bound by debt to Queen Aoife of the Morini, but would serve her gladly for love alone. It was she who gave shelter to me and to my kin when we had nothing. Now, by her request, in the view of all ages and of the gods, I come to be her voice.

"My queen would have me tell you that she has no wish for war—nor does she wish simply to avert battle. It is long since time that the rift between the two kingdoms was healed."

"I see." Branwen's face, which had been open, was now like stone. "And to what does Aoife credit this sudden revelation? For all her reign, her soldiers have harried my folk when we dared venture into the midlands. She has not offered us an end to our exile...not until we rode on Dun Druim. So, tell me, emissary, what has changed her mind?"

"I am new to these lands, your grace. I cannot claim to know the truth of my own queen's mind—I can tell you only that she sees devastation in war, come to both our peoples."

"To her own, you mean." Lugh's voice was harsh. "Aoife sends you to bargain against a war she cannot win. Tell me, emissary from a far-off land, why should we not take what is rightfully ours?"

"Because the Morini are both enemy and kin to you," Miriel said simply. I felt myself smile. Had she not cried those words to me in despair the night before? And now she turned it to her advantage. "The line dividing the kingdoms cannot erase the obligations of blood, nor can the half-clans of either Cornovii or Morini lay whole claim to the lands in the east. To set our armies at each other's throats would be to ask kin to kill kin."

"Hmm." Branwen settled back in her chair. "And what say you, Gwydion?" The question was sudden and sharp, and Fidach raised his head, startled. He paused to choose his words.

"In the spirit of friendship between our people, I think a truth must be spoken that we would all gladly forget: in the last war, kin did kill kin. Blood debts are owed now that can never be repaid. The Morini drove your people into harsh exile, your grace, but was it not the Cornovii who slaughtered three hundred at the Battle of Cathair Reul?"

"And the Morini who killed as many on the road to Abhainsal," Branwen said readily.

"And the Cornovii whose archers sought out the unarmed in their flight from Dun Sragh. Shall we go on, your grace? I cannot tell you that our home is not fairer, that our soil is not richer—for it is. But if we call each other to account for the crimes of our past before we make peace, we will all be dead of blood debt."

I did my best not to cast Miriel a quick look. These were not the words of a man trying to turn on his own people. Surely they were not. Was this a plot between Fidach and his mother to sow discord in the Morini court? Or was this all a show, a pretense at seeking peace while he turned on all of us?

"Honestly spoken." Branwen had no such reservations. Her eyes had found Morwen's, and whatever she saw there, she nodded slightly. She sank her chin onto one fist and studied us. "And you? The third emissary, who reminds us of a shadow, who says nothing and watches everything. What say you?"

I swallowed hard. I had not been prepared to speak, and with the eyes of all upon me, my heart pounded. I could not afford to ruin the peace negotiations before they were begun. As Fidach had, I took a moment to compose myself.

"Your grace, I am Catwin. I have no clan, and would have no kin but for my oath of fealty to the Lady Miriel. I am no politician, your grace, but I can tell you that I have seen my fill of war. I have known the fear of the powerless when kings fight, and I would see a world without it."

Branwen's eyes found Morwen again, who nodded. She plainly believed in Morwen's powers, but I knew it would not have taken magic to hear the pain in my words.

"Interesting," Branwen said. She looked at the three of us, and her face was unreadable. "We judge that your offer is made in good faith, and we agree to bargain with you. Perhaps you can guess the conditions of our peace."

"I would not presume, your majesty." Miriel looked at Branwen gravely. "The years have bred misunderstanding. To assume would be disrespectful."

The whispers flowed, and I thought I saw Lugh's lips tighten. It was as with the Lady, I thought—Miriel's mother. The woman had so hated me that nothing would satisfy her but my destruction. No action Miriel could take would endear her to the queen's consort, lest it be to fail utterly.

"Very well." Branwen pitched her voice to carry. "You have seen the land of our exile, emissary. We have made our home here, but we will accept no peace unless our people may farm the midlands."

"I hear your demand." Another evasion, as Fidach had advised her. "We will respond on the morrow."

"We seek also to fell lumber in the forests to the east." At this, Lugh looked sharply at Branwen, but her eyes did not waver from Miriel's.

"Indeed, your grace." Miriel had noticed the sudden tension in the hall, but she was too clever to acknowledge it until she knew what it meant.

"Very well, then." Branwen's voice was smooth and kind, but there was steel in it. "You shall bargain with our emissaries, and see if we can reach an accord."

She smiled, and Miriel curtsied, but three hundred soldiers stood at our backs, and the word hung in the air.

If.

Chapter 11

Our rooms were small and dim. A peat fire sputtered in a small hearth, opening into both rooms to spread its meager heat. Old cloth hung in the windows to protect us from the damp, but even so the stones dripped and the air was chill. Miriel was shivering violently, and though we were not coughing yet, I knew the air would be good for none of us to breathe.

Creaking ropes held up the straw pallets on our beds, and the old woolen blankets were at once fiercely itchy and not quite warm enough. The tiny bedroom, at least, meant that we would be close to the fire, even if the smoke made us cough.

Miriel looked over at me, and I knew she was thinking of the diplomats' quarters in Penekket: sunlit rooms of marble with finely wrought iron braziers and crystal lanterns, velvet window hangings in deep blues with golden thread. There were brocade couches to sit upon, priceless bowls holding fresh fruit and sweet rolls, and hot baths in copper tubs. In Heddred, such rooms as this would go only to the lowliest servants.

"Are they making a point, do you think?" Miriel asked softly. "Or is this truly the finest they have to offer?"

"Dun Beal was only built within the last two generations, and all they have is stone and driftwood." Fidach dragged his fingers between two of the stones. "They've used straw in the mortar. They'll have nothing in the way of treasures or finery. If I guessed, I would say Branwen lives much like this."

"You are certain?"

"It is not so different from how we all once lived." Fidach looked almost amused, but I detected a hint of pricked pride. "Stone huts, straw roofs. It is not, perhaps, a *courtly* life, but it is enough. When you have food, anyway."

"She said they wanted lumber," Miriel said contemplatively, having had the good sense to extricate herself from the prior topic. "For houses, d'you think?"

"Not very likely." Fidach settled into a chair by the fire. It was a well-made piece, if old, cut high at the back to hold the heat. We seated ourselves in the other chairs and I looked to Fidach, who was staring into the flames.

"So what for?"

"That, I cannot say. These halls are not luxurious, but they are enough. There is ample stone, or she would be requesting the quarries. Lumber, though... It isn't fuel they want, for they have peat. I would think fields would be her greatest request. And flocks. Lumber makes no sense to me, unless it is a bargaining chip to make the rest seem better by comparison. The main thing..."

"What?" I asked, when his voice dropped off, and he shrugged.

"They're dying here. This place is killing them. It is a crueler exile than I ever imagined."

"And so?" Miriel asked, her voice light. Her jaw was set, she did not intend to give way to sentiment now.

"Branwen must know that. Lugh will know it. I think he would resolve it by taking our lands forcibly, and he only brought us to bargain because he knew Branwen would want that. So the question is....what does Branwen want?"

"You have an idea," Miriel observed.

"Better lands," Fidach said promptly. "She knows they can't survive here much longer. I assume she will ask for the midlands, and then she will have to move the court—it would be foolish to leave her people within striking of us, and have her here, so far away. Lumber. She wanted lumber..."

"Lugh did not like it that she asked," Miriel observed. "We must find out why. Perhaps tonight, while we are at the banquet..."

"Oh, no," I said when she looked over at me. "No, we don't want to do this."

"Do what?" Fidach asked.

"Catwin, it's the only way."

"I was made to spy on *nobles*," I said desperately. "Nobles in Heddred! I'm not a servant here, I can't just wander about and pretend to bring food or carry messages. I can't slip away in the middle of a banquet. And I can't spy on them. Miriel, look at these people."

"Yes, look at them." Miriel was implacable. "They're hungry and they're cold, and if we bring them back to the Morini—don't interrupt me, Fidach—then they will have what they want. But we must get past Lugh first."

"You want to make them Morini?" Fidach demanded, as soon as she had gone quiet once more.

"It's really the only way this will work. Think ahead. You said they would need to move into the midlands. If we give them fields on Morini land, they will be closer to us than to their leader. As you say, Branwen would move the court, and for what? So the two courts can sit more closely, spitting insults at one another? Could we not simply make them Morini instead? One throne, one queen?" Fidach only looked at her, and Miriel tilted her head. "Don't you think your mother would be pleased if we reunited the tribes?"

"Only if she still ruled them. I warned you: you may have to choose between peace, and my mother's throne."

"Give them a war both you and your mother claim you cannot win—why, you will not tell me, but you insist on it—and your mother's throne will not be secure then, either."

"You agreed to bargain for it."

"Do *you* want that?" Miriel asked him bluntly. "You, who will never take the throne even if your mother keeps it? Is this what you want, her power over peace?"

"It isn't *about* what I want," Fidach hissed. His eyes were narrowed. "It hasn't even been about what I want. I want not to be whispered about by my own tribesmen, I want peace, I want not to live in the shadows—but I am bound to my mother's line by honor and blood. What I want has nothing to do with this."

He pushed himself out of his chair and strode to the door.

"Where are you going?"

"To the banquet, where we all should be." His eyes were like chips of ice. "You swore an oath, cousin. We all did. What we want is of no concern."

He was gone, and Miriel shed her cloak with a regretful shiver. I watched her while she moved. I knew that faraway look. Miriel had learned to pay attention to things others might not notice: stray words, strange inflections.

"What do you think?" I asked her, as I held open the door, and she looked at me almost blankly.

"I'm almost starting to think he's telling the truth about all of it. You remember my uncle, Catwin—with him it was always oaths and honor and truth. But they were weapons to him, tools. When Fidach speaks about it...he means something different."

"Different how?" Our feet carried us towards the roar of a crowd. Flickering torches lit the halls, and we walked single file to avoid them.

"I don't know. We keep hearing more, and the more we hear, the less clear all of it is. We're missing something, Catwin. Something important."

"We'll figure it out," I said, with more confidence than I felt. "We always have."

I shook my head for silence when she opened her mouth. The great hall was before us, hundreds of citizens who might hear our words, see our fear. Fidach waited in the doorway, a dark shape, his face unreadable. Miriel hesitated, but only for a moment: her chin came up and her smiled flickered to life. Her hair, even brushed out only with her fingers, gleamed in its curls.

"You will be a shadow, then?" she asked me, as we drew close to her cousin.

She had trapped me with my own words, but there was no triumph in her gaze. She stopped at the doorway to the great hall and stared up at me. I saw fear, true fear. Miriel was often angry, fiery, passionate. Fear was rare.

"This isn't *like* Heddred," I told her. "We aren't your uncle's servants anymore. We don't have his protection."

"We need something," Miriel said, and I could have sworn there was desperation in her eyes. "Information, anything. Please, Catwin."

"I can't just spy on them," I hissed.

"You'll need to," Fidach said, to my surprise. "Lugh is too changeable to trust, and most of them have no interest in peace—you've seen that. Peace treaties are not made with logic alone. If you want peace, you'll need to find someone in this court who supports it. Someone who will make Branwen agree to leave my mother on her throne. Whoever knows more secrets about their enemy, wins."

"What if we can't have everything your mother asked for?" Miriel asked him bluntly, and his face did not flicker.

"Then we will be returned to our lands, and the war will begin. My mother's signature is needed for any treaty. Unless you can think of a way..." His voice trailed off and I saw something flicker in his face. He cleared his throat. "Come. Drink little, and speak no more than you have to. Catwin, do not try to leave until after the banquet is over. They will notice."

He turned to smile and lift his hand in greeting as we walked through the doorway. On the dais, Branwen and Lugh lifted their mugs to us, and gestured to three seats, split along the length of the table: one at Branwen's side, one at Morwen's, and one at Seiysell's. I noticed then, for I had not, before, the glint of Seiysell's eyes, the arch of her nose. Branwen and Lugh's child, I would stake money on it—and so Lugh had children by the queen, and his place on the dais was not simply for his rank as emissary. Branwen had chosen a party as bound to her as we were to Aoife.

I sat next to Seiysell and tried to manage a smile. When she poured something into my mug from a flask, my eyes nearly watered from the smell of it.

"Whiskey," she said mischievously. "Never had it?"

"Er..." I had, and all of a sudden I knew why Fidach had advised us to drink little. The people of Priteni did not drink smooth wines, light and sweet on the tongue. They did not drink port, or even brandy. No, they drank whiskey, and it made my throat burn and my head spin. I lifted my mug and took a cautious sip, hearing Seiysell's laugh when I choked on the drink.

I watched the crowd. Mercifully, banquets in Priteni did not seem to involve speeches, but toasts were exchanged between tables, and one or two proposed by Branwen and Seiysell at ours. For all her easy good humor, Seiysell kept a sharp watch on the hall itself.

"You're not even going to ask, are you?" She appraised me.

"About what?" I asked, my heart sinking.

"About the treaty. About your chances."

"I thought—" I stumbled over my words, and then found an excuse. "I was perhaps mistaken. In my land, it would be rude of me to ask you while you ate."

"Hmm." She looked at me, nonplussed. "And what would you like?"

"To be able to go home and sleep in my own bed," I said promptly. I might not have Miriel's skill in conversation, but I had learned a bit by watching her. Seiysell laughed, but her eyes were still watchful. I quieted, and looked down into my glass. "Truly. Truly, that is what I want. I wish I could find words to make people forget, on both sides."

"Ah, yes." Seiysell looked down into her mug. "You're not from Priteni."

"No. So I suppose I don't understand. Anyway, that's what I want."

"Peace," Seiysell said, and there was a hint of bitterness in her voice. "You really want it. Well, I wish you luck with my family, then. You don't understand who stands in your way, and honor forbids me to tell you—but it isn't who you think."

She spoke little for the rest of the meal, her eyes fixed on the crowd, turning her head every so often to listen to Branwen and Lugh speaking with Miriel. I saw her appraisal, detached, and the near complete dismissal of the crowd below. Few looked up at the high table, and fewer still seemed to watch Miriel. What did it say that the common folk did not have any interest in the peace delegation?

I knew exactly what it meant. But was that what Seiysell spoke of when she told me that I did not know who opposed us?

"So?" Fidach asked, as we walked back to our rooms. Guards trailed us at a discreet distance, but Fidach kept his voice low. He held his arm out for Miriel to hold. A beautiful family, I thought: Miriel like a little doll in her perfection, Fidach fair and handsome. One would have to know them both to see the faint irritation in the set of her head, and the tension in his mouth when he looked at her.

"So we need to know more," I said glumly. "Seiysell as

much as admitted Lugh doesn't want peace. Him, and other people. She said someone here opposes us."

"She might be wrong," Miriel said, an attempt to cheer me.

"She's not," Fidach muttered. "You heard him."

"He's only one of three delegates." I could hear Miriel's irritation in her tone, and I held back a sigh. The last thing we needed was to be fighting amongst ourselves.

"We should go to sleep," I told her, and I tried to smile. This was not the same, I told myself. This was nothing like Heddred. This was for a cause we believed in. This was not the idle games of nobles, but a war that could destroy two tribes. "We'll need our rest if we're going to persuade Lugh."

I lay still in my bed as I watched her fall into a fitful sleep, and turned my head slowly to watch Fidach's chest rise and fall in the sliver of moonlight that came through the shredded drapes. Fidach, who seemed so innocent while he slept.

I pushed myself up on my elbow cautiously, and took the time to study his face at last, while he might not see me. His breathed slowly, deeply, and his full mouth settled into a calm I had never seen from him before. Seeing him at rest now, I realized how guarded he had always been—even sitting by his mother's throne, even when he walked alone outside the gates of Dun Druim.

Now, asleep, he looked not so much angry as afraid. I knew the lines cruelty made in a face, and I did not see them.

Ally or enemy, I did not have time to wonder. I pushed myself out of bed and made my way carefully across the floor, avoiding the creaking boards I had noted as I first paced out the room. *Always know your surroundings.* I kept saying I was no shadow, and yet Temar's voice was echoing in my head. I hesitated, but my body seemed to move without my own volition. I leaned close to listen at the door, for the clank of armor or weapons, or the shift and breath of a guard. Nothing.

I lifted the latch and slipped out of the room.

Chapter 12

A castle never truly sleeps—Temar taught me that. In the deep hours of the night the watchmen may gamble and the kitchen maids doze, but there is no true safety in the night for a Shadow, for its very silence and stillness are a trap. The single footstep upon a stair, the glimpse of a blonde head or a family crest on livery, may be seen that much more easily. If one spies in the night, one must do so carefully.

One must also spy for good purpose, and I wondered what I could hope to find here. My task in Heddred had been to watch anything and everything, preparing myself for confrontation that might never come. I was trained to notice and remember even the smallest things, and I had the luxury of time—the long game of marriage and children and thrones. Here, I had little time, and no way to coax out the secrets I might otherwise have won from servants with smiles and a shared place in the world.

A quick journey to the great hall found it dark and silent. The stillness meant there would be no indiscreet, drunken tongues wagging. This was not a land where the lords sat long over dinner and the servants snuck the carcasses away to sell in the city. The lords went home early, to homes as meager as their peasants had, on bellies nearly as empty. A long, slow look around the hall showed it to be a much more pleasant placed when there was no one here.

Pleasant was useless to me. A spy seeks discontent and strife above all, for they expose pride and thwarted desire, and those in turn promise mistakes. And where to find discontent and strife in this unfamiliar, silent court?

I sank into the shadows as a patrol came through, a man and woman clearly accustomed to finding nothing on their rounds. I snatched a quick glance and then settled into stillness, eyes closed so they would not gleam in the darkness. The paired footsteps receded, but I stayed still to ponder my next move.

Wandering aimlessly was as good a plan as any. A silver ring in my pocket would be my excuse if I was found: I had dropped it in the great hall, the only souvenir of my dead father, and after I had found it, I could not find my way back to my rooms.

The great hall sat directly off the courtyard and the stables, and the castle formed an immense ring around both hall and stable yard. I made my way quickly across the hall from our wing, and peered both ways. Turning right would bring me towards the stables, I was relatively sure, and turning left would bring me to the back of the castle, lying furthest from the road. There, unless the Cornovii built differently from all others, would be the royal family.

Perhaps I should have listened to the little voice that told me this was a bad idea, the voice that told me to go back. I could curse myself now to think how blind I was. *You don't understand who your enemy is*, Seiysell said, and there had been no malice in it—but the words wormed within me nonetheless.

Tell them they don't know who they're dealing with, either, I might have said, but that would be pride, and Temar had taught me never to tip my hand. Never warn the enemy, he would say, and what if the enemy was Seiysell herself?

I shook my head and tried to keep my eyes open and my thoughts on the task at hand. Fidach seemed to be correct: these corridors were no richer than those where we were housed. The walls were the same rough hewn blocks, and below my feet was not even the meanest carpet, but instead straw. Whatever luxuries Branwen might have in her chambers—and I wondered if there were any at all—she walked from her throne to her rooms each night through a potent reminder of her people's poverty.

I walked quietly out of habit, studying the hallway for points of egress and hiding places. After so many years away from Penekket I felt faintly ridiculous, but I could no more stop observing than I could stop breathing. I was glad I had done so, for angry words rose behind me with flurry of footsteps, and I took off like a frightened rabbit. I only just managed to wedge myself behind the sparse cover of a weapons stand before Lugh and Branwen came around the corner.

"They are liars," Lugh hissed through his teeth. "Do you not trust your own truthseer? Was that not why you sent her with us?"

"I *sent* her to fight the prince if need be, not so that you could twist her words and start a war!" Branwen stopped in a whirl of skirts and crossed her arms, and Lugh turned back to her angrily.

"You sent me with soldiers."

"As a show of force! A precaution. You heard the prophecy as well as I did. If that man had any training—"

"He didn't," Lugh said curtly.

"Even Morwen didn't know that," Branwen snapped, and Lugh lifted his shoulders in an angry shrug. "What do you want me to say?"

"I want you to understand the danger you're in. That you won't be fooled. She nearly fooled *me*, the one with the dark hair."

"She's polished through and through, but surely that is no reason to distrust her. Her desire for peace seems sincere."

"Seems, yes!" Lugh leaned close to her and Branwen stepped back when he might have reached out to take her hands. She lifted her chin, and Lugh fell to pacing. "She *seems* pleasant. She seems ready to offer us the world, doesn't she? And the prince seems to be an honorable man. But who sent them? Ask yourself that."

"Well, you're proof enough that a courtier and a queen need not share all opinions," Branwen said acidly, and I bit back a laugh.

"Why will you not heed me?" Lugh demanded of her, and any trace of humor vanished from her face.

"I might ask the same of you. I am your queen, and I sent you to save us from this place. I sent you to make a true peace. I strengthened your hand with bowmen and riders, for we agreed that this would need a show of force. But we agreed, too, that war was our last resort, did we not?"

Lugh looked away from her, and Branwen paced around

———

79

him, her hair gleaming red in the torchlight.

"We did," Lugh said at last.

"And you returned with more than we could have dreamed for a bargaining chip! Why do you insist on telling me there can be no peace when we hold Aoife's son in our castle, when their emissaries are so young and untried? Why do you think this is over when you have not held one day of negotiations? What poison has been put in your head?"

"It is no poison but truth, and I seem to be the only one who can see it! I am trying to save you, *your grace,* from making a terrible mistake."

"Here, now." The voice was cool and calm, and both Branwen and Lugh turned sharply to look. So consumed were they with their argument that they had not heard footsteps, but I had, and I tensed. Morwen stood behind them in her customary gown of white, her eyes appraising them coolly—and were she to look only a little farther afield, who knew if she might catch sight of me? Branwen and Lugh were too angry to have noticed me yet, but Morwen was calmer, and more dangerous for it.

Branwen recovered first. She bowed deeply.

"Gwydion."

"What's this?" Morwen looked on them both as if they were squabbling children.

"Talk some sense into your brother," Branwen ordered, and her voice echoed harshly off the walls.

"Would you please tell your queen that—" But the slam of a door cut off Lugh's words and he slumped against the wall.

"You were fighting?" Morwen asked delicately, as if she had not seen them in the thick of it. More a courtier than I had guessed, and now I was afraid. My legs were beginning to cramp, and I pressed my lips together in pain. I must not move, not even an inch.

"She's taken in by them," Lugh said, and his voice was full of muted anger. "You all are. So young, so earnest, so pretty. They're snakes, the lot of them."

"You seemed to like their chief emissary well enough when first you saw her." Morwen's eyebrow was raised, and Lugh shot her a look that was nothing short of venomous. "What can possibly have changed in a few days?"

"I liked her well enough before I saw what he was," Lugh growled. "Lying, *lying* to us in Glen Tuam, on sacred ground."

"She wad been bidden to lie. You can hardly fault her for doing as she was told by Aoife."

"I can't fault her for the words she speaks? She is an emissary, those words are her whole purpose. She was sent to bargain, and every word out of her mouth has been a pretty lie, presented with a smile, a curtsy—" His voice was thick.

"For the love of all gods, brother, what do you think her capable of? She's gone out of her way to bow to your demands. Her companion hardly does anything but bow, and the prince has been nothing but courteous. They've gone out of their way to put us at ease."

"Yes, exactly, lulling us into a false sense of security."

"Don't see shadows where there are none," Morwen advised him, and I felt a chill. "They left their army. They sent Aoife's only child. These three are young, they are seeing how we live. Surely you can show them what we need to survive."

"To survive! Is that what we have come to?"

"Yes." Her voice was like a whiplash. "It is all we can hope for. You are my brother and I have faith in you, but even you cannot gain us more than dregs from this."

"Is that what you see in your visions?" He was practically snarling now. "For they are wrong. You are wrong, to think so little of me."

Morwen sighed, and looked down at her hands.

"Forgive me. Perhaps it is only despair that speaks. I am growing old, Lugh. I have never seen anything but this life, this..." She took a deep breath. "But who knows. You may be the one who can achieve the impossible. And if the worst should happen, if it should all be a ploy, we have them hostage, all three of them inside our walls. And Dun Beal is strong, brother—there is no way in when the gates are closed."

It was the very worst thing she could have said. Lugh, whose face had calmed, was at once alert. Morwen had forgotten that she spoke to a warrior. His head would be spinning, as mine was—for was this not the perfect setup? All of them penned in

—

here so that their horses were no use, and three emissaries who might slip away to leave the gates open? But where I knew we had planned nothing of the sort, Lugh would have no such assurances. I cursed Morwen's foolishness in all the languages I knew, and even she saw what she had done.

"Lugh..."

"What? You will tell me not to worry after you have stumbled upon the perfect plan?"

"A perfect plan means nothing if it is not the plan they mean to use," Morwen said tentatively. "So Aoife is an oath breaker..."

"Yes, so she is! And you told me yourself the dark-haired one was lying. And the prince..."

"Is an ally worth cultivating," Morwen said. "Or might be, if you would stop scowling for a single moment, brother."

"If they attack us..."

"I should not have tried to speak with you. Go and sleep, and in the morning we will speak again." She swept away, and Lugh sighed, lifted the latch to the door of the rooms he shared with Branwen.

When he was gone, I crept out of hiding and gasped at the pins and needles in my legs. My escape must be swift, I reasoned, for Lugh had the look of a restless man to him. I eased out from behind the weapons rack, its rattle now overloud in the abandoned hall, and shot at once into the shadow of another doorway when Lugh wrenched the door open again to look up and down the hall.

"Who's there?" he called, and I froze with a breath half-drawn. If he walked down the hallway even a few steps, I was lost. "If there is someone spying..."

"Lugh." Branwen's voice was like ice, even as faint as it was from her room, and he cast an angry look over his shoulder before withdrawing.

I practically sprinted through the castle to my rooms, tumbling through the door and sinking to the floor, drawing deep breaths in as if I might drown. Never had I been so close to being caught, and so vulnerable with it. In that one terrified moment, saved by Branwen's ill temper alone, I had known that this was not worth it. No matter the discord I might see, no matter the mystery of Lugh's hatred, we would need to find another way forward.

The stakes were too high.

Chapter 13

Fidach and Seiysell were right, of course. Lugh had no intention at all of letting the peace talks succeed. Whenever Miriel tried to offer suggestions, the consort was quick to twist them. Whenever Fidach spoke, Lugh managed to remind Branwen that Fidach was living proof of Aoife's duplicity. When I did not speak, his glare to me told me that he was only waiting for his moment to strike at me.

"Why do we hear that the Morini are massing in the midlands?" he snapped, on the first day of negotiations.

"The midlands..." Miriel said thoughtfully, tapping her mouth. "The only reason I can think you would hear that, my lord, is that you sent scouts into Morini territory."

"It was necessary to know that we were not being followed. I would expect any treachery from your queen."

"Oh, indeed," Miriel agreed sweetly. "And now that you know the army is only waiting, and you are not being followed, surely we may proceed."

When Lugh narrowed his eyes, I bit my lip and Fidach shifted uncomfortably in his chair. Neither of us had Miriel's courage in negotiations. Where I would fear to interrupt, not wanting to give offense, Miriel slid her words like a dagger. Where I had seen Fidach turn conflict into a joke many times in the Morini court, poking fun at himself so as to lighten the mood, Miriel took the conflict and turned it back tenfold.

Morwen leaned over to murmur something in his ear. Her face was calm, and she smiled at us, but he bridled at her words instead of calming to them. His eyes narrowed as he surveyed us.

"Tell me this is not the first stage of a counter-offensive."

"It is not." Miriel inclined her head. "So long as we are kept safe and no further incursions are made into Morini territory, you have nothing to fear from our army."

"While your army waits, there can be no bargaining."

"Was this not begun when your army rode on Dun Druim?"

"It was begun by your queen's treachery. Until we have—"

"Were we not brought here to bargain in good faith?" Miriel snapped, and I saw Lugh smile to see her temper at last. He inclined his head.

"Yes. We did offer that."

"Seiysell did," Miriel corrected. "And after you've spent half the morning arguing that my petitions weren't presented in the correct verb tense, you've somehow managed to forget one thirds of your delegation. Go. Bring Seiysell. We will wait."

"Are you sure that you should have lost your temper?" I asked, as Lugh sent a runner to fetch his daughter.

"In this case, it seems there is nothing to lose. Morwen keeps trying to hold him back, I think, but even she can't manage it. He's determined."

"Don't say that. Branwen is pretending to be cold, but you're holding her interest. *She* thinks your suggestions are valid."

"Such negotiations are no time for whispers," Lugh said loudly. "You see, your grace? The pale one does not speak at all to us, only pours poison in the ear of the emissary."

"Why *do* you not speak, Catwin?" Branwen looked at me with interest. No doubt it was a fair question, from her perspective, but I could feel only resentment.

"Your grace, I was trained to protect, not to speak."

"You speak well enough to the envoy," Lugh observed. Branwen's eyes did not leave me. She nodded at his observation.

"If I misspeak to Miriel, it will cause no war."

Branwen smiled at that, but Lugh leaned forward, narrowing his eyes.

Are we sure she has no magical talent?" he asked Branwen, and her brows drew together.

"Of course I don't have magic!" I said, and the two of them looked at one another.

"Oh? For I hear you move without sound, appearing and disappearing in a blink. I hear you have been seen in the corridors like a shadow at night."

"And whence did you hear this, my lord?" Miriel inquired. "For it hardly seems like a warrior to be unnerved by rumors and whispers that a young woman can move quietly."

"She is sneaking about!"

"Is she? You say you hear this and that, but what proof have you that these are not your own rumors that *you* are pouring into her grace's ear like poison? Hardly a moment ago you suggested that it was magic, so that you might spark fear in her grace's heart. And yet, did you offer any proof then? No, for there was no proof to give. Shall I offer you a litany of the times such power might have helped her, and she did not have it at her disposal?"

"It is not beyond Aoife to send another mage into our midst. She is poison, that woman. She is an oath-breaker. She has no honor."

"And now you move to yet more accusations, without offering any proof of any you have yet given. My lord, either you seek to discredit us or you have run mad. For your sake, I will assume that it is the former."

"You hear her? She insults me." Lugh turned a scowl on Branwen.

"Both of you will cease your accusations," Branwen said flatly. "I will not have them here. It does us no credit."

Miriel was wise enough to stay quiet, but I saw her bridle at the injustice. Even Fidach shifted, uncomfortably, in his chair. When the door opened, it was the runner, returning alone.

"My lord, the lady Seiysell cannot be found."

"We will have to continue without her," Lugh said.

"We will not."

"Every moment that you delay, the Morini army draws closer!"

"You said yourself that your riders saw them stop at the midlands." Miriel's hands tightened on the arm of the chair. "It is not we who are delaying. We are the ones who have met and exceeded the requests of your queen."

"Who has betrayed the treaty," Morwen murmured, and Lugh smiled triumphantly at Miriel.

———

"You see? Aoife may never be trusted while she breaks the very treaty by which she keeps us imprisoned on these shores."

"A treaty we are willing to overwrite to free your people from this poverty. A good consort to the queen would perhaps think his people's safety and prosperity the most important thing."

"I do! I think of it always. And *you*—"

"Me!" Miriel flared up. "I am not Morini. I hold no blood debts to you, I am owed nothing. I stand neither to gain nor lose by whatever happens here, unless war claims my life. Catwin and I are your best hope for a fair treaty. I wish for peace!"

"It is certainly the envoy's wish for peace," said Morwen's voice, from the doorway. She looked nonplussed at Lugh's discomfort, but exchanged a small nod with Fidach.

"A peace which deprives us of vengeance," Lugh said, and Fidach's head came up.

"Yes. Vengeance. The same vengeance my mother withholds from her generals. The battles three generations back ended whole bloodlines. There is still debt on both sides, my lord. But while my cousin would see the debt wiped out with peace, you would see it wiped out with blood. And are you truly ready for the Cornovii to be called to account for their crimes?"

"What crimes we committed have been atoned for ten times over while our children starved!" Lugh's hand hit the arm of his chair. "And your kin sit in warm halls living a soft life, fed on crops from our fields and meat from our herds!"

"And so it is time to be ended! The fields will be *yours*, the herds will be returned to your families. But you do not want that, emissary. You want vengeance. And so I ask now: did you lie when you brought us here to bargain? Did you have any intention of allowing your queen to agree to peace?"

"He need not allow me to do anything," Branwen said, and her voice was like ice.

"To be queen is to be a captive," Miriel said. She spoke softly, but all eyes turned to her. "Lords always outnumber a monarch, and the common folk outnumber the lords. All it takes is desperation for the scales to tip. You know that your lords might not accept peace."

"We would be right not to do so," Lugh cut in. "What good has peace brought us?"

"This would be a different peace," Branwen suggested, and Miriel nodded.

"A peace forged in shared prosperity. What we have now is not peace, my lord—it is starvation and blood debt. We know that any true peace must be built on the safety of your people as well as the Morini."

It was an offer of friendship, and Morwen put her hand on his arm, looked into his eyes—but Lugh would have none of it.

"Listen to her lies. Do you think we will be so easily taken in?"

"She does not lie," Branwen opined, and Lugh turned a blazing look on her.

"You cannot see it. You will not see it. And you always thought me short-sighted."

Brother," Morwen said gently, and Miriel and I exchanged a quick look. That Lugh was Branwen's consort, we had known. Morwen was another matter. "Your suspicion is well-earned, and no one can doubt Aoife's lies, but the woman who sits before you is no Morini, and the prince has made true offers of friendship."

"You are blinded by his talent," Lugh shot back. "And by her charm. Ask yourself why she has a bodyguard—an assassin who has been sent to kill kings. You saw that in her past."

"I was not sent," I said. "If you knew the story, you would know that the man was no king himself, but an oath-breaker who defied his king. He was leading his army to their deaths as well as the death of our people. And I did not kill him even so."

Truth, and yet it was not enough.

"Look well on those they send to bargain with us," Lugh said, and his finger shook as he pointed. "A half-breed who is living proof of Aoife's treachery, a temptress who speaks in riddles, and an assassin. How can you trust them?"

"This is the man you send for your peace envoy?" Miriel asked Branwen baldly. "A man who will not listen even to his own truthseer?" Her own thoughts on magic, she had set aside. *All that matters is that they believe it.* She would use it to twist the knife.

"I will not stand here to be insulted." Lugh stood and disappeared in a swirl of his grey cape, and Miriel stared after him thoughtfully.

"We will resume on the morrow," Branwen told us.

"And if Lugh will not bargain?"

Branwen appraised Miriel coolly.

"You may think me a fool for choosing Lugh," she said. "Lovestruck, you would say, perhaps? But I chose him for a purpose. You speak to me of peace and I would like to believe you—that is my weakness. Lugh, though he seems set against you now, has ever been fair and just. Morwen, I sent to temper him, and Seiysell, to remind him what he bargains for. Any peace you make, bargained for by those three, will be an answer to the decades of suffering the Cornovii have endured. Remember that, emissary. This will not be painless for you." She stood and swept to the edge of the room, but turned with her hand on the door hangings. "And remember. You may not wish to force Aoife's hand, but the treaty is clear."

Miriel sat very still as the Cornovii left the room. Her blue eyes were looking into the distance, and her jaw was set; I could see her trembling. One curl had tumbled free of her upswept hair and it lay delicately on her neck.

"I'm not sure we can do this," she said finally.

"Find the key to what Lugh wants..." Fidach suggested lightly, and Miriel shook her head.

"If we give him that, he will only find something else. Did he not say his people were starving? And yet he will not take the fields. He makes no sense, first saying one thing, then another. After today, I almost think the only thing that would satisfy him is if we all put our heads on the block."

"Perhaps." Fidach gazed after the queen and her consort.

"What we need is for Lugh to fall," Miriel said to me in Heddrian, not trusting the open doorways.

"What we *need* is for the court not to listen to him. Make him a martyr, and you fan the flames."

"He's fanning the flames as it is."

"Then we take their resolve. Morwen and Branwen:

—

89

they're the keys." I switched back to Pictish, pausing to consider my words so that Fidach could understand and none outside the room could. "And there may be more. Not all the court desires war," I said. "They cannot. It is not possible. We need to give them a voice."

Chapter 14

A solution should have been easy enough to find. Between the three of us, we were able to watch the court, compare our stories, share what Morwen or Lugh or Seiysell might have let slip, or what we'd heard from a chambermaid in the hall. A division might have been easy to find, were we not so divided ourselves.

"They're hiding something, all of them, every one of them," Miriel paced around the room. She was shivering violently, even with the blanket wrapped around her shoulders, and in the nights, I could hear her coughing.

"You distrust everyone you meet, don't you?" Fidach asked wearily from his place by the fire.

"You have not lived as I have."

"Well, you have not lived here!" Fidach glared at her. "Why must you insist on believing that this is Heddred? It isn't."

"And this isn't some bickering at a winter feast!" Miriel shot back. "It's not a dispute over a bauble, it's survival. Lugh's playing to destroy the Morini. If Seiysell hadn't stopped him, he would have left us at Glen Tuam and gone for Dun Druim."

"So tell Branwen you want Lugh removed as emissary."

"Haven't you been listening?" Miriel demanded. "It won't help. Branwen wants something as well, and for all I've thought, I can't figure out what it is. I've offered land, lumber, safe passage to both, I've all but given her the keys to Dun Druim and she won't do more than glance at the treaty. Seiysell's young, but she's intelligent, and she's passionate—and that's dangerous. I don't know which way she could swing. And Morwen..."

"What of Morwen?" The defensiveness in Fidach's voice was plain to hear. "She has taken your side against Lugh every time. She sees the truth of your words, and yet you doubt her."

"She looks at me like I'm already dead!" Miriel burst out. "She stares and stares, like she's seeing a ghost."

Fidach swallowed and looked down, and I took note of the tension in his shoulders, the white lines by his mouth. Miriel took one disapproving glance and swept to the table, where her notes—in Heddrian, for what little protection it afforded us—were spread out over the table. I watched her push aside pages and pages of lineage, her memories of the Morini court and what we had managed to learn of the Cornovii lords. Beyond that lay her observations, tiny facts she had gleaned about those who influenced the court.

"Who's that?" I asked, and Miriel shrugged.

"Cadman? One of Lugh's brothers. The other is..." I saw her look away from the paperwork deliberately, trying to test her memory. "Talyn. Cadman is a warrior, has two children, but that hardly matters, none of them are in line for the throne. Talyn is unwed. Lugh doesn't like to talk about him, that's all I know."

"Aeden?"

"Seiysell's twin. Likes music. No contender for the throne. The next in line beyond her is probably Bran, and he's only eleven."

"Connor's twelve," I reminded her, and she shrugged.

"Seiysell is Branwen's favorite in any case. She's very....light-hearted. Always laughing with someone. It reminds me of court."

"She hardly speaks during negotiations," I said softly. Seiysell rarely appeared, apparently busy with her training as a soldier and her duties as heir, but when she did, she sat quietly, her eyes flicking between all of us as if she would learn the secrets of bargaining.

"Which means she's either a coward, or clever." Miriel narrowed her eyes at the lists. "She hardly speaks at all, and Morwen spends so much time trying to calm Lugh that she hardly speaks to us, either. Talyn is one worth cultivating. We need a way to seek him out."

"You could ask to meet him," Fidach suggested acidly.

"And why would an emissary ask to meet members of the consort's family?" Miriel asked. Her eyebrow was lifted.

"Surely you could come up with something. Being so

---

clever about court life."

"What I need is time," Miriel said promptly. "I need months and months spent watching this court so that I can pick my moment and align the players perfectly. So that no one sees what I am doing."

"Well, you don't have that. As I pointed out to you earlier."

"You were the one who told us to look for secrets, were you not?"

"These aren't secrets, they're bargaining chips. They're giving you nothing so you give more and more. We could consider simply asking Branwen what she wants. Bypass Lugh entirely."

"Wouldn't that be a breach of etiquette?" Miriel asked, and Fidach laughed, not warmly.

"No more than sneaking around after the emissaries' families. Family, I guess. Lugh's done well for himself."

"And it looks like he's willing to use all of it for this war," Miriel said softly. "If I had to guess, I would tell you he's planning to march."

"What?" Fidach asked, startled out of his chair.

"He doesn't want peace at all. He's blocking our suggestions, but offering nothing in return. We can all see that. But what's the endgame? Even he must wonder. If it's not peace, it's war, and if it's war, he needs to make the first move. Your mother moved troops to the midlands. He needs something to top that."

"No." Fidach moved for her urgently. "No, you can't be serious. He wouldn't—I mean, it's...it wouldn't be done."

"It's what I would do," Miriel said simply, and Fidach stared at her.

"You'd truly do it, wouldn't you? If my mother had sent you to destroy them—"

"If she'd asked it, I would have asked a great many questions as to how she could justify killing civilians," Miriel snapped. "I am not a monster, Fidach. But it's different for Lugh. It's different when your people are starving. I'd never advise him to do it, but at least he has a reason."

"It wouldn't work," Fidach said.

"We should probably plan for it," I opined. "Find a way to get a message back if we need to."

"It's not going to happen," Fidach said flatly. "That's all. It would be to break all rules of warfare among the tribes, and more than that—my mother has time to prepare and pick her battleground. The Morini will have scouts, will be spread across the border."

"So?"

"So, to defeat them, Lugh would need information. The sort of information only one of the lords would have. Something to show him where she's weak."

"Do you have that information?" Miriel asked, and any shred of good humor died in his face.

"What are you suggesting?" he asked coldly, and Miriel cross her arms over her chest defiantly.

"They're all kind to you. They seek your company out. They ask questions, don't they? Friendly questions, I have no doubt. Morwen, so trustworthy. Seiysell, so young. Even Branwen asks things that *might* mean nothing."

"And you think I would just tell them our secrets?" Fidach demanded. "That is what you think of me?"

"I think you have no idea the game they're playing!" Miriel whispered back, her eyes darting to the door. "You like to pretend that intrigue is something only Heddrians play at, but it's in this court, too, and you're out of your depth."

"You're seeing enemies where there are none," Fidach ground out. "You're *making* enemies."

"I'm keeping you safe!"

"Can't we just come up with a plan?" I asked, and they both snapped their heads around to look at me, the same straight nose, the same set to their mouths. "Miriel, Fidach is a warrior, he knows well enough what not to say. Fidach, Miriel's worry in Seiysell and Morwen is...well-placed."

"And her worry in me?" Fidach demanded.

"Is also well-placed," Miriel spat out, before I could try fix it. I shot her a glare, and she glared right back. "Oh, don't be so soft, Catwin. He has to learn sometime."

"I am not a child," Fidach shot back, and I sank my face

into my hands.

"Listen, both of you." I took a deep breath and gathered my courage. "A plan and a failsafe, that's all we need. The sooner we're done with this, the sooner we can return to Dun Druim and you two never have to speak to one another again. Until then..."

"Until then, Fidach will watch his tongue and trust our enemies less."

"Our enemies! When did it become our enemies? You're not Morini. You're bargaining away things my mother's lords will never accept."

"Then tell me what they *will* accept, if you know so much. Give me the treaty that will resolve this! Or leave us in peace, to make our own plan."

They glared at one another and I leaned with my back against the door, listening for spies outside and despairing of this. If we could not even trust each other, what could we trust? Fidach broke first. He bowed, a shallow motion, mocking in its courtliness and brevity alike, and then he pushed his way past me and out the door.

Chapter 15

I could not find him the next morning. He was not in our room, nor in the great hall to break his fast. Lugh claimed not to have seen him, and invited me to go search for my friend. His narrowed eyes and oversweet words told me that it was a challenge. No matter what the others said, Lugh would always be convinced that it was me he had heard in the hallway all those days past.

I had no interest in arguing, not least because he was quite correct. I gave a quick bow and made for the stables, half-afraid Fidach had taken his horse and ridden for Dun Druim in his rage—although, I realized, that would at least make him loyal to Aoife.

Lugh had, I was sure, assigned people to follow me, but no one to help me search. Still, a piece of silver meant it was not difficult to find a guide, and a maid led me through the back halls. She did not speak, either when she accepted my coin or when we walked together, and I wondered at that. A maid might be expected to engage a noble visitor with coin—which was what I now realized, uncomfortably, I was. In Heddred, even in Dun Druim, a maid would be hopeful of another coin, offering the best cuts of meat at dinner, perhaps, or a secret about a lord.

Had she been told not to speak to the foreign retinue? Was she one of Lugh's servants, a woman who would hate me for my connection to the Morini? Or did she hold me responsible for her hollowed cheeks and her pale, meager life at the ends of the earth? She might well, and it galled me to think that it was not a poor assumption. Was I not well fed? Had I not profited from the fact that the Morini held the plains?

I did not know you lived like this, I wanted to tell her. *Until I saw your army on the horizon, I did not even know of the Cornovii.*

I did not say it. What would it change?

—

96

We traveled through corridors dim and dark, only slits in the heavy walls to guide us, and the very stones themselves seemed to seep cold. Almost I might think this was Dun Druim, left abandoned and without the glow of torches. The layout of the place was similar, corridors flanking the main hall, a wing of nobles' chambers, but this place was nothing but ruins, for all it was new.

The maid left me without a word at the stable doors, sketching a bare curtsy in my direction before leaving with the same, purposeful stride. She did not hurry, nor did she look back. I frowned at her retreating form, and pushed open the door to the stables.

Fidach was not there. His horse, a roan, stood stabled next to my own and Miriel's, and I felt my breath leave my body in a whoosh. Sighing with relief, I walked over to peer into her stall. Fidach was not seated in the hay, as I might have expected. His saddle and bridle shone rich against the salt-greyed wood of the stables, and a quick glance showed that our horses were by far the healthiest in the stalls, their ribs not showing through their sides. Fidach's mare tossed her head and whinnied at me.

"Where do you think he went, girl?" I stroked her nose and she snorted at me as if to wonder why I asked such a silly question. I hopped up over the wall and took a brush down from the wall. In the excitement, we had not stabled our own horses— and I expected they might prefer someone familiar.

I considered as I brushed. I was certain that Fidach had not gone to the hall. I realized now that unexpected depths lay behind those blue eyes. Fidach was not, perhaps, a man without ambition. He was a man who must be courted, carefully, in order to ensure his loyalty.

I struggled to frame my thoughts. Fidach was an enigma, a man I had avoided for his connection to the Duke. A small cruelty, I saw now, after the scorn of the court at Dun Druim. We had never had much to say to one another, it seemed to me. All very well for Miriel, his cousin and nobly born, but what could a servant, a woman with no family and no childhood and no place talk about with a prince?

In my haste to avoid any shadow of my former life, to shy

away from courting the favor of royalty and keep from remembering the cold eyes of the man I had killed, I had let a man of unknown mettle come close to me and to Miriel. No greed, we said to one another. He had no ambitions to the throne, we said to one another.

And I had never given him another thought. It was pride. It was foolish and dangerous and it would have killed me in a moment in Heddred—to think that such a man, so close to the throne, might have no ambition at all. For certain, Fidach might have been a man who was born without ambition at all, and yet a man kept forcibly from the throne was nearly certain to desire it in some measure. Had I not learned with Wilhelm, that those closest to power may see its ways and be drawn in even so? If I had paid attention to my own teachings, if I had watched more closely, I might know where he had gone. I might have an idea of what he intended.

I might know what he would do, when driven away by Miriel, when she might have verged on tipping her hand and telling him that she knew he was playing a deep game.

And if I had learned more about him, I might understand why I felt so conflicted in his presence, so drawn to his humor and openness, and so wary, now, since I had learned of his lies. I was reminded powerfully of my first days at Miriel's side, when I had been drawn to her and hated her equally. Only it was different with Miriel—she and I had ever been on the same side, kept together out of necessity. Fidach had nothing to fear.

You swore me an oath, Miriel reminded me, and I had run to teach her a lesson, or so I told myself. I had run, as well, so that I would not have to look at her and think on how deeply I had failed already. We came to a foreign court, hoping to broker peace against all odds, and I did not even know who rode with us.

Miriel, I reflected, was not helping.

"She didn't have to yell," I told the mare, and she flicked her tail at me. I opened my mouth to speak again, and jumped as a stable boy appeared silently beside me.

"She said you might be lookin' for someone." His words were accented strangely, but I could make them out. I nodded, and he flashed a smile. She, I took it, was the maid. I nodded, and he raised a brow at me in query. "The Morini prince?"

He made a gesture, instinctive, at the name of the Morini—and then flushed, embarrassed. A curse, I gathered, not so different from what the people of Heddred might do against a witch.

"Yes, the prince. Fidach." Always name the enemy, Temar taught me. People were much more apt to kill *the Prince, the Queen, the Duke*—but a name made it murder, a name made it real.

He nodded, waiting, and I flipped a piece of silver up to him.

"Went to the sea shore with Talyn."

"Talyn?" The name was vaguely familiar on my tongue, but I could not place it. The stable boy nodded.

"Aye, the consort's brother. You speak funny."

"Aye, I do," I said, mimicking his accent as I had learned long ago, and I saw his eyes widen at it. "And maybe if you take me to Fidach and Talyn, I'll tell you why." There was a chance he might push me off the rocks at Lugh's order, of course, but I did not judge it likely. Opportunistic, I had judged in the first moment of seeing him. Not malicious. Not an assassin. And indeed, as I had bargained, my story was too good to pass up. He beckoned me and I hoisted myself back over the wall.

"Should we ride?"

"There's no need, if ye're up for a climb." He led me out a side door, the horses whinnying their protest at our backs, and out to the walls. The guards watched us go with thinly veiled dislike, but no one moved to stop us. It occurred to me that Lugh might well have decided to keep us watched. Wait to see if we broke the rules. Miriel and I, I thought, must be very careful to follow Fidach's lead. If he had gone to see the shore... Well, I would have to trust that he knew what he was doing.

I would be watching Fidach very closely from now on. That much was certain.

The stable boy led me across a small plain of dirt and rocks, a few straggling pieces of grass being the only relief from brown and black. I thought of the perfectly-tended forest outside

Penekket, even of the fields of wildflowers that bloomed outside Dun Druim in the summer, and pressed my lips together. This land was buffeted by sea winds, the soil poor and sandy. How desperate would I be, if I had been raised here?

The air whistled eerily around me as we approached our protection from the sea: a great hulk of black rock, the peak of a gently sloped hill. Dun Beal nestled into the hollow of its peak, a castle of black against black rocks, and the lonely sound of the wind the only companion. I was reminded of Voltur, a castle maintained in the harshest lands, with few luxuries and ever-present cold; I shivered.

A path had been cut into the rock of the mountain itself, skirting around the edge. It was no easy climb, but a welcome diversion after days of riding. I chose my steps carefully, looking down so as not to force the stable boy to speech. If he had something to say, silence would bring it out.

"The lords say ye're here kill us all," he offered finally, and I took a moment to smile up at him.

"Our lords say the same thing about you." He laughed at that.

"For truth?"

"For truth. They told Queen Aoife you were not to be trusted, but she sent us anyway." He looked at me suspiciously and I held out my hands palm up. "I swear it."

"On your mother's honor?" he asked, with the drama of the young, and I tried to keep my face from flickering.

"I never knew my mother." Best to focus on that one small sadness, known for so long that I could not imagine a life without it. Best not to think of Roine, dying at my feet—and wonder if, at the end, she had found it in her heart to be grateful that I survived. "But I would swear to it if I did," I added, trying to keep my voice light.

"But what about the prince? Lugh said—" He broke off as we came over the rise and I gasped aloud.

Seashore, the stable boy said, and a shore there was, with dunes and grass waving in the wind. Gulls wheeled above, and the sea stretched away in a stormy grey-blue under thick clouds, but nothing beyond that was at all familiar. The shore lay far below, down a steep drop and across half a mile or more of sandy ground dotted with patches of grass and white flowers, and amongst the sand rose tall spires of black rock. Moss and lichen adorning their sides, and I even saw the nests of sea birds on their sheltered sides. It was as if pieces of the mountain had decided to stride, long-legged, into the sea. I could see spires out in the water, lapped at by waves, and toppled columns where the ceaseless lap of the tides had worn away the stone.

"Seven gods, that's beautiful."

"Seven gods?" the boy asked, and I frowned before I remembered. Threes were sacred in Priteni and so there were nine gods here, three of three; Maid, Mother, and Crone; Hunter, Mage, and Advisor; Life, Death, and Chaos—that last which some knew as luck, and others as cruelty.

"For my people, there are seven."

He watched me to see if I was joking, and I only smiled. At length, unnerved, he pointed at a small ledge below.

"There's your prince, then."

Fidach stood with his green cloak billowing back in the wind, the ornate hood pushed back and his head held high. At his side stood a man who must be Lugh's brother, Talyn. He was gesturing out at the water intently, and whatever he spoke of, he was passionate.

I would not have disturbed them, for to see Fidach listening instead of talking was to trust him a little more, but he turned his head and saw me. A word, and the man in white stopped talking. I made my way carefully down the steps, faintly slick with moss and recent rainfall.

"Did Miriel send you for me?" he asked neutrally, his face a polite mask. He did not want to expose our fight to the world, but I knew it might well be all over court before the night's end. Who knew who might have lingered outside our door, and heard raised voices?

"No," I said simply, no more inclined than he was to show a crack in our unity. "I came to find you. And to see the ocean as well."

We stood aside as the stable boy edged down to stairs and made for the ledge. I watched him peer cautiously down and shudder, then bow deeply to the man in white.

"What lies there?" I asked, and Fidach knew what I meant without looking. The only structure on the shore was impressive, indeed, a large wooden building with a dock stretching out into the water.

"Something we might be able to use," he said carefully. Then, as the wind shifted and our voices would not be heard, he spoke quickly, taking care not to lean forward and make it look as if we were trading secrets. "It is a passion of Talyn's, and Branwen's as well. Legend says there is an island far to the west, and they have made great boats to sail for it and see if they might establish a new home, away from the Morini—but it has been months since they launched the boats, and no one has returned. Lugh has never been in favor of the plan. He wishes only to retake what was lost."

"The lumber." My mind leapt into overdrive, and I looked back over my shoulder. "We must go tell Miriel."

"Must we." His look said he had no intention of doing so, and I sighed. Too much, too quickly; I must pretend that there was nothing to forgive, and no suspicion in my heart.

"I ask you to forgive her."

"Why should I?" A simple question, and one I could not answer well. I sat down on the steps and pondered the shore, uncomfortably aware of him watching me.

"You know, I hated her when I first met her," I said finally. "For months and months. And then off and on for years." He gave a snort of laughter.

"Really? I'd not doubt it to meet her, but you've always seemed...devoted."

"Really," I assured him.

"While you two were dancing and drinking and—what *did* you do in that court?"

"I...don't think you want to hear about all of it. I'm sorry. Maybe I shouldn't have mentioned it. But Fidach, here's the thing—she'll never betray the Morini. She would never turn the Morini over to slaughter. She'll fight for peace, just like she promised."

Miriel would have known if this was the right note to

play, I thought miserably. It seemed right to me, for if he was true to Aoife then he would find us agreeable, and if he was not, he would not think we were betraying the plan. But his face was set, I could get nothing from it.

"Yes," he said flatly. "She'll do what's right for them. I just don't think she knows what that means yet, the power she has."

"She's not one to abuse power, I promise."

"It not that, it's...not important. What's important is that she doubts me."

"She's afraid. We keep learning new things, the two of us. It's hard to believe there aren't more."

"I won't answer for my mother," Fidach said stubbornly, and I looked up at him in the shifting light.

"We're all here to answer for your mother." *And maybe for you.* "It isn't just you now." I looked over and wanted to ask if he would do it—if he would really stay, and take his mother's choice away. But I could not bring myself to say the words. I did not want to hear his answer. "I just mean to say, Miriel is quick to anger, but she's quick to laugh, too. Surely you've seen at least a bit of that at Dun Druim."

"She frightens me," he said frankly. "She's like a windup toy. Like a pretty doll my father made and then left to rust. I don't know what she might do."

I stared at him, chilled by his assessment, half understanding it and half offended. I wanted to tell him that he knew nothing of Miriel. She was more than a toy, even if her uncle had treated her like one. But what words could I say? I opened my mouth and closed it again, and then my eyes widened.

There was something on the horizon.

"What?" Fidach asked, and his voice was weary. "No lies, Catwin."

"Fidach..."

"What?"

I put my hand on his arm and pointed, trembling. Where there had been nothing but iron sea and leaden skies, there was a flash of white.

There was a ship.

Chapter 16

We made for Dun Beal at a run. As we slid down the stone steps and pounded over sandy ground, Talyn and the stable boy yelling towards the walls, I reflected that it had only been a week since I had done the same at Dun Druim.

This, I hoped, was no invasion—dark humor, but I'd had little enough of humor in any form, and from Talyn's excitement, I knew what this was. This was the ship, returned home after its journey to foreign shores. And after Fidach's hurried summary, I knew what we wanted: for there to be land to settle, for the court to fracture. Who would hope for war when land lay free for the taking?

"I'll get Miriel," I said in an undertone, as we ran into the main hall. Fidach grabbed my arm.

"Stay in the room. I'll watch, and report back."

"I want to see. I want her to see."

"If this goes poorly for Lugh, you don't want him to know you saw it," Fidach said shrewdly. "People never forgive you for seeing them fail, do they? And he has no use for you—or her, either. He needs me, though. Stay clear, and I'll come back to tell you how to prepare for dinner tonight."

A branch point: trust, or doubt? Every instinct told me to run from how much I wanted to trust him. It would be so easy to call him an ally, my thoughts said. He meant no harm, they said. He seemed so open and free of guile, as if the struggle for power in the Morini court had never touched him. And still, he had fooled us once, seeming to be nothing when he was now the cause of a war—a war *he* had started with this pretense, for no reason I could understand. I wavered, and he saw it.

"Catwin." His voice was soft when he said my name. "Just this once. Trust me just once."

This is how it begins, I wanted to say. *And then it becomes a habit and you have power over us, and I cannot let you have power over us.* But I did not speak. I only nodded, and went, and kept my eyes down so he could not look into them and know how deeply I was troubled.

Miriel was standing by the window when I entered. She would know it was me, for I had taught her to recognize my footsteps, but still she did not turn around. She was standing ramrod straight, as perfect as she had been in the days before, when any hint of laziness incurred her uncle's wrath.

I had thought that these mannerisms were softened by time, worn away by days of ease and trust. I had hardly seen as the set of her head grew less precise and her movements began to flow into a truer elegance: a woman instead of a girl, with a home and safety where there had been only fear before. What I thought now, as I saw her with her hands clasped behind her back and her chin raised stubbornly, was that she looked so very young.

"Miriel." It took conscious effort not simply to bow and wait for her to speak. How did one move forward out of this maze of the past? I could nearly see the bustle of Penekket city behind her.

"What?" she asked at length, when I did not leave and did not say anything further.

"Fidach found something that may help you."

"Are you our go-between now? Do you carry our messages?"

"Miriel, please..."

"When I woke in the morning, you were not here," Miriel said simply. "You went to him. I will not forget that, Catwin."

"Oh, spare me. You baited a man you should never have baited. What were you afraid of, Miriel? That he might find it more to his liking in the Cornovii court, so you decided to hurry matters along?"

"I reminded him where his duty lies." Her eyes flashed.

"Because he did not know already?" I cried. "Neither of us saw what he was hiding, all these years. And we still don't know! What chance to we have of learning it if we lose his trust now?"

"You never saw anything at all. At least I knew there was something to see."

"Is that what this is all about?"

"Were you not supposed to build your own web of bribes? Stable boys and maids and lords? Should you not have gained Fidach's trust on your rides out together? All the times you went and he followed you, did you think I did not see?"

"You're still seeing shadows everywhere you look," I spat. "In your own kin, in me. We were safe! We had found a haven. Who could have known?"

"*I* knew," she shot back. "We never stay safe for long. You should have known someone would come for us. There's war everywhere, Catwin, always someone trying to win. You never stay safe unless you wield power of your own."

"So what would you have us do?"

"What we must, what we would *always* have had to resort to in the end: we play the court. Fight Lugh, and we will lose. Play faction against faction...and we have a chance. Did you really think we could escape this?"

"Yes," I admitted, after a pause.

"Then you're a fool," she said simply, and she turned away.

"Fidach knew," I mused. I let the insult pass over me like water. Insults from Miriel were to be expected. If I could just let it go, forget it...

"Of course Fidach knew. He's playing his own game, isn't he?" A good reminder, and one I should not have needed. I shrugged my shoulders. "Don't go soft on me, Catwin. You fail me now, and we have no one to catch us. Not even my uncle."

I was in no mood for her lecturing. I needed no more voices telling me to be ashamed for failing to be a Shadow, warring with the voices that cried out that this life should be behind me. I was not meant to be a Shadow any longer—Temar had meant me to be free when I came at last to Priteni. I had tried to cast the voices aside so that I might be...what?

A weapon unused became not a ploughshare, but a rusted sword.

"Wait." I hated that Miriel's commands could still stop me in my tracks. At least the mix of hatred and hope felt familiar—more familiar than anything in this court.

"What?" I waited with my hand on the latch.

"You said Fidach found something."

"And you wanted to know nothing," I threw over my shoulder. I turned only my head, and watched her. "So while you sit here alone, I'll go and serve him instead, and save all our necks."

I meant it to hurt, but I did not expect her face to go pale, as if I had just slapped her. I did not want to hurt her more, I truly did not, but the words were already on my lips: "So who failed, Light or Shadow? Who was supposed to charm Lugh, and Fidach? Who was supposed to gain the favor of the queen and keep us safe?"

We stared at one another, accusations and wounds harsh in our blood, and neither of us could move to apologize. Miriel held herself as still as I had ever seen, trembling, and I was frozen with my hand on the door. I only barely managed to move away as running footsteps approached and the door burst open.

Fidach. He stopped when he saw the two of us, our masks left aside and pain there for him to see. But Miriel shot me a furious glance and raised her chin.

"What is it, cousin?" Her voice was smooth as silk, the courtier's voice I remembered.

"Has Catwin told you the news?" He looked at her as if she was a snake that might bite.

"No." Her voice was like winter, and Fidach foundered, out of his depth between the two of us.

"I..." He looked down at the floor. "I don't know where to start. Lugh's younger brother, Talyn, unearthed a text three years ago. It spoke of an island to the west, with some farmland and forests, and he wanted to send a party to establish a colony. Branwen was in favor, she had no wish for war. Lugh hated it, and when the ship they sent disappeared, some people said it was him. But the ship has come back, after years away. There's a banquet now. The court is in an uproar, and Lugh is not best pleased."

"That *is* interesting." I could see Miriel's mind working furiously behind those blue eyes, but her tone was a bored drawl. "Catwin, you should have told me."

She swept past me on her way to the door without a glance, and I bit my lip against a retort. Miriel had always been good at this, baiting me, making me look incompetent when we both knew any defense on my part would look weak. I bit my lip and looked away from Fidach as Miriel drew him away, linking her arm through his.

"So, tell me. Now I must pretend I know nothing of all of this, yes?" A glance over her shoulder, her dark head silhouetted against Fidach's, and her eyebrow raised. *I'm courting power now, Catwin. Do your part.*

I let them go, went to the saddlebags in the corner, and extracted all the money I had kept. After the banquet, then, I would begin my work in earnest. No half measures. No stopping at the first sign of trouble, as I had done that first night. I leaned on the windowsill when I was done, watching clouds scud across the sky and the grey-black of the mountain rising behind Dun Beal. I wished Temar were here.

I know you wanted me to be safe, I told his ghost. *But there's no safety anywhere. Not for us.*

Fidach had called me truly free, but I was not. I never had been. I told Miriel that we needed to find a new home, and the truth was that I could not even escape our old one. I was lost in the past, a shadow even of myself.

Chapter 17

The banquet was already raucous by the time we arrived, our little party met with roars and cheers. It was good humor borne of their luck. There was a land across the sea, perhaps cold in the winters, perhaps with mountains that spit fire and pools of water that smelled of rot and could burn a man's flesh from his bones, but a land they might call home, with free land to farm. The emissaries of the Morini no longer mattered at all.

Lost in my thoughts, I had to run to catch up to Fidach and Miriel. In the glare of the court's attention once more, Fidach was lifting his hand and greeting, and Miriel was smiling and curtsying to the hall. For the first time, I felt almost invisible—no one would focus on me when Miriel was trying to charm them. She waved when they cheered, and when a servant brought her a mug of ale, she hoisted it, smiling at their words.

"Fidach?" she asked, a sweet smile still on her lips. "Are they cursing me, or is it a joke?"

"A joke," he said, smiling despite himself.

"What do I say in return?"

He leaned down to whisper a phrase in her ear.

"Are you sure?" Her smile never wavered, and he nodded. "Then say it again."

He repeated it, and she called out the syllables with all the projection she could muster. The crowd fell silent, and then laughter burst forth, good natured, men raising their tankards to her and woman blushing as they laughed.

"What did you have her say?" I hissed from his side, and he bit back a laugh.

"You don't want to know. But see, it worked."

"I knew I should have learned better Pictish."

"Come along." Miriel looped her arm through mine and dragged me into the hall. "We don't have any time to waste. Remember, tonight is about convincing them that this island is a good idea, and that *we* think it's much too dangerous to send the Morini. They mustn't think they have competition. Yes?"

"Very well. Do you want to try charming Branwen?"

"Talyn," Miriel said under her breath, and she dropped into a curtsy in front of the throne. Lugh sat at Branwen's right hand, near-entirely overlooked and looking ill-humored for it. Miriel's curtsy might have been just for him, her face grave and the bow of her head respectful, and for the first time since we had met him, Lugh had a smile on his face as he looked at Miriel. For a moment only, she was the only one not toasting his younger brother, and it was enough for a spark of kinship.

The consort's good humor died when Miriel came up gracefully and her smile went to Talyn like an arrow. She gave only the glimmer of a backwards glance as she swept in the younger man's direction, and I swallowed at the surge of fury in Lugh's eyes. At his side, I saw Seiysell reach out to place her hand on her father's arm, and whisper something in his ear.

"I hope you know what you're doing," I said to Miriel through gritted teeth, my own attempt at a smile. "You had a chance of making him an ally..."

"Don't be a fool, Catwin. There was never a chance of winning Lugh."

"So what was all that? What were you doing?"

"Lighting fires," Miriel said, with one of her elegant little shrugs. Her eyes sparkled up at me through her lashes. "Try as I might, I can't see any pattern in him—so I shall go for a new target now, and let Lugh make a fool of himself. He is like a bull. He can't be controlled...but he can be baited."

"This doesn't sound like a very good plan."

"He was going to charge around wreaking havoc no matter what we did. We're just trying to aim him in a particular direction before he charges."

"And what direction is that? Miriel..."

But she was gone. A quick glance showed Fidach in close-headed conference with Morwen. He was making some of the gestures I had seen when he summoned his magic to him in our rooms, and I wondered if this was yet another lesson. Still, he wore his iron collar and ring prominently, a potent reminder that he was no threat to the people in this room.

I sank back into the shadows at the edges of the room to watch the dais. Branwen made a fine show of lifting her goblet to each cheer, but her eyes often drifted to where Fidach sat, and her gaze was narrowed in speculation. In the raucous cheer after a toast, she leaned across Lugh and issued an order to Seiysell. I saw the younger woman's mulish response and a hissed exchange, but fiery as the younger woman was, she would not defy her mother and her queen before all the assembled. She plastered a smile on her face and moved to sit next to Fidach, leaning her head into the conversation with Talyn, and Branwen sank her chin onto her fist to watch.

Information-gathering, or match-making? I felt a stab go through me at the thought. Instinct screamed for me to end it, and end it now—for all Fidach seemed not to want his mother's throne, it would be a strong man indeed who would not waver if the crown was held out in front of him. And we could not afford for Fidach to waver.

I glanced in Miriel's direction, but she was deep in conversation with Talyn. No way to signal her or call for her attention without disrupting this; I could only turn back to watch. We would need to know everything, watch this as it began. I took deep breaths, trying to sink away from the surge of panic. I must see clearly. Seiysell leaned towards the prince, but her slumped shoulders and wandering gaze showed that she was bored by the conversation. Fidach had leaned back courteously to include her, but his gaze was fixed on Morwen.

It was hardly the makings of a love match, but that mattered not one whit. If Branwen was bold enough to ask for a marriage between the royal families, I knew, with a sick, sinking feeling, what Miriel would say: *very interesting. Very interesting, indeed.* Uniting the royal families would displace Connor, and yet...Aoife's bloodline would be on the Cornovii throne. It was a short leap from there to a shared kingdom once more, the suggestion Fidach had claimed neither side would accept.

If there was any comfort to be taken from this, it was that Fidach seemed unaware of it entirely. Had he set his sights on a crown, I was confident I would see it. I could tell Miriel, at the least, that this had not been Fidach's plan. And yet....

As if sending my gaze, his head came up, and I looked hastily down into my tankard. I did not want him to know what I had seen, and what I wondered—for when Fidach did realize what was happening, what might he do? It would depend, I realized, entirely on what Branwen wanted from the match. I filed that away, and drifted to Miriel's side, stealing small glances at the throne. Nothing was happening, I reminded myself. Nothing yet. It was only idle talk and a mother's speculation. We would talk of this later.

Indeed, for all the cheering and toasting, it seemed an uneventful banquet until Talyn rose to speak. He had been in close-headed conference with Miriel, who had beckoned Branwen over to their side. In the presence of both queen and advisor, Miriel sank into silence. She nodded sagely at Talyn's points, and countering Branwen's worries when the queen frowned. When the evening ended, Branwen would remember an impassioned request to send Cornovii to Innis Tearmen, and she would remember as well that it had been Talyn who spoke, and Miriel who was cautious.

I was not the only one who watched the queen and the shipbuilder as they talked, laughed, and as Talyn even spread out a map on the table. Left alone on the dais, Lugh's mood turned from sullen silence to rage. I could see him growing angrier with every toast and song. Miriel's ripples of laughter from Talyn's side made him wince. He looked over to Morwen for counsel, but she was engaged in speaking with Fidach. By the time he finally broke, I had been waiting for it for several long minutes.

It was Talyn that did it. Flushed with drink and success, he stood and pushed his way between Miriel and Branwen to go to the dais. Lugh, lounging back in his chair sullenly, stiffened at once, and I found myself reaching for a knife that was not there. No words had been exchanged, or blows, or even a glance, but the air between the brothers was charged.

"My fellow Cornovii!" Talyn called, and they turned and hoisted their tankards to him, the hero of the day. I could see it hit him in a wave. How often had he sat at the outer tables, forgotten, while Lugh had their cheers and their love? For two years he had watched his dreams fade, lost beyond the horizon while the men flocked back to his brother, the warrior, the consort, the golden one. Now Talyn basked in their praise and spread his arms to welcome their cheers.

"The ships have returned!" he cried, and they shouted their approval. "Across the sea lies a settlement near fields of black stone, great hills carved by the gods, a castle to rival Dun Beal and fields richer than any we have seen before!" A dream, and one they loved. The people cried out and Lugh's fingers tightened on the arms of his throne.

"Our future has come at last!" Talyn cried, and Lugh made to stand. A sharp glance from Branwen and he settled back, but I knew it would not hold. Talyn turned to meet his brother's eyes in open challenge, and then looked back to the crowded all. "Our future can be won with ships and plows, not with your sons and daughters dead on a battlefield!"

The hush was sudden, and complete. The people could smell the challenge in the air. I watched them, as I knew Miriel was, trying to note how many faces looked hopeful, and how many looked angry.

"You were promised revenge," Talyn said. "And it sounded well enough, did it not? But now the emissaries are here, and we barter over the same lands and scrabble for scraps like the dogs. Is this what the Cornovii have become?" He swept his eyes around at the crowd and the people were frozen. A few looked to Lugh, and some to Branwen. They did not know what to say, whom to support.

"Enough," Lugh said. A few people looked away hastily, but Talyn would not be cowed.

"There comes a time when we must stop looking to the past," he called. "When we must become more than our enemies! When we realize that the cost of the midlands too high, and Innis Tearmen are ours for the taking. Can anyone here, anyone, tell me why we should set our sights on lands that are well-defended instead of sailing to our own land, far richer, and building castles to rival the Gwyddu's?"

It was then that Lugh broke. Talyn spun as his brother's

hand dragged him around, and the older man sent him stumbling backwards with a contemptuous push.

"And you think the Morini will watch us sail away and let us be?" he asked Talyn with a sneer. For all his raging, Lugh was the better courtier by far; he made sure that his voice carried throughout the entire hall. "No! Your sailors built a castle that is indefensible. The Morini will come to follow us, and take our new home, and drive us away to the edges of Innis Tearmen until we starve once more. We will never be safe until our enemy is—"

Miriel moved into his line of sight. It was enough, barely; Lugh broke off his words and turned away, cradling his head in his hands.

"People of Dun Beal, hear me." He faced away from them, but his voice echoed off the high stone walls. "The ships have returned, and I am as glad of it as you. Is it not a nice dream to sail for a new land of fertile fields and an ocean's worth of peace? Do you not wish for that as I do?" He turned back to them and I saw the lie shining plain in his face. But the people were nodding hesitantly, pleased to see the queen's consort admit to the same dreams. "But how will we feel," Lugh asked them, "the first time we see white sails on the horizon and know that our enemy has come to fight us? Ask me, then, when they will stop coming for us. I will tell you! Never. Never, until Cornovii or Morini are dead."

"Or bound together once more," Miriel said bravely. Lugh rounded on her with a snarl and she held her ground. "You are not two tribes but one, consort. You fight like brothers who learned to hate in the schoolroom. The only peace you shall have is when you reconcile, for to kill a brother brings only curses upon your house."

"There can be no peace with your kind," Lugh said, drawing himself up. "Is not your prince proof of it?"

"Our prince is proof of Morini honor, I should think," Miriel said clearly. "Proof that great power did not lead Aoife to attack you and destroy you. Now he comes and binds himself in iron to resolve this peaceably—as peaceably as your brother would resolve it, seeking prosperity instead of battle."

"You think I do not see your hand in all this?"

"Me? It was not me who sent the ships, but your queen. It was not me who brought them back safely, but the gods. You stand before us as emissary and swear that we can never have peace, but the only one who stands in the way is you."

"*Enough.*" Branwen's order was only barely enough to keep Lugh's fists at his sides. "Enough. Tonight is a night of joy, not of accusations. Tonight is a night when we think on what could be."

And with a chill, I saw her gaze drift to Fidach, with Seiysell at his side. As the diners rose to make their way back to their quarters, I let myself disappear into the crush. The crowd shielded me as I moved slowly and surely across the great hall, and only Miriel, her eyes darting across the mass of revelers, saw me go. Our eyes met, and she nodded. I had sworn my oath, and she called it in now. In truth, there had been no other option than this.

Dun Beal had one more shadow now.

Chapter 18

My path was slow, but my steps were sure. It had been a fool's question to ask if there were divisions to exploit in Dun Beal. There always were, and we had not even had to seek them out—Talyn and Lugh had driven them into the open, and the lords would even now be taking sides. What we needed were pressure points, and the only questions to ask were whether I could find them quickly enough, and whether Miriel could exploit them.

And, of course, whether Fidach would turn on us. Mild-mannered Fidach, who had hidden his deception so deep that I could see no flicker of it in his eyes. Pain, yes. Fear, yes. But not lies. Fidach, who would soon realize he had a crown within his reach.

My steps slowed and I stopped to think. Could he possibly, truly believe that he was a mage? It would explain the honesty I saw in his eyes, or hoped I saw. Dreams might seem real, a foretelling. A man might believe he knew the future, might even see things that his conscious mind could not comprehend—and think, later, that he had foreseen events yet to come. It was possible.

I wanted Fidach to be telling the truth. It was then that I realized the truth, and the knowledge was unwelcome: I could not trust my eyes when I watched him, for there were things I wanted to see, and things I did not want to see. Oh, I was not child enough to wish for magic—though I thought, amused, that it would make the battle to come somewhat easier—but I did wish for Fidach to be neither liar nor enemy, but friend.

I must face this, I thought to myself. If I could not accept it now, then I would be deceived by myself. My bias would blind me to what I observed. I must understand that my belief in his honesty might be no more than a wish, however dearly held. I had been blind already, where Miriel had been clear-eyed.

I knew, however, how I had fallen into the trap. It was simple enough: if Fidach truly believed in his powers, then he was no liar, destabilizing the Morini court for reasons I must try to discern. Instead, he would be only a young man in pain, believing his so-called magic to be the cause of war, and a piece of himself that his mother could never accept. A young man desperate for approval was dangerous for certain, likely to follow anyone who would give him the slightest bit of love. Still, it was better than a prince, a man some might call the rightful heir of the Morini, holding secrets and telling beautiful lies. We did not need any more enemies.

I was trained to be above such things. I steeled myself to uncertainty and set off again down the hallways, my steps soft and my ears pricked. I walked slowly and tried to look at everything and nothing at once, and expect nothing at all. I wished desperately that I was a servant once more so that I could walk seen-and-yet-unseen with my livery as a camouflage to noble eyes.

At first I pushed the thought away, thinking it no more than regret, and then it gave me an idea. The kitchens had been a place of refuge for me in Penekket, where nobles went to cut across the palace unseen and cooks gossiped with maids about the habits of Those Folk Upstairs, as they called the nobles. If I were to speak of what I had once been…perhaps it would be enough to gain the sympathy of these servants now. I followed my nose and hoped not to run into anyone who might recognize me.

The kitchen was evident not only by the scents of dried fish and baking bread, but by the clatter. I poked my head inside and saw the familiar sights of children turning spits, bakers with flour up to their elbows, piles of vegetables to be chopped and peeled. A wealth of food, perhaps—for half as many people as I knew filled the halls upstairs. In Dun Druim I had seen barrels upon barrels of potatoes and onions, rows of plump chickens to be plucked. Here, the vegetables were small, and the spits held fish and goats. If this was the most Dun Beal could provide for the royalty, it was a poor land indeed.

The flurry of activity was such that I thought I might slip

in unnoticed, but I was sadly mistaken. As soon as I entered the room, a hush fell. My eyes found the head cook at once, for the other servants looked to him—seeking guidance, or merely waiting to see what he would say, I could not yet guess. He said nothing at all.

"Might I just—" I bit my lip. It was easy to playact at being unsure, when that was precisely what I felt. "I wondered if I might just sit for a moment. It's such a crush." My gesture indicated the nearby roar of activity in the hall. "I won't be any trouble, I promise."

"You sound like a Morini." The words were not friendly, and I swallowed. Back away now, or press forward? The Duke was not here to offer the threat of vengeance for a murdered servant. I had no protector, for the shield of diplomacy would hardly count for anything here. Who could say what might befall me in the dark corridors of the palace? Lugh would undoubtedly pin the crime on one of the servants and hang them as a show of friendship to Aoife, clearing himself of guilt—but the servants had not thought so far ahead yet. I saw it in their eyes.

"I am not Morini," I said at last. Truth. Let it show in my face, sound in my voice. "I am from a land beyond the southern ocean. Both me, and the emissary with hair like night. I was her servant once, and she freed me when I helped her escape her uncle."

It was a risk to admit to being free, but no more a risk than coming here alone, skulking about in the shadows for information—and the hint of Miriel's story hung, temptingly, in the air.

"You were a servant?" The head cook's disbelief was plain. A few of the others laughed, as if my lie was pitiable.

Now came the moment when I must take their loyalty. Any less, and they would run to Lugh. I considered all I knew about the emissary. What I could use. Did not every servant resent their master?

"My mother cast me out when I was not even a day old. Our village lay in the shadow of the Winter Castle, and their midwife, Roine, raised me. Our home was called Voltur, up in the mountains. The ground is like iron the whole year through, but in winter, it is so cold you can hardly imagine. The snows drift higher than a man—whole villages can be lost. The wind drives ice like knives. It can cut into your flesh."

It was guards and soldiers who taught me to tell stories, not Temar. In the long evenings at camp, wine scarce and women scarcer, guards and soldiers would spin tales they all knew word for word, and to liven the telling, they would add flourishes to the tale and drop their voices low. I leaned forward a little now, hunching my shoulders as if the story was a great secret, and despite themselves, they leaned in to hear it better.

"My patron was the Duke of Voltur. A great lord, but born common like me. The other lords hated him, and so he must always be the best, the most ruthless, to keep his power." Did I see a flicker of recognition in their eyes? Was I speaking now of Lugh? I could only hope. "He had designs on the throne, but how to take it? He thought to use Miriel, his niece—the beauty upstairs, who came with the Morini prince."

"Aye, she'll have ensnared him now, eh?" A man called out, and there was the knowing chuckle of servants, who watched the nobles pine over one another. *Nothin' stupider than a noble in love,* Donnett used to say. He liked to pass on his wisdom to me after our bouts of sparring, for he had no children of his own to teach about the world. *And they're always fallin' in love, too. It's how they pass the time.*

"Ah, no, for he is her cousin."

"How can that be?"

This would take some embellishing. I paused, as if to draw out the tension, while my mind whirled furiously.

"In his youth, the Duke of Voltur sought power beyond the seas. He was a man of fierce wit and great beauty, but a fool as all men are when they see a pretty woman." A few of them grinned. "Well, he came to Priteni himself, and he was beautiful enough that Queen Aoife had her way with him—him, lost and washed up on her shores like a prize." They hooted with laugher and one woman put her hands over a child's ears even as she held back her own chuckle.

"But he would never make a king, so she turned him away no matter how much he spoke of power and glory. He went back to Heddred, to Voltur, and there he won great battles, all the while thinking he might have been king. It began to consume him so that nothing would do but he gain the throne.

"He thought to have Miriel seduce the Boy King so that he might rule her, and thus the throne, from the shadows. For that, he used me. I was a girl with no family, see, no one to miss me if he took me from my home. He brought me all the way from the furthest reaches of the land to the great court: Dun Warden." Yes, that would do. "There, I was to protect the lady, Miriel—take any blade for her, eat any poison, help her ensnare the king."

"And did you?" They were eager for the tale.

"Yes, but not for the Duke. He was a harsh master. When Miriel did not dance to his liking, he would beat her until no inch of her skin was still pale—save that one might see at the neck of her gown. He wanted power more than anything, and he would accept no failure. He would do anything—anything. When the king had worked for peace for years, the Duke did nothing to help. War would help him, you see. He thought he would lead an army onto our soil and assassinate the king, but we uncovered the plot, she and I."

"Did you kill him?" piped a young boy from where he had hopped up onto the edge of a table. A woman pulled him down gently, but still he peered up at me. I looked at his young face and wished with all my heart that I could be so young as to think such stories were simple. So naïve as to think I might kill the Duke and not still, years later, regret it. *It is easy to kill,* I wanted to tell this boy. *And difficult to live with.*

But such words did not make a good story.

"Aye." They all gasped, and I spread my hands. "What else could we do? He wanted to destroy Heddred with war, let armies burn its fields and kill the people on their farms. And what good to any of them, I ask you? Farmers care nothing for the battles of nobles, though they tell us all it is for our good, that we should hate their enemies as our own. Miriel slipped poison into his food on the eve of battle, fearing that the war would destroy us all."

For a moment, I thought I had gone too far. That they would see what I was doing. But even the head cook was waiting for the next piece of the tale.

"What happened then?" he asked, and I swallowed and looked down. *Always tell a piece of the truth with your lie.* I could still remember Miriel's tears, our first nights in Priteni. She knew that Marie had borne Wilhelm's child, that the two royal cousins would forge a marriage of some happiness, if only to give themselves peace in the years to come. It had been bitter, very bitter, indeed.

"With the warmonger dead, the armies went home. But to kill a noble...cannot be forgiven. We had to leave." A somewhat tortured narrative, but true in its own way. When had the Duke ever worked for peace? So concerned had he been with who would lead the troops that he never thought to work at ending the war entirely.

"Is that why you helped the lady escape?" a woman asked, remembering the start of my tale.

"Yes. Even though the king would have been killed, himself, he had to punish her. We were banished. We would have been killed if the king had not loved Miriel. She had done what she was bid, you see. He loved her and could not bear for her to die—but he could not keep her at court, either. So we ran to Priteni.

"We did not think we would ever reach your shores. In our land, they think Priteni is a myth, that it is only the shadow of clouds on the ocean, but we knew the Duke's story and we arrived safe."

"And now?" The head cook looked at me, and I laughed bitterly. It was easy to show anger, when I could rage at Aoife for sending us here with secrets behind her words. As well drop us into a nest of vipers.

"And now we dance to another noble's bidding. To be sure, Miriel would never have come just for Queen Aoife. But the Morini lords, they told her that she should send an army and destroy the Cornovii—and Miriel could never bear that. She begged Aoife to let her come here, and see if she might bargain for peace."

"But she's a noble."

"Aye, but a rare one. I might have killed her a dozen times, or left her to die on the shores of Heddred, if she was like the man who raised her. But she cared for me when I was only a servant. I owe her my life, and I can never repay the debt. How could I abandon her—especially now?"

"She'll have a hard time of it, bargaining with Lugh," one of them said, and though the head cook shot her a sharp look, the others nodded in agreement. "It's true," she told the man, and then looked to me. "It's true. He wanted peace once, but not anymore."

"No," I argued. They frowned at me. "Surely not. He can't. I heard from another that his own brother—Tal..." I frowned, pretending to seek the name in my memory, hoping the tales of Lugh and Talyn's fight had not yet made it here. "Talyn? Aye, Talyn. They told me that Talyn seeks a land beyond the seas. How could Lugh seek war when he would have peace? How were ships sent, if not with his blessing? Is he not the King?"

"Lugh's not the *king*," a woman said, as if explaining something to a child. "He's a consort, only. He does not want anything with Innis Tearmen. He wants the old fields back, our farms that were taken."

They were not allies, not yet. I must be cautious. I fashioned a frown.

"So Talyn acts without the blessing of Branwen? He is a brave man. In my land, we say that such bravery is much like foolishness." They laughed.

"Talyn has the blessing of Branwen," the head cook explained. "She gave him the whole east wing of Dun Beal for his maps and his model ships. Lugh was fit to be tied, but it's his queen and his brother—how could he speak against them?"

The east wing, then. I bowed low and ducked my head, then looked up as the roar of a toast shook the floor, coming from the great hall.

"I must go. I thank you all, truly—I might have said something to embarrass myself. If I thought Lugh had sent the ships, that he liked them..." I shook my head. "I cannot thank you enough. And please, tell no one what I told you of Miriel. I would not want to embarrass her."

They chorused that they would not, and I backed out of

the kitchen, well pleased. By tomorrow, every servant in Dun Beal would know the story of the tragic beauty who had come to secure peace, and in another day, all the nobles would hear whispers. And I? I knew to go to the east wing of the palace, to the see the man who so discomfited our adversary.

So it was the Talyn, returning late from a night of feasting in the hall with his supporters, found me seated in his chambers with my dagger laid by my feet. I stood when he entered, hands splayed to show I meant no harm, and he stood by the door with his hand on the latch. A cautious man.

I studied him for a moment: black hair, pale skin. Eyes like sapphires. With his delicate features, he might be a match of Miriel. He waited for me to speak, and I did not hesitate. I had composed my speech while I waited.

"I have a proposition for you," I told him.

Chapter 19

I shook Miriel awake in the small hours of the night and held my hand over her mouth for silence. While I waited for Dun Beal to sleep, I had named myself a fool for beginning this again. My heart cried out that I was no longer a Shadow, that Miriel should never be so cruel as to ask this of me. I remembered her words before she left for the hall. I remembered the look over her shoulder. It had been habit, and no more, that brought me back to her side. And still, had I not goaded her? Had I not sought out Fidach, who was working from the shadows as well?

We were goading one another onwards, she and I, using sharp words as a poor stand-in for the Duke's terrifying anger. Even as I shook her shoulder, part of me wanted to cast aside this new scheme and let her run it, if she was so determined.

The flash of relief in her eyes changed everything. No matter that it was replaced at once with anger—I had seen it. Even when she pulled me close to ask where I had been in a low hiss, trying not to wake Fidach where he slept in his chair in the next room, I could feel my anger ebbing.

"Come with me."

"Where are we going?"

"The kitchen." I allowed a smile to tug at my lips. "You were hungry and I am accompanying you, like a dutiful servant should."

"Help me tie my gown." She had not smiled at my weak joke. I laced the gown tightly, hoping for some sort of response, but she was absorbed in pinning back her curls. I might not be there at all.

"The servants think you're one of them," I said in an undertone. I made a careful knot at the top of her laces to keep the dress in place. "I have them thinking the battle is nobles' business and you wanted to spare them that—like with Ismir. They think you quite tragic and wonderful."

Miriel turned and appraised me coolly, her features still in the sliver of light from the door. We both waited as the faint sound of a patrol grew louder and passed by, pausing by our door. The guard waited for some minutes, clearly having been told to watch for misbehavior from the Morini delegation— exactly the sort of thing we were up to, of course—and Miriel and I both stood still and silent, not wanting the creak of the floorboards or our whispers to give us away. When he moved on, Miriel gave an imperious lift to her little pointed chin.

"Tell me who we're going to see." She kept her voice low, lest Fidach hear her, but her tone was still purposeful.

"I'd rather not have you know if someone stops us."

"As if I can't keep a secret? Why aren't you telling me?" She leaned close, her face hardly an inch from mine. "Is this some plan of Fidach's, that you think I'll dislike?"

"It's Talyn," I spat out, knowing my voice was harsh and not caring. She was scared, nothing more, her sharp words betrayed by the pallor of her face, and even so, I could not quite forgive it. I resolved to let her wonder if it was Fidach's plan. "Can we go now?"

"What have you promised him?"

"That you want peace as much as he does, after having spoken to him all night. That you found Lugh's display shameful."

"Hmmm."

"I told him that maybe you could persuade Aoife to give lumber and supplies to fund the expeditions—that if people were to go, perhaps they might cede the land left behind. Does that pass muster, my lady? Is that good enough for you? Is a man with the ear of the queen and kinship to Lugh a good enough wedge to drive through the court?" My voice was like acid, but Miriel did not flinch.

"Yes," she said, after a moment. "I think that may be good enough."

We walked through the halls in stony silence. Miriel, for all her imperiousness, still knew my signals to draw into the shadows, or stop at once, and she obeyed them instantly. The patrols that passed nearby, clad in leather instead of mail and carrying daggers instead of spears and swords, walked more softly than guards in Penekket. The stakes were higher, and we both knew it. No protector, and once we had passed the kitchens, no excuse.

Talyn, whatever his reservations, had gone out of his way to welcome Miriel. His chambers were lit well with candles and lanterns, rolled maps were laid neatly on one of the wide tables, and he had poured two glasses of what was, if my watering eyes could be believed, very fine whiskey. I watched, dispassionate, as Miriel made a very fine show of misunderstanding his gesture that she drink the draft in a single gulp. She sipped, coughed prettily, and then sat with the glass cradled in her hands.

Much more impressive was her instinct. Many an academic could be easily charmed with honeyed words and bright smiles, but Talyn was not such a man. The younger brother of a man gifted in statecraft, he resented such talent, distrusted it deeply. Where it had taken me nearly an hour of cautious discussion to discern this, realizing that my feeble attempts at diplomatic pragmatism were doing more harm than good, Miriel realized it in an instant. At the banquet, in the clamor of the hall, Miriel had been all smiles and Talyn had bowed to convention. But here, all flirtatiousness was gone. She was grave and quiet.

"Catwin told me you might wish to speak more about the ships," she said, leaning forward.

"And what did she say?" He was distrustful by nature, I saw now. The ships had a place in his heart that other men might give to a wife. They were his life's work, and he would never let us endanger them. "You know, I had wished to be at the docks tonight to assess the damage."

"Catwin said the same you said at the banquet, my lord— that you desired an end to this war, so that the Cornovii could go forward instead of back." Miriel did not answer his jibe, only spoke low and calm. When I saw his mouth press shut in a grimace, I saw she had touched on the sorest point.

"All they will hear of is taking back the lands," he said bitterly. "Of course, I suppose *your* queen would be pleased if we broke off our attack. That's why you're here, isn't it?"

"Of course," Miriel agreed equably, and his eyes flickered

at her honesty. "I was sent to make peace, my lord. You may look at me and see only a noble lady, but I have seen wars fought. I have seen the cost. I wish neither for war to engulf my new home, nor for either of our people to live with burned fields and dead sons."

"So you do not come because you wish for a new land. You come to see if it all might be arranged without fuss."

"Has Catwin told you our tale?"

"Some of it." His glance flicked over me where I stood, guarding the door, and then moved back to Miriel. It was plain enough that he trusted no one who had a bodyguard.

"I spent nearly all my life under the guard of a man who cared for me only as a puzzle piece," Miriel told him. "I was a pawn, nothing more. What I wanted for my life did not interest him, and it was my greatest defiance to read books he would not have wanted me to read, speak to people he would not approve of. I had a passion he could not understand, for the people to rule themselves. I was never brave enough to tell him, and when he discovered some of it, he nearly killed me.

"If you want me to share your love of sailing beyond the horizon, I am afraid that I will disappoint you. It is not my dream. But I have known dreams I would fight for, do anything for, risk my life for—that, I can understand."

"Hmph." He poured more whiskey and narrowed his eyes at her. They were so alike, I thought, little copies of each other. Where Lugh was a warrior through and through, Talyn was shorter, delicate, pale. He would never have won fights in the schoolroom. Where Lugh had a quick charm, Talyn had a quick wit. If Miriel had been a second child overlooked by the Duke, left to pass the time how she chose instead of schooled in charm and flirtation, she might now be as dour and contemptuous as Talyn.

She did not press him, but leaned back in her chair and took a cautious sip of whiskey, showing a tiny wrinkle in her nose at the taste. A little piece of vulnerability, but none of the mannerisms of the Heddrian court. She was cautious in her flirtation. He saw reserve, but I saw her searching for an opening and suddenly I felt weary. *It's the same thing all over again,* I had told her, and it was true. Talyn thought himself clever, but he had no chance against Miriel. She had learned to be patient.

"So you admit this is self-interest." Grudging respect, but disbelief. I wished he would hurry up and let her charm him. I was tired, and only slightly amused that I was so jaded.

"I don't *like* fighting other people's battles for them," Miriel said with sudden vehemence. "I'm not *from* Priteni, none of this is anything to me. I just want everyone to go home and stop making war. If that means bargaining for the Morini fields, then I'll do it. If it means giving Morini lumber and grain to send the ships, and let our people explore Innis Tearmen as well, I'll do that. All I want is to be able to sleep at night without fearing there's a horde of soldiers bearing down on me. Is that so much to ask? Can't we all just *live*?" Whisky tipped over the edge of her glass and she brushed at it with her hand, looking down to avoid meeting his eyes. A spring coiled tight, her whole body set with frustration. Doing such a perfect job of seeming out of control, and afraid. "I came here because I thought maybe you would help. Maybe I'd finally found someone here who understood."

Her Heddrian accent had come out strong now. She looked close to tears, a woman out of her element, frightened. She was passionate—interweaving little lies with the truth so perfectly that even I could not always see where one picked up and the other left off.

Talyn did not have the first idea what he might do to placate her. Miriel had always known how to push people into comforting her—myself as well, I thought sourly—and this was no exception. Faced with a tearful maiden, what could Talyn do but apologize? Accused obliquely of caring nothing for his people, what could he say but that he wanted peace for them? He opened his mouth to speak, and was mercifully spared the task of trying to find words.

"And Lugh won't even *hear* of a joint expedition, he wouldn't speak to me of the ships, and I don't understand why not!" Miriel said, her voice rising so that Talyn looked towards the door in alarm. I had leaned back to listen for guards as she began her tirade. She knew that I would signal her if she needed to be quiet.

"He doesn't understand." Talyn's jaw was taut. "He *won't* understand. He says it's unjust that we should have to look for a new home, when our rightful home was stolen from us, and he won't see that war will kill us as much as the Morini. I heard him tell Branwen that he hoped Morwen was wrong, that you would not try to bargain for peace. He wanted to sweep across Morini lands and have done with it."

"Morwen foresaw the bargaining?" Miriel asked, her eyebrows raised in interest. I saw her give a little shake of her head, an inner reprimand for such gullibility, but even Talyn, with his charts and his calculations, was taken in by the stories.

"She was how they knew the prince was a mage in the first place," he said, as if it hardly mattered, and Miriel shot me an alarmed look. I felt a moment of cold fear in my stomach. How *had* they known? We were verging from hope and dream into improbable coincidence.

But I shook my head at Miriel. A disgruntled courtier, looking for coin. A spy sent, pretending to be from one of the outer homesteads. Information followed money, it *always* followed money. I had seen it my whole life and never thought it magical before. Leaving aside the question of how Morwen had foreseen a delusion that Fidach had so carefully hidden, I shrugged my shoulders at Miriel, shook my head again to comfort her. A brief moment of comradeship, the two of us against a whole country that seemed to have gone mad.

"And he says Branwen won't hear of it, either—she seemed so interested at the banquet, but he said not even to *ask*..." The most daring play yet, for I was certain Lugh had said nothing of the kind, but I need not have worried. Talyn, already resentful, would be only too willing to believe that Lugh was trying to sabotage the plan.

"He said that?" At last, an opening taken; he was furious. "It's a lie. Branwen blessed the venture from the start. If it weren't for him speaking against it, we would have had the ships back a year ago now. Even he couldn't persuade her against it in the end, but he keeps trying. He'll tell her now that it's too dangerous, too long a journey."

"He was lying?" Even I thought Miriel might have gone too

129

far. She was the picture of injured pride, but Talyn did not notice. He had pushed himself out of his chair, was pacing angrily. He barely spared a glance for the young woman by the fire.

"Of course he was lying, he always lies."

It was too soon to ask for his help; both Miriel and I knew it. A gesture of her fingers, and I hissed softly, jerking my hand for silence. Talyn stopped, his eyes on the door, and I put my finger to my lips.

"We should go," I told Miriel urgently, and she pretended to waver.

"But if we could only persuade Branwen—"

"It's too dangerous," I repeated. I could see the repressed amusement in her eyes, and hoped my own was not showing. Talyn would tip into paranoia, spend his energy to persuade Branwen all over again, placing pressure where Miriel could not. Now it was a challenge. "Lugh will never accept peace if he learns we're for this."

"Catwin, I can't just—" I made a show of pulling her away.

"We can't risk it," I told Talyn baldly. "Not with Lugh for an enemy. Not with his lies. I'm sorry." And I took Miriel's hand and pulled her away before Talyn could speak. He stood, shocked by the abrupt departure, and we crept back to our rooms, exchanging only a look of mutual approval before we went to our beds. Talyn was not an ally, no—he was a man desperate to win support. We did not have to speak for the expedition to Innis Tearmen. Talyn would do it for us, and Branwen would face not the requests of an enemy, but the support of her own people. I tried to focus on the victory we had made, and not on the twisting in my gut, the sense that we were slipping back...

"Catwin?" Miriel said, when we had both begun to drift to sleep at last.

"Hmm?" I thought I heard Fidach stir on the other side of the wall.

"Please be on my side," Miriel said. Her tone was dreamy, so open that I wondered if she thought herself asleep. I lay still, too afraid of waking her to say anything. "Please, just one more time."

I hate this, I wanted to say, and I knew she would come

awake at once and push herself up on her elbow to stare at me.

What choice do we have? She would ask.

I would have no answer for her.

Chapter 20

Try as Lugh might, there was no denying that the expedition to Innis Tearmen had been a success. He might speak of danger, but the ships had returned. He might speak of an uncertain future, but the sailors who had brought the message spoke of a colony under way and their brethren healthy on plentiful fish and berries, caribou roaming the hills and grass where cows and sheep might graze.

Lugh might say that now was not the time for excitement, and indeed, he did. He said it loudly and gravely, and no one—I was delighted to see—paid him the slightest heed. That the ships had been gone for so long only heightened the drama of it, and the next day, the entire court turned out to make their way down to the seashore and toast the return of the ships.

The winter winds whipped around us as we walked down, a great mass of courtiers and servants. Someone had seen fit to get heavy cloaks for the members of the diplomatic party, and so we walked in comfort. The cloaks, Fidach had noted drily, were so bright a red that they might be seen at several leagues; Lugh clearly did not want us sneaking about when we reached the docks.

But we had no intention of doing so. Miriel made a show of walking with Lugh, trying to engage him on matters of a treaty as if this detour to the docks was an inconvenience.

The court was in too fair a mood to take much notice of the intruders—even Fidach and I were greeted with a certain warmth—and so Miriel's choice was noted only by Branwen, who seemed pleased not to conduct the outing under her husband's scowl, and Talyn.

As the day began, he strode at the head of the party and pointed out the features of the boats to all assembled. Crates of strange, black rock and plant specimens were unloaded, and toasts were drunk. It was Talyn's moment of triumph. Yet as the hours progressed, his glances towards Miriel became more frequent, his glory in what he had achieved diminished by the loss of an ally. As Miriel continued her close-headed conference with Lugh, I watched Talyn's temper rise.

"Why do I think this is why you returned late to bed last night?" Fidach murmured in my ear, and I jumped. I had not heard him come up behind me.

"You move too quietly," I said, and he smiled.

"A fine accusation, coming from you. So am I permitted to know why our friend is antagonizing the shipmaster?"

I looked over to where Miriel was still, apparently, hanging on Lugh's every word, and threw caution to the winds. Even as I did it, I knew I would earn her wrath later—and yet, would we even know of this opportunity without Fidach's help?

"She cannot speak against Lugh," I said simply. Fidach frowned for a moment.

"So she speaks to him?"

I felt a stab of hope, and named it for what it was, thrust it down sharply. Either these were the words of a liar, or of a man who did not grasp well how politics worked. If the latter, we did not have much to fear from Fidach's plans, no matter how nefarious—and I noted, with a mix of amusement and relief, that Fidach had left Seiysell's side to come speak to me.

"And as you noted, certain people are displeased with Miriel's choice of conversational partners." I shaded my eyes to gaze across the shore.

"Why?" Fidach asked. "Surely she cannot have taken him to her bed."

"That's not the only way to catch a man's interest." I sighed at him. "She let it known that she might be an ally to him. And now, she shows that she might not be. We should not speak of this here."

"Indeed." Fidach studied her, and then looked over at me. I tried to stand still as I felt his gaze pass over my face. "But why do I feel you will make some excuse and we will not discuss it at all?"

"I don't know why," I said, looking away from him, trying not to betray myself with sudden stillness. I attempted a smile.

"Why would you say that?"

"Catwin, why do you mistrust me?" He was not taken in, and I did not answer, for I did not have any idea what to say. Miriel was so much cleverer at these things than I was. What could I say that would not trap me, would convince him? Already I had lost the window, had hesitated too long, and I did not want to look over and see those eyes. It disturbed me, how I could not find the deception there.

"Do you deny that your motives might seem, to us...complex? Divided?"

"Of course I deny it." I cursed myself. Fidach was a warrior, and as such, I had thought to be open with him. I had forgotten that he was also a man of honor, to be mortally offended at any suggestion of disloyalty.

"We have lived different lives," I said softly. "Miriel and I have been betrayed by friends and family alike, given up as sacrifices to others' ambitions. That was our whole life until we came to Priteni. We have seen nobles conspire against each other and their king. We would be shocked by no one's betrayal."

It was again the wrong thing to say.

"You would be shocked by each other's betrayal," Fidach observed. His eyes had gone cold, paler than the sky above.

"We have spent six years with no one but each other to trust."

"And two years knowing *me*. Is that not enough for you to see that I am no oath-breaker?" He was genuinely angry now, and I swallowed. I had nothing to say, and that was enough to show him what I thought. He looked out at the sea. "For all of what Miriel said, I thought to trust *you*."

"Thought?"

"Before you started sneaking out in the night. Catwin, we have no one here but each other. Can you not tell me what games you're playing?" I hesitated, and he took my arm, trying to make me face him. "They're my *family*, Catwin. My home. I cannot just trust them to you without a second thought. Can you not understand?"

It was a cruel question to ask of a woman who did not have either. I pulled my arm out of his grasp.

"What do you want me to say?"

"That I can trust you," he said passionately, and I felt cold inside.

"You've just told me that you can't."

"I see," Fidach said. He settled back to look at me. A look showed narrowed eyes. He had gone as cold as I was. "I think I shall go join Miriel's discussion, then. We should make sure we're all working for the same peace, after all."

I did not try to call him back when he strode away. I had just tipped our hand to our most dangerous enemy, and yet all I could think was that I had hurt him. He had not asked a true question when he spoke of mistrust, and so my honesty had come as a surprise. He rode with two others who trusted each other, and spun schemes, who did not love the Morini as he did, and who did not trust him. I thought that he must feel very alone here.

And then I thought myself a fool. Fidach was a danger to us, nothing more—one of the few people who knew beyond a doubt that he was no mage. He was a liar, and all that remained to be seen was why. No matter how open his face, how honest his tone, he could bring us nothing but grief.

I saw Miriel cast me a sharp glance when he joined the party, and I only shook my head and turned away. The day was bright and sharply cold, and so I drew my cloak about me as I wandered, staring up at the cliffs and thinking about home— although I no longer knew where that was.

Distracted I might be, but I was still a Shadow. I heard the quiet steps behind me and was ready when a hand tapped on my shoulder. Talyn, I guessed, and so I was surprised to see the queen herself when I turned.

"Studying our defenses?" Her voice, as always, was light and courteous, but I knew the warning there. I pondered saying that she need not try to frighten me, as I had seen her army and was frightened enough by it, but instead I only shook my head and looked up at the mountain.

"I was homesick. I grew up in the mountains."

"In the land beyond Priteni, if the gossip is to be believed." She plainly did not believe it in the slightest, and I tried to hide my smile. Perhaps she had heard it from Fidach, or perhaps my story to the servants was spreading.

"A land called Voltur," I said. The word did not fit with the Pictish I had learned. It felt strange on my tongue now. "It was not an easy life—not even a happy one, but I still sometimes miss the whistle of the wind."

"Truly?" She was trying not to let herself be taken in.

"I think what I miss more is being a child. There were no games to play except stealing pastries. Things were not so...complicated."

At that, Branwen laughed. She shaded her eyes and pointed up the cliff side, to the tiniest hint of a cave.

"Do you see? There is a path, very slippery. When we were young we would dare each other to the cave, and steal pasties from the kitchen when we returned. At the time we thought it great fun." She sobered. "We stopped when Lugh fell and broke his arm. I think the lot of us were whipped—and we were the daughters and sons of great lords, so no one had ever dared before. But my father certainly did."

"He told you that you were not grown yet?" I suggested, and she shrugged.

"Something rather like that. He told us that we were not our own, me most of all. He reminded us what happened to lands that had no lords to rule over them." I thought what Miriel might say about this and I bit my lip, but Branwen did not see. "He would not stop until we recited the whole tale of Evrard the Bonebreaker."

"I haven't heard that one."

"No? He sailed from across the seas and built a great kingdom, but took no wife and made no heirs. When he passed, each of his lords claimed the throne, and in time, war claimed every one of them. The last of Evrard's kin took the last longship home across the ocean, and Priteni had peace from its invaders...but it was a peace that broke Evrard's people."

"There have been invasions before?"

"Not many. Few survive the north seas and fewer still can forge the waters to the south. Those who do arrive are weary, and easily beaten back. Evrard's men put fair, tall warriors in our women's bellies, and then left us in peace. I think we got the best of the bargain, do you not?" She touched a hand, self-consciously, to her own fire-red hair.

"Very practical."

"You are sad, child." She had seen that the humor in my eyes was fleeting. "You look alone."

I would not be led into confidence.

"I have Miriel," I said.

"And why, if you are from a far-off land, would you come to bargain for the Morini? For oath-breakers?"

"No one deserves to fight for the battles of kings, no matter how righteous." To say anything of Aoife was a trap; I did not try. "Miriel and I have no stake in this, beyond wanting to keep our heads attached to our shoulders. I think Aoife hoped we would see more clearly."

"I am surprised she had the courage to send the Gwydion," Branwen observed. "A fine warrior, and a stronger mage, if Morwen is to be believed. Did she not think we might take him from her?" She looked back to me and her gaze sharpened. "Or did she think it a worthy trade for her throne? No, do not fear. I will not force you to answer. But think well on the woman you bargain for, emissary. Think well whether you wish to defy her now. And know that a woman with peace in her heart might find a warm welcome in the Cornovii court."

"I will never have peace," I said without thinking. "I have seen too much."

I bowed and made to leave. I was suddenly desperate to be anywhere else. I did not want to know what else Branwen might stay. It was like a nightmare. And indeed, as I tried to leave, she put her hand on my arm to stop me.

"And there is one more thing." Her jaw was set. "I thought perhaps it would become clear to you in time, but it has not. You will tell Miriel I asked for this, yes? Very well: Aoife must hold to the treaty by which she keeps us exiled. No family of the line of Gwydion may rule. If there is ever to be peace between us, there must be honor in Dun Druim. Aoife must cede her throne...or her son."

"I..." I could not think what to say. Branwen tried not to

smile, but there was triumph in her eyes.

"If you will excuse me, it is time to reconvene the court in Dun Beal."

I walked back to the castle alone, hearing Miriel's cries behind me and letting her think that they were lost in the shriek of the wind. Too much, it was all too much. I had managed to keep the shadow locked away inside me for two years, and now it threatened to spill out and engulf Priteni. Was it me? Had I brought this upon us?

"Catwin, what is it?"

"She wants to keep Fidach," I spit out, and Miriel stopped dead, then ran to catch up.

"She..."

"Yes. I noticed last night, I should have told you but there was no chance—she wants Fidach to marry Seiysell."

"She said that?"

"No. 'Aoife's throne, or her son,' were the exact words."

"How did we not guess?" Miriel murmured, and I fought the urge to run my fingers through my hair.

"I can't do it," I told her baldly. I did not look over at her. "It's all games again. I want to trust all of them, Branwen and Fidach. I think I even trust Talyn. I trust them and don't trust them. Sometimes I think I'll never trust anyone. Except *you*," I added, at her hurt look. "Of course not you."

"Sometimes I wonder. You haven't looked pleased."

"And you have!" I burst out. "Like you *like* this. You're back as you were, being feted and adored."

"Being hidden entirely from myself. I do not like it anymore, Catwin. I am only good at it." We walked through the corridors in near silence. Our chatter in Heddrian had drawn some raised brows. "When this is over, we'll go. I promise. We can go on Talyn's ships."

It was a joke, but it hit both of us with sudden, painful certainty. A new home. Somewhere across the seas, away from old scores and blood debts. A fresh start.

"I want that," I said to her, and she nodded.

"Me, too. We just have to live long enough."

I was still smiling when I opened the door, and saw

Fidach standing, waiting for us.

"Hello," he said. His knife was naked in his hand.

Chapter 21

I did not even think. I launched myself at Fidach, driving my shoulder into his gut and hearing his surprised grunt as he went over backwards. The knife clattered away onto the floor and I caught its faint gleam out of the corner of my eye. Could Miriel—?

She was at the door with her hand pressed over her mouth, trying to hold back the screams. *Keep it secret.* That this should be her instinct, no call for help, was horrifying to me. At the desperate jerk of my head, however, she flared into motion. She was the shadow, quick and dark, and the knife was gone from my vision. I got an arm free and hurled my own after it. I was not ready for this to be a knife fight. I had avoided Fidach, I reminded myself in despair. We had never sparred; I didn't know what he could do. Safer not to know what he could do with grappling, instead of with a knife.

Of course, that meant he did not know what I could do, either. That was something. We rolled and I dodged his fist, driving my own up under his sternum. He deflected a second punch and wrenched my sideways, and I grimaced: with so much more reach, and more bulk, he had an advantage I couldn't shake. It would take quick cruelty, and I didn't know his aim, yet.

Enemy.

Enemy was not enough anymore. Not with Temar, not with Fidach. My wrist slipped away from an attempted lock, but he was stronger than I was. If I was not willing to be cruel, it was only a matter of time before he caught me and we both knew it. As we rolled and he settled on top of me, I drove my hips up and sideways. When he hit the floor, I was scrabbling away, between him and Miriel. Was it her he was after? Had he made some deal with Lugh?

He must have thought I was going for the knife, for he threw himself, desperately, after me. He brought all his strength to bear and I was dragged across the rough floor. Fingers closed around my neck.

"Enough!" It was fierce whisper. I blinked as the hands fell away from my throat. With one knife at either side of Fidach's neck, Miriel held him in place. Her nod directed me away, and she stepped back quickly. Fidach and I had not taken our eyes from one another. He backed into the corner and I sank into a crouch. "What is the meaning of this?" Miriel asked him in a harsh whisper.

"You're asking *me?*" he demanded, and I almost laughed at his expression. He looked at me, and then at her, like a child who had been caught stealing sweets with his friend. "Did she not tell you what we spoke of?"

"No. She did not." Miriel's voice was dry and weary. "Catwin?"

"*He* said he couldn't trust us!" My turned to feel caught out. "He said we were playing games with his family's future."

"You *are.*"

"We—"

"Stop it, both of you." Miriel stepped between us and swept an imperious glance at us both. "Stop looking at the knives and go sit."

She held the knives behind her back with one hand and pointed to the chairs by the fire with the other. I sat cautiously, still poised to move, and Fidach lounged back with the appearance of cat readying itself to leap. Miriel made a show of sitting elegantly, and then gave each of us a look.

"Tell me what you though we were doing," she said to Fidach.

"Bargaining in secret." He probed at a loose tooth and glared at me.

"Yes, indeed we were. And?" He stared at her, silent in the face of her honesty, and Miriel leaned back in her own chair, clearly enjoying this. "The question, of course...is whether you fear that we'll betray your mother, or ruin your own plans. So which is it?"

Fidach made a motion, hastily cut off, stretching his fingers out for a knife that Miriel held out of reach with a deceptively delicate curl of her fingers. Her eyes narrowed.

"You know," Fidach said, "I fought my way through the Morini court to stop them saying things like that. They were all more Morini than I was, more loyal than I was, not stalked by the ghost of a conqueror's fate. I never expected to be called a traitor to the Morini court by two women who have not a drop of our blood."

"You can stop trying to get her sympathy, you know." I smiled with genuine humor. "You're not doing very well." He shot me a look of pure fury and Miriel sighed.

"Perhaps what Catwin *means* is that you have not yet addressed my question."

"I should not have to. I am a prince of the Morini. You are outsiders—it is your loyalty that should be questioned."

"Oh?" Miriel lifted one brow, perfectly composed. She sat with her spine ramrod straight, and so managed to look down her nose at her cousin. "Let us speak of loyalties, then. We owe our lives to Aoife's hospitality, and we have no ties to the Cornovii court. *You,* however..." She rose from her chair and her skirts swirled around her as she began to pace. She held both knives in her hands. "You have divided loyalties. On the one hand, your mother. A woman who will never let you rule, as perhaps you believe you should. Simple enough, but all you would have had to do was drop your pretense and you could have the throne—which means you must be playing a deeper game than that. Or you could be truly deluded, of course, but you seem quite sane to me. And on the other hand, you have the Cornovii court, a place where your supposed *talent* is greatly desired, and your blood might well give you the throne. You have them all vying to keep you here with greatest honors, don't you? So was this your plan all along, cousin? Provoke a war with your mother's enemies and destabilize her throne? It would be revenge, wouldn't it?"

She had paced all around Fidach's chair as she spoke, and now she stood just out of reach to look down at him. Her eyes were narrowed, and I could see why: the prince looked utterly bewildered. He was, I thought with a certain awe, the best actor I had ever seen.

142

"What I can't figure out," Miriel said, and her voice was at once light as any courtier's, and as cold as a Voltur winter, "is *why*. Why you hate your mother so—and why you have planned such an elaborate revenge. And how, in the name of the seven gods, you've managed to hide it so well."

For a moment, he couldn't seem to speak at all. His jaw worked, and nothing came out, and Miriel finally threw the knives to the floor, stamped her little foot. It was a tantrum, and I wanted to laugh—but she was near incandescent with fury.

"Stop it! Stop acting! Stop *playing* with me!"

"What do you *mean?*" Fidach asked finally. His voice broke on the words. He looked to me, and back to Miriel. His demeanor was so bewildered that I had to clench my hands to keep my sympathy at bay.

"I mean," Miriel said, through gritted teeth, "that for reasons I cannot understand, you have decided to pretend that you're a mage. I don't know why, I don't know what game you're playing. And I hate that, Fidach."

"What do you *mean*, I'm pretending to be a mage?" Fidach asked. He stood so that he towered over her, and in her anger, she did not look the least bit afraid. Her hands were clenched, and I thought for a moment she might strike him. He took a step towards her, and she did not flinch.

"I mean just that," she said bravely.

"Do you honestly think," Fidach asked dangerously, "that I would pretend to that? Do you think I haven't prayed to the Nine a hundred times to take my powers away? Do you not think I would be happier as a true heir? Do you think mages were *welcome* at Dun Druim?"

"You're serious," Miriel whispered, and his hands clenched as if he wanted to take her by the shoulders and shake her.

"Of course I'm serious." He spoke the words with exaggerated courtesy. "Why on earth would you think I was pretending? Don't you think Morwen could see through it in a minute if I was?"

Miriel looked at me. I looked at her. Both of us looked at Fidach, and back to each other. I saw her wondering if we should run, and I looked behind me to measure the number of paces to the door. It was too much, too absurd. We were in a diplomatic party with a madman. At last, Miriel spoke.

"But Fidach..." Her voice was gentle. "Magic is not real."

He has started pacing and now he stopped, comically.

"Not *real*?"

"I know you've been told stories all your life, but there's nothing to fear." Miriel's face was kind. She could afford to be kind now that Fidach was not a willing enemy, for neither of us could doubt him now. "We'll find a way out of this for you. We'll show that you were mistaken. Morwen...we'll find a way around Morwen."

He walked back to his chair and sat. He was shaking, and I wanted to go to him, take his hand while he heard this—for the first time in his life, heard the truth. It had hit him hard. He sank his chin onto his face and gazed into the fire for a long time and I moved to take Miriel's hand, squeezing it. She squeezed back, biting her lip as she watched him. Finally, Fidach looked up at us.

"All this time. You've been travelling with me for two weeks, and the whole time, you've thought me a liar—or a fool. You thought I was speaking children's tales and myths to my own ends. *That's* why."

I met his eyes and nodded. I was trying to be gentle, and to my surprise, he laughed.

"Oh, Catwin..." He stood and went to the saddlebags. He thumped their sides so that the dried mud cracked and flaked onto the ground in a little pile. Miriel shot me a look and I shrugged helplessly. Fidach motioned us back, and then pulled his hood back up, over his head. His eyes drifted closed, and his hands lifted. Miriel exclaimed and I saw the noise disturb his concentration, but his face quickly sank back to its look of concentration.

When I saw what Miriel was pointing at, however, I stepped back and ran into the table. The loose earth Fidach had freed was rising towards his outstretched fingers. Each piece drifted like dust motes in a shaft of sunlight, and the whole mass of it swirled in a cone below his hand. *The call of earth.*

His lips moved on a single word and the wind rose

outside the windows. A tiny breeze swirled around him, lifting his cloak, and then tangled in the hanging earth, whipping it into a spiral. *The call of storm.*

Fidach's other hand was held palm up. His eyes squeezed shut with effort, and the air above his hand began to shimmer. An image was becoming clear, I realized now, and Miriel recognized it before I did. She put her hand to her mouth, and I shrank away when I saw what this was. Twinned images: Temar's face, staring down at me as he held my arm wrenched behind my back, and in the other image, the two of us together, across a courtyard. My memories of the night I had been chosen as a Shadow—and Miriel's.

The call of time.

Fidach looked opened his eyes and stared at me, and I saw his lips form the words he had told us all those nights ago, on our path to Dun Beal: *Most mages have one. A rare mage will have two. The rarest have three.* Then he let the magic go with a breath, and Miriel ran to catch him as he staggered.

"It's real," she said softly, brushing a lock of hair away from her cousin's face as he leaned his head on her shoulder, eyes beginning to drift shut. "It's *real*." She looked up at me and I saw her lips move. *It's real.*

I sat down on the floor with a jolt. I was shivering now, convulsively. I had learned to sneak and observe until many would have said I knew magic. But everyone knew—

—that was, it was completely certain—

—magic wasn't *real.*

Only, apparently it was.

Chapter 22

"It's real," Miriel said again, sometime later. That seemed to be the only thing either of us was capable of saying—or even thinking. The evening had passed in a haze of dancing and toasts in Pictish, the whiskey slowing my thoughts until the words became no more than a jumble of sounds. Fidach sat quietly, and though Morwen pressed him to see why he was so exhausted, he evaded her with answers about his journey, worries about the peace talks failing. When I murmured as much to Miriel, she only shrugged. Her eyes on Fidach's face were still watchful, wary.

No business had been done, not with the whole court celebrating. Lugh, sullen, would not be drawn out again after the fight the night before—and Miriel was too shocked to try in any case. It was all we could do to sit in the banquet hall silently, for I wanted nothing more than to take a horse and ride for the south shore, take a ship, escape this land with its ghosts and magicians. When at last we staggered to our rooms together, it was in silence. Fidach, looking at our shocked faces, suggested gently that we get some sleep. His gaze searched mine, and I only nodded. I could not think of a single thing to say.

"So what do we do now?" I asked in Heddria as the two of us climbed into our pallet beds. That managed to break her free of her daze.

"Sleep," she advised, with a firm nod. "He was right about that, at least. In the morning, it will all be clearer."

Her advice made sense, but I was unable to follow it. I played back every memory of the past week, and my mind drifted to the times I had found Fidach wandering alone outside Dun Druim. How guilty he looked. What he had been hiding. It seemed that I had only just slipped into an uneasy dream when, at dawn, Miriel sat bolt upright, looked at me, and said simply:

"Morwen."

"Bloody hell." I sank my head into my hands, and cut off

---

my next words as Fidach stirred in his sleep. My dreams had been of storms and rising earth, and too-vivid memories of the first days I had known Temar, when he had been a man who smiled at me with the promise of my destiny and I had known nothing of what was to come. I would wake with tears on my cheeks, and when I closed my eyes once more I would see Fidach's face twisted with concentration as he twisted earth within the air.

I was exhausted after a night with hardly any sleep. I did not think I could face the fact that we now had a mage for an enemy.

Miriel looked over to Fidach, who did not seem to have awoken, and then drew the covers about herself and beckoned me out of the room with her. She went to the chair by the fire and curled into it, and I mused that only she could look so dignified with a woolen blanket trailing behind her like a makeshift cape. She motioned for me to join her, and I sat with my arms drawn around my knees. The fires burned low and smoky here and my eyes burned.

"So," Miriel began, and I finished her sentence for her: "What do we know?"

It was always the question, for everything came back to knowledge. A court was a machine of near-infinite complexity, a beast ready to turn on anyone for its next meal and yet willing—if gentled—to be led anywhere. Miriel could charm and dazzle and seduce, and I, well, I could find their secrets and offer to pin their deals on their enemies. People were malleable if only we could figure out what they wanted. They key lay in knowing where to press, where to encourage, where to spark anger, and to know that one needed information or extraordinary luck. Preferably both.

I wasn't sure anymore if luck was on our side: catching the Cornovii invasion before it occurred, but then being sent into danger ourselves to resolve it. Finding a potential ally...and learning that the stakes had been changed greatly. No, luck was not to be trusted. We needed information.

"It's real, and the treaty *was* broken. Our beloved queen should have ceded the throne, yes?" Miriel had ticked off the first two things, and I nodded at her raised brows.

"We know Morwen at least has the Call of Time," I suggested. Miriel frowned at me. "We couldn't figure out how they knew about Fidach," I reminded her. "Or how they suspected they might find us at Glen Tuam."

Miriel only blinked, a delicate flutter of her dark lashes, and held up another finger. She did not look pleased to be factoring magic into her calculations.

"We know that Branwen supports Talyn," I said, and Miriel nodded.

"But Lugh does not." Two more fingers.

"Still, Talyn is his brother. That can bring pressure to bear. Lugh might make a misstep."

Miriel nodded and we sat and stared into the fire, stomachs growling. We were fed the same as the warriors—indeed, the same as Branwen and Lugh, but the food was not plentiful. I suspected they were trying to make a point.

"It all comes down to what my cousin will do," she said at last, and as if on cue, the door to the inner chamber opened and Fidach emerged.

"Good morning," he said courteously. I nodded, my eyes resting on him warily. He wore the iron torc, as if to flaunt his status and his goodwill. "Did you sleep well?"

Our eyes met, and at once his question seemed ridiculous. Why bother with formality when he and I had been at each other's throats mere hours ago, deciding between restraint and the killing blow? I remembered my own fear at his strength, and the strange surge of joy—to be *acting* once more, defending, matching wits with a worthy opponent. I knew more about him now. It disturbed me to find that I trusted him all the more for having fought him, and yet I knew he had failed to strike where he might have. He, too, had held back. We smiled slightly at one another, and for a moment I had the foolish thought that we were not courtiers together anymore.

"We don't have time for pleasantries." Miriel's voice was not icy, but weary, and it pulled me back from my flight of fancy. "Sit. Did you know what Branwen was planning?"

"No." Fidach looked between the two of us.

"She is demanding you as the cost of peace," Miriel said flatly, before I could find a gentler way to say it.

"Me?" Fidach was aghast. He rubbed sleep out of his eyes and shook his head as if he might have misheard, and looked at me again.

"She says that the treaty must be upheld," I told him. "She called your mother faithless for keeping you. She...well, I'm sorry, but she doesn't think well of Aoife. I think it's genuine. She thinks it was cruel for your mother to have hidden you. But she says she cannot trust Aoife unless she does not have you."

Fidach slumped back in his seat.

"I should have known she would ask it," he said softly. He looked down at his hands, where a golden band was fashioned into the shape of a dragon. "I realized before I went to sleep last night. You said taking the throne. She would never make me her heir, not over her own blood."

"No, but she might wed you to her heir," Miriel suggested delicately, and I could have cursed her. "A true mage-king."

"No," he said instantly, and at our looks of evident disbelief, he shook his head. "I mean, yes. It makes sense. It makes too much sense. But I could not...." He would not look at us, and I looked away, trying to calm the racing of my heart. He was not pondering the alliance. That was very good, if hardly important; Fidach's feelings might not be consulted at all.

"But then what?" I asked, and Miriel nodded.

"Catwin is right. If they could not keep you here as an heir, would they....?"

"No, they would never put me to death," Fidach said. His mouth quirked at my expression. "Certainly not such a valuable commodity. If the Cornovii could not bind me to their line, they would claim me for their own another way. It would be the only way to guarantee that I was no longer able to do my mother's bidding. I would be severed from her line, no longer her son in the eyes of the gods."

"A ceremony can neither take loyalty...nor give it," Miriel said, and Fidach flashed her a small smile.

"Indeed not. But the distance between the courts would drive a wedge. It would mean I was no longer my mother's advisor. And they would not be cruel to me, Miriel. They would take me as one of their own. Indeed, I would likely still be a prince. They would...treat me well."

"What does that mean?" Miriel asked sharply. Both of us had heard the change in his voice, yearning.

"You know what it means." His face was stubborn. "In this court, I would never be asked to hide what I was. I would not be asked to live without magic. I would be celebrated for what I was."

"Fidach..." My voice trailed away, but Miriel was not so circumspect. Her lips had tightened at the mention of magic, but she did not address it.

"Will this be a problem?"

"What do you mean?" His voice had grown dangerous, but she did not shrink from it. She matched him.

"You know exactly what I mean. You rejected it at first, but perhaps now you are reconsidering. Do I have to worry about you taking their side, forcing us to a peace your mother will not like, giving your blood to the Cornovii? You say you should have known—well, did you? Did you plan this?"

"Of course not!"

"No?"

"The marriage, no," I said, and Miriel gave a tiny nod. Fidach frowned at me, and I lifted my shoulders.

"I was watching you."

"Of course you were." He was annoyed, and I flushed, looked down at my hands. He did not expect my spying, and that made it different, somehow, from Heddred. In Heddred, where everyone had known they were watched, all the time. Here, it seemed a breach of trust.

"So?" Miriel asked, when he did not answer.

"No, I am not planning to betray you all." His voice was tight.

"And your mother..."

"What does it matter what my mother wants?" Fidach hissed. "She has sent us on an impossible mission. Even if we secure peace—and we will not—she will never be able to force the lords to agree. The blood debts run too deep."

"Then persuade them to let the blood debts cancel each other before what you said comes true and we all lie dead!" Miriel shouted. My anxious look at the door recalled her to herself and pressed her lips together angrily.

"Do you truly think we can accomplish that?" Fidach hissed.

"There is always a way," Miriel said, wholly assured, but her words only angered him.

"Well, now there is. They have named their price, and it is *one* life. Should we consider it, then? Is that what you are saying?"

"No. Out of the question." Miriel's voice was flat. She shook her head at him once, emphatically. "We return to Dun Druim together. I don't know the whole of your mother's plan, but I know it was not to give you up."

"I would not be killed! They would treat me well, I would be a prince, I would advise Branwen—"

"Yes, you would, and make heirs to rival Connor! And you think your mother could accept that? How long until you realized you were priming their army for another war? How long until they had you bound to help them against your own kin?" She shook her head again. "No, Fidach. We cannot allow that."

"We may not have a choice," Fidach warned her. "Much as I do not seek this marriage—and I don't, stop looking at me like I'm a power-hungry maniac—I don't see a way around giving me to the Cornovii one way or another. You play with fire if you cede Morini farmland, and that's the only other thing we have to give."

"Your mother will have to accept it. A good bargain," Miriel said sharply, "leaves both parties unhappy."

"Well enough, but giving them farmland doesn't make *you* unhappy. Just giving them me." He raised a hand to cut Miriel. "If you would just consider—"

"No. We'll rewrite the damned treaty if we have to. But I am not leaving my family here, Fidach. I will not return home to tell a mother that the cost of peace was her never seeing her son again. We will find a way out of this."

"I don't think we can! Morwen says—"

"Morwen! How many secrets have you spilled to her?

151

How far did she worm her way into your affections? Did she turn you, or were you already turned—or, worse, are you trying to gain their trust so you can stab them in the back? I won't be made a fool of, Fidach. I'm here to bargain honestly."

"I know what I'm doing. Don't you dare lecture me."

"I'll lecture you if I damned well please! You put us in danger, you and your mother both."

"Will you still bargain for peace?" he asked her, his voice dangerous.

"Will *you*?"

He moved nearly as quickly as she did. He was out the door and away before I had a chance to call him back, and the door slammed in his wake.

"Some peace delegation we make," Miriel said sourly. She sank into one of the chairs and stared at the flames moodily.

"I'm going after him." I reached for my cloak, and she looked over at me sharply.

"You'll stay here."

"Why?"

"Do I need a reason? I seem to recall you saying that you swore an oath to me and I am telling you to stay. If you must know, I need your mind to help me untangle all of this."

"I'll bribe the stable boys and talk to the maids," I said impatiently. "I'll do it as soon as I get back. But right now, we need someone to follow him and see what he's up to. We need to make sure he doesn't get in trouble."

"What is it to you if he does?"

"Well, for one thing, he's the only person in this court who's even possibly on our side. Isn't that worth anything to you?" She only looked at me, and I sighed. "You didn't have to antagonize him. Even if he might be an enemy. Especially then."

"No? I should just have let him play the spoiled prince and spin his own plots? He'll ruin it all if we're not careful."

"If you think this is petulance, then we can win him back. What?" My brow furrowed as Miriel looked at me accusingly.

"You're taking his side."

"I am not."

"You are!"

"Fine. I don't think you should have yelled at him. But that's far from taking his side. Miriel, you need to be gentle."

"Why? What does gentleness accomplish?"

"This is a game of loyalty, isn't it?"

"No. It's a game with hidden rules and hidden goals. I said I'd broker peace, and I will—but not for Aoife, and not for Fidach. And I won't keep coddling him while he runs around courting disaster!"

"Oh, like you're one to be lecturing someone about that!"

"What does that mean?"

"It means I picked up after you while you ran into trouble for five *years* in Penekket! While you courted treason, and courted Wilhem behind Garad's back. While you defied your uncle, I had your back! I cleaned up your messes!"

"And what about your messes?" she spat back. "Temar? Loving the man who would have done anything to see my uncle on the throne? How many beatings did I take for secrets you spilled? How much did we both pay for your trust?"

"We're only *alive* because of Temar! He bought us peace with his life. He picked me for you—what d'you think would have happened to you if you'd been brought to Penekket without me? What if he hadn't spared my life after the Duke found out you'd been seeing Garad?"

Miriel swallowed.

"Go, then." It was a challenge, a dare. Her look said that she did not think I had it in me to turn my back and go.

I turned on my heel and left.

Chapter 23

I found Fidach up on the battlements. He was a dark shape against the sky, his cloak billowing in the wind while he sat perched on the roof of one of the watchtowers. He turned his head to the sound of my progress as I climbed and moved to let me share a perch on the slope of the roof. The height was dizzying; I could see the faint glint of the ocean from here, sun on water.

"I used to climb like that back in Voltur," I told him, to break the silence. He had not answered, and so I tried to set him off-guard: "It was an old castle, and there were chinks in the stone, so you could climb anywhere if you put your mind to it—but Roine said I would break my neck."

"The woman who raised you?" He had turned his head idly.

"Yes." I took a piece of straw from the roof and twisted it.

"You never speak of her." He looked over in interest, and I realized my mistake. I did not want to speak of this.

"You and I never spoke much to start with," I pointed out. A deflection; I saw him smile.

"True. But Miriel said something once, and then looked like she wished she had not. I've wondered, that's all."

"What did she say?"

"I had asked about her mother and father, thinking she must have left them—that you had both left behind your families. She said that they were both dead, and when I expressed my condolences, she said she had been lucky." His voice changed. "Unlike you," he finished softly.

"You don't know the story, do you? Miriel never said?"

"No." He looked away, a deliberate gesture to let me get ahold of myself, and I blinked back tears.

"Well, then," I said savagely. "You might as well know. She took me in because she heard a prophecy that her betrayal of someone she loved would bring about a revolution and end the monarchy. And when a woman in the village gave birth, and said her daughter was born to be betrayed...well, Roine took me in. And raised me." I didn't want to say it. I likely did not have to say it. The words came anyway: "And then, during the invasion, she came to kill me. Four times she tried to see me killed. Miriel saved me, actually, the last time."

"Yet you speak of this woman fondly."

"She is my mother," I said, and saw a frown on his face. "Until the end...well, I have more good memories of her than bad. She loved me, you know."

"But she would have killed you."

"I can love her without forgiving her," I said, and my voice came out all broken. "I...." *I have no words for this.*

He nodded, and looked out at the sea, and I had the absurd desire to tell him that I was sorry I had killed his father. It would be a lie and the truth all rolled up into one. How long had the Duke held an entire tribe hostage? And yet, he was a husband who had never come home, a father who had never seen his son. I opened my mouth to speak, and what came out instead was,

"Why did you go along with it? Your mother's plan. Why did you hide what you were?"

"What else could I do?" he put his head in his hands. "You know the court. You know who would take the throne if she had to give it up—they would never have asked for your help, they would be riding on Dun Beal with an army. They would have done it years ago. It was...better...to stay hidden."

"You don't think that."

"I do." He would not look at me. "The Gwyddu nearly destroyed Priteni: the people, the very earth itself. They called storms down to destroy crops and sank riverbeds, raised cliffs. That is what happens when magic walks with power. And I believe it, you know—my mother is the best the Morini have for a monarch."

"But the price is your happiness," I said passionately.

"I am one man," he said, as if he had long repeated it to himself in the dark watches of the night. "One man, against all the Morini."

"Please don't stay," I whispered, and he looked over at me in surprise.

"What?"

I flushed and looked down at my hands, shook my head.

"When Miriel says that," he observed, "you say nothing. Do you come to bargain on her behalf?" There was a touch of pride in his tone, something prickly I could put no name to—and yet I had heard just such a tone in Miriel's voice. It was oddly familiar.

"No. I didn't even intend to say it. It just came out." He laughed, then. "Honestly."

"I didn't doubt you. It's just odd, after the past few days— well, my whole life, really—to hear someone tell me the truth." His smile died when he looked back at the sea. "But why shouldn't I, Catwin? It's the solution to everything. My mother keeps her throne, we have peace, and I...will be allowed to be a mage."

"Is that what you want? To leave your family behind?"

"What family? There is my mother, and Connor, and my aunts." He looked over at me and saw me white-faced at the dismissal. To me, it was a wealth of kin. "I apologize. That was...I didn't think it through."

"I only meant...family is more than that." I couldn't seem to find words. "You don't really know what it is to be homesick, but it's everything, your highness. The people you see in the halls and smile. The way people greet each other on the holy days. The way snow piles against your window, your seat in the hall. Home and family aren't just a building and blood."

"You want to go back to Heddred, don't you? And stop calling me, 'your highness.'"

I ducked my head at the order.

"Sorry. And I don't want to go back, that's the thing. There was nothing for me there. No family, nowhere I could live. Temar..." I swallowed. "Anyway, it still hurts. So if you do have those things, I think it would hurt more."

"You know you have family among the Morini," he told me. "Any of the warriors would have been proud to march at your side."

"And I at theirs," I said automatically, and then realized it was true. "I would, truly. But I don't want to march to war at all."

"I know. I'm just beginning to think that we may not have a choice."

"Miriel will find a way. She always finds a way."

"Tell me about her. About...the two of you. My mother won't speak of it."

"Any story of the two of us is a story of your father. I'm not sure you want to know."

"I do." His voice was strong. "I have to, Catwin."

"I don't think your mother ever knew him like we did," I said desperately. "Please remember that."

"I'll try." But his eyes were said. "The rest of them knew."

"People always like to say they knew. They suspected this or that, they saw through the lies. Well, most people don't, not really." I smiled humorlessly. "They'll all say they knew about you, you know."

"I suppose they will." He laughed, and looked down. "Please. Tell me."

"Very well." I wrapped my arms around my knees. "He wanted the throne for himself. That was his bargain with Temar—Necthan—he thought, but really it was to put his *blood* on the throne. Temar tricked him, he was always working to have Miriel wedded to the King. Your father would just have had her as the king's mistress, a forbidden lover who could turn his head while your father staged a coup."

"Somehow I think that doesn't tell all of it," he said flatly, and I sighed. *I would want to know*, I told myself, and still a piece of me whispered: *but he doesn't understand.*

"It doesn't."

"Tell me." His eyes met mine, both of us stubborn. "Catwin, if I cannot ask you as a friend, I will command you as a prince."

"You don't need to do that." I threw away the twisted piece of straw. "But for what it's worth...it's not the prince I don't want to tell. It's the friend."

"Thank you."

We stared at one another in the sunlight, and I could feel

the mistrust clawing for a place in my heart. He was so honest, so hurt. I had trusted Miriel like this, hadn't I? The stakes were different here. I had to remember it, and I was afraid that I could not. I looked away and cleared my throat.

"Your father was willing to do anything to get the throne. Anything. To win the war with Ismir, he tricked a general into defecting. The prince who lost killed himself, the defector's family was murdered…. But your father was made a lord. He married his sister to a nobleman and locked her away until she gave birth and he could see that the child was trueborn. That was Miriel. He never cared for her. I think he even hated her, because he hated her mother, and he hated her because he needed her. I think Temar was the only person he didn't hate, and that's because he thought he had the upper hand. But he always knew Miriel might turn on him, and he couldn't forgive her for that. He tried to frighten her, and…he did."

"But he gave her you."

"He gave her me," I agreed. "It's easy to say he shouldn't have, but that's the same as people saying they knew he was trouble, isn't it? I saved Miriel's life more than once. With me, she secured the king's hand in marriage, and the love of his heir— and when the king was assassinated, she escaped. No, that wasn't me," I added sharply when Fidach opened his mouth. "I wasn't an assassin. Most of the time."

"Except for my father," Fidach said. I looked over at him, and he tried to smile. "I know why you did it, you don't need to say anything. I tried to hate you for it when you first came, but the more I learned of you…"

"Fidach, I truly am sorry." What did you *say* to someone whose father you had killed? My words were as inadequate here as they had been with Aoife. "I regret it every day. It isn't easy to live with."

"But you would do it again."

"Yes," I admitted finally. "He was going to turn the army on itself and kill the king. It would have ruined Heddred. He would not have ruled kindly. Miriel would have suffered for it, and Temar, and all the people who died when he mutinied."

"He would have done anything for a crown, you said."

"Yes."

"And yet he wouldn't even come back to see me." Fidach's jaw was clenched. "I was his *son.*"

"Fidach...." I could not begin to know how to comfort him.

"Go on, say it's a mercy." A dare. I shook my head, and he sighed. "What was my uncle like, then? You loved him, I can see it when you talk about him. He must have been..." His voice trailed away.

"He saved my life. He saved Miriel's life, although she'd never admit it. They hated one another. You know, I think if he'd thought about it, he would known I was as untrustworthy as Miriel."

"Untrustworthy?" Fidach looked over at me, surprised out of his black mood.

"I suppose. Temar—Necthan...he was absolutely loyal to the Duke. To your father. You know this, yes? And your father made me loyal to Miriel."

"No one can make you loyal."

"I'm not sure of that. He made me swear an oath, and I would never have thought it would come true, but it did. Sometimes it feels like he made me from nothing. Anyway, your uncle and I—we weren't always on the same side. I betrayed him, he betrayed me. He was desperate to get Miriel on the throne to fulfill the bargain, and I was desperate to keep her safe. But he spoke for me when the Duke would have killed me, and he didn't come for me when Miriel and I ran away, and at the end..." My voice broke, and I clenched my hands in the straw. It was over and done with. I did not want to cry about it anymore; the fact that I did, sometimes, I did not even tell Miriel. "At the end, I told him I was going to go assassinate the prince of the invading force. Their army didn't want to fight, they were just all scared. And Kasimir was crazy. Temar talked me into going together, the two of us. We knew we weren't going to make it out, but we thought it was worth it."

"And?" Fidach reached out to take my hand, and I clenched my fingers around his without even thinking. I stared out to sea and watched the moonlight blur and shift with my tears.

"He went without me."

"Catwin." I looked away. I wanted to be a bird, fly away into the night and leave all of this behind. I had never told this story to anyone; Miriel knew, and she never spoke of it. If Aoife knew more than that I had killed her husband, she knew of it from Miriel, and to her credit, the queen never asked me about Temar. I had not known it would hurt this much to say aloud. "Catwin, I didn't know."

"How could you?" I wiped my hand over my nose and grimaced. A handkerchief appeared in the corner of my vision. "Thank you."

"I'm sorry I asked."

"You don't have to be."

"I am. My uncle, my father...your mother. I should not have forced you to tell it."

"I chose to." I sniffed and looked up at the sky. I could not face Fidach just yet. "A friend once told me that speaking of things chases the shadows away from them. I hope it's true."

"Mayhap." He withdrew his hand and rested his arms on his knees. "But kingdoms, I am afraid, are built on lies and half-truths, and it seems that courts are made of shadows. And where does that leave us, Catwin? You and me and my cousin—Lugh lying if he says he will ever accept peace, my mother lying about me, and Branwen in the middle, trying to claim me like a prize. Where does that leave us?"

"We can break the treaty if we have to," I told him. The bitterness in his voice tore at my heart.

"I hadn't thought of that," he admitted. "I never thought it was—well, all the more reason for me to stay here. Catwin...don't argue with me. You know I'm right. And you know it's not likely Miriel will find something better. Catwin?"

I *was* looking at him now, shaking my head. I pressed my lips together to keep silence until I could think of the right thing to say, the pace to put pressure. It seemed easy with everyone else. Why could I not see where his fault lines lay?

"Miriel's right, you know," I told him finally. Too blunt, but I did not know any other way, and Miriel's quick wit had earned her nothing with Fidach. He went to look away, and I put my hand on his arm. "Please just listen. You say that Lugh will never accept peace. Yes? That means even if we leave you here, he'll march on Dun Druim someday. He'll have had years to turn your head. It wouldn't be weakness for you to fall to that, Fidach. There's pain, and loneliness, and fear, and remembering the slights and the whispers at home. You'd be all alone here, and he'd force you to help him—or he'd kill you. Neither of those serves anyone but Lugh."

He bent his head.

"What do you want me to say, Catwin? That I won't stay? We both know it's not my choice to make. My mother might even…"

"What?"

"Don't you think she might bargain me away?"

"No," I said, because it was the right thing to say. I reached out to take his hand, and squeezed my fingers around his. I was not sure of my words, and I did not want him to know it.

"King of the Cornovii," he said glumly. "It has a ring to it. That, or Queen's Advisor, I suppose."

"Oh, don't be like that," I said, and saw his mouth curve slightly. "We'll get you out of this. We're in this together. For peace."

"I see." His smile died and he looked down at his hands. "Come on, then. Let's go back to Miriel."

Chapter 24

And yet, as the days wore on, we made no progress at all.
We spent long hours closeted with Lugh, Morwen, Seiysell,
poring over maps and bargaining sections of forest and
farmland. Branwen stayed away, ostensibly to conduct the
business of the kingdom and allow her delegation to lead, more
likely to avoid the incessant stalling that we had resorted to:
Lugh would not settle for less than nine of every ten farms, and
Miriel would not agree to cede Fidach.

"Can we not at least discuss it?" Fidach pleaded with her
in our rooms, and she turned her face away from him where he
paced. I watched the tread of his boots. He walked as softly as a
hunter, with the grace of a warrior. Fidach always moved as if he
should have a blade in his hand.

Miriel shook her head. The peat fire lit her hair red-gold,
making her a creature of fire and earth, not the statue of blue
and ivory she had become here at Dun Beal. She sat still and
silent while Lugh spoke. She no longer smiled. And at rest,
during banquets, her eyes rested on Fidach as if she would strip
his flesh away and see into his soul, measuring him as a weapon.

I tried not to think about where I had seen that look
before, but the Duke's eyes haunted my dreams, cold as chips of
stone. I remembered the way he stared at Miriel, entirely
unmoved by her beauty or the shared blood in their veins. Only
the Duke had ever been so cold, as if he could see nothing but
clockwork inside others; even Temar had been kinder to those
he spied on. Now Miriel watched Fidach as if he were a bridge, a
strut that might fail and bring our peace plans tumbling down.

"I do not bargain in lives," she said simply. "It is barbaric."

"Perhaps it is my choice," he shot back, and Miriel shook
her head.

"Only if you stay once bargaining is concluded. Stay if you
will, but I will not allow it into a treaty. I will not go back and tell

a mother that I signed away her son."

"I would have thought…" He dropped into a chair and studied her face, and at last Miriel turned unwillingly to look at him.

"Yes?"

"I would have thought you would be more ruthless," he said at last.

"Why?" Miriel's wariness faded into curiosity, but Fidach seemed to think he had said something wrong.

"It's nothing. We should get back to negotiations."

Miriel, who knew that Fidach often leaned close to speak to me as the negotiations wore on, who often sought me out in the evenings to ask about the nobles and learn my thoughts on the day's bargaining, looked at me for answers. I shook my head blankly. I could not think of what he might mean. Fidach would know that his father and uncle had trained us—but even after my story on the rooftop, I did not think he knew what that meant. The stories the courtiers told behind their hands at Dun Druim were wild in their inaccuracy, with Temar as a saint and the Duke as a madman, and Aoife had never known what either man became.

What Fidach expected of Miriel, I could not say, but he was correct that the Cornovii wanted him above all else. Every impossible bargain Lugh presented was tempered with the sly suggestion that perhaps different terms would be better for all. Seiysell, no less mulish than Fidach about being bargained away, made no such concessions, but her voice had little weight. When Morwen sat by Fidach, the consort would watch them with a look of naked greed on his face—a pair of mages, more power than Aoife would ever be able to summon. Mages to raise the earth or call storms, tell him the truth of his subjects' minds. It was not difficult to see what Lugh wanted.

Morwen, however, was the slyest in her interest. Always one to speak reason when her colleagues made impossible demands, she nonetheless spoke often to Fidach, and kindly. She listened while he spoke, her eyes fixed on his face, and dinner often found her at his side, leaning in to hear his words over the din of the great hall. Fidach was at ease in her presence as he was nowhere else, and even if she did not look on him possessively, I could not help but think that Morwen was turning the prince's mind subtly, irrevocably, and entirely on purpose.

Conversation, I might have matched. If not, I then Miriel, who was well-trained in the art of appearing to be a perfect ally. But Morwen had two things neither of us could claim: magic, and knowledge of how to use it. After his mother's prohibition on his magic, Fidach was drawn to Morwen like a moth to flame. When the dinner platters were cleared and it was time for singing or dancing, Fidach never even looked up from his close-headed conferences. When Miriel looked over to gauge our support for a treaty item she had proposed, more often than not Fidach and Morwen would be speaking together, low, and he would not even be aware of Miriel's gaze on him. And when we spoke of the day's negotiations, secure in our own room, Fidach would speak only of Morwen.

"She is not sure of the war," he told us once.

"Is that so." Miriel's voice was anything but pleasant, but Fidach did not notice.

"She did not think it would work when they rode out the first time, for she said she saw no ill intent in her visions of me then. Now, with you both, she is even less sure. She thinks that Lugh will ask too much and you will leave."

"*We* will leave," Miriel said icily, and although Fidach nodded, he was hardly listening. He was poring over a diagram Morwen had given him, and with a murmur and a sketch of a bow, he left us to ourselves in the room.

"He's going to her again," Miriel said, as if she were a wife, and Morwen a rival.

"Can you blame him?" I dropped into the chair he had vacated and looked at her. She was huddled miserably into her own chair, eyes near bruised from her exhaustion, shivering in the drafty room, but even in her pitiful state she managed to look furious.

"I didn't say I blamed him," she whispered fiercely. "But he should know better. He shouldn't go."

"Miriel, we don't know anything about magic. No one he's ever known has known magic. He has to be trained."

"Why would you give your finest weapon to an enemy to train?" she asked sharply. "Fidach is our advantage."

"And more of one if he has training."

"*Less* of one if he defects."

"Miriel..."

She sighed and sank her face into her hands.

"You don't want him to leave, either."

"No, but..." I did not know what to say.

"We need rest, Catwin. You most of all, trying to keep track of both of us. Get some sleep."

"Aren't you going to sleep?"

"I can't rest yet." She arranged her skirts and gave me a sweet smile, tired and stubborn all rolled into one. "I'll be there soon. Go, Catwin. A tired spy is a spy who makes mistakes, and we can't afford any of those. I will follow soon."

And yet, when I woke hours later, it was to the sound of voices in the outer room.

"—nothing for *you*," Miriel whispered passionately. "Can you not see it?"

"Lugh, yes." Fidach's voice was flat. "Do you think I'm a complete fool? I can see that. Even Branwen does not care for me at all. But Morwen never speaks to me of leaving the Morini."

"Of course she doesn't," Miriel snapped. "Lugh plays for your affection, Branwen tries to trap you with duty. Morwen only shows you what you might have if you stayed. They won't rest until they have you."

"Then why can't you let me stay? Here, I will be privy to their plans. From here, I can stop the armies before they march. I would be a voice for *peace*, Miriel."

"You would be alone," Miriel said flatly. "You have never been alone before in your life, Fidach. You don't know what it means. In time, you would start to sympathize. You would not even see it happen, but you would become their weapon and you would move against us."

"You think I am so faithless?"

"I think you are human! *I* know what it is to be a commodity, traded between noble families. Without Catwin, without an ally, it would have destroyed me. You think you are

---

165

doing this for us—"

"I am doing it for you! So the Morini can be safe. So you and Catwin can go home. Connor will rule after my mother, and I—I will know that I did something useful with my life. I will be her agent here, I swear it."

"Can't you see the lies you're telling yourself? You want to be a mage, you want to be accepted for what you are. Well, they'll never trust you any more than the Morini lords do."

He did not answer her. I heard his footsteps and the door creaked open, then slammed behind him. There was no sound for a long moment; Miriel would be staring at the door, listening to his tread recede down the hall. Her mind would be whirling, planning her next move. She walked slowly back into our room.

"Catwin?"

I said nothing. I did not know what to say to her, this woman of steel and fire. Fidach was our ally, *should* be our ally. And as we saw him slipping away, neither Miriel's pleas nor my quiet could bring him back. For the first time, I was beginning to taste true despair.

Chapter 25

"Talyn's their focal point," Miriel said the next night as she pinned up her hair. "Willing or unwilling, he's the going to be their leader."

As more and more specimens from Innis Tearmen were unpacked, the Cornovii were finding a land rich in iron, copper, herbs. Wool from the sheep seemed healthy, and Talyn walked about looking at once as happy and defiant as Lugh looked sullen and forbidding.

Miriel scowled at her reflection in the little mirror we had. Between Talyn's success and the entertainment of the peace delegation, we could expect yet another night of whiskey and singing. We were attempting to look as presentable as we could in our road-worn clothes, and it was not going well.

"Lugh said—"

"That he wants to talk with us over dinner. I know. Why he suddenly wants to talk now, when he would hardly speak to us at negotiations, I have no idea." Miriel paused, thinking. "He's up to something. But what, I won't know until I speak to him. Anyway, it will hardly be urgent. Talyn's the one we need to court again, now that the people are showing their mood."

She put her arms down and turned in front of the polished metal plate that served as a mirror. There was no hint of her fears now, for there was no room for such things in the performance of the court; I, miserable in my doubt, wondered if I could ever learn to do this as well as she could.

I watched her turn her head prettily, practice her most flirtatious smile. Her shoulders came up, a gesture of innocent pleasure and joy, and then she dropped them and extended her neck elegantly. A grave look at the mirror—the serious emissary—and then her spontaneous smile, dawn breaking, a young woman in love.

"Fidach, what kind of dances will there be?" She turned,

twisting her hips so that her skirts would flare around her. "I should like to practice, if you'd—Fidach?"

"Must you do that?" He was seated by the fire, looking fixedly away, his hands white where they gripped the arms of the chair.

"Do what?"

"I told you." I could see muscles twitch at his jaw. "I told you not to behave like that."

"Oh, for—" Miriel marched over to where he was standing, and he avoided her eyes. She moved, patiently, until at last he looked up at her. "You may not like how I came by these skills. *I* don't like it. But I have them. We might as well put them to use."

"And scream all your secrets to Morwen in the process? Your whole mind is laid open right now! I can see everything!"

Miriel, practicing her walk towards the mirror, froze. She turned back slowly, her jaw set. Fidach had warned us, of course, on the ride to Dun Beal. A warning neither of us had heeded, thinking it no more than imagination and dreams at best, and lies at worst. In the whirl of diplomacy and intrigue, we had not yet realized just how far the world was shifted. It was bad to think that the stories of mage kings and storm weavers were true, but far worse to know that two people, in the hall, were no less than truthseers.

"It wouldn't be so obvious to me if weren't kin," Fidach was explaining to Miriel, "but Morwen is watching you. She has more training than I do. She'll know what to look for, and Miriel..." His voice trailed off when he laid a hand on her arm and she jerked it out of his reach.

"Don't. *Touch*. Me." Her teeth were gritted.

"I'm trying to help," Fidach said. I saw annoyance in the set of his head.

"No! Stay out of my memories!"

She stepped forward and I was between then in an instant, pushing her back and pulling on his arm to lower it.

"Miriel. Fidach." Who might be outside the door, listening? Who would be watching when Miriel arrived at the banquet, white-faced and shaking with anger? "Please, now isn't the time."

"He's prying through my memories and he hasn't the right!" Miriel shot a furious glare at me, at my hand on Fidach's arm. The accusation was plain in her eyes.

"It wasn't on purpose!" Most people were petrified in the face of Miriel's anger, but Fidach was not most people. I wondered now if the Duke, terrifying and cold in his anger when I knew him, had once been as fiery as the two of them: Miriel white-faced now, and Fidach her match, narrowed eyes and clenched fists. "You might as well walk up and scream them to me. They're everywhere on you, I can see his face, I can hear his voice—"

"Don't *speak* of it!"

For a moment I thought he might lunge at her, and then he sank his head into his hands and dropped into the chair. Miriel swallowed and looked away. Her hands were clenched in little fists, the same false bravery she had used with the Duke. *We both know you can hurt me, but you'll never see it.*

"I'm sorry," Fidach said at last. "It isn't your fault. You couldn't have known. No one was supposed to know what I was. I wouldn't have seen it if we weren't blood to one another. I see it with my mother. Some with others, but it's like whispers." He looked up at her, and she drew away instinctively, putting the chair between them. Her fingers closed around the back of it as if it was her last link to reality.

"I don't like you seeing into my mind," she said softly, and he shook his head.

"I don't like it, either. I grew up being told that my father was a monster who would have ruined Priteni given half a chance. They were always watching me, they thought his fate would find me and I would become as he was. Do you know what it's like to be watched as an enemy when you're a small child?"

Their eyes met.

"Yes," they both said, the twist of his mouth showing me that he had seen the truth of her words. Miriel moved, finally. She came to sit on the floor by his feet, and I despaired to see how many mannerisms of the court had returned to her. She sat in a beautiful swirl of cloth, her head raised elegantly, her spin ramrod straight, and she held his arm. He put his hand over hers and they tilted their heads together, cousins, both knowing the spite of others for their kinship. I, who had never known kin at all, withdrew to watch.

"You never knew him," Miriel said softly, and Fidach shook his head.

"Only in others' words and my mother's memories. I could see hints of it sometimes, things she missed, things she told herself she didn't see. But she loved him—sometimes I think he really loved her. It was easy to pretend…"

"Until I arrived." Miriel had long ago learned to search out the reasons others might hate her, and she saw it quickly now.

"Until you arrived. And I saw what he was, or what he became. Every time I see it, I wonder—he never knew I existed, but what if he *had*? Would he have come back for me?" Fidach's face crumpled. "Would he have done the same to me? And then sometimes I think I'd rather he had…because that means he would have cared enough to come back."

He looked up at her with his face twisted and Miriel bit her lip against the words he wouldn't want to hear: that he would never have wanted her uncle to find him, boy child that he was, a bargaining chip to pass on the Celys name, a warrior to lead troops.

"How could you bear to see me?" Miriel asked finally, and he squeezed her hand.

"I could learn not to see it, if I knew when I might see you—the hall at dinner, or festivals…. And you never held it against me—you, of all people! What did the rest of them have to complain about? It was Necthan that sacrificed his life, it was you who got beaten—and you, Catwin." His blue eyes found me and I swallowed at the memories as they flooded back. "None of the rest of them had anything other than suspicion and dislike, but you, who had real cause to hate him….you didn't hate me for my blood."

"Blood means nothing," Miriel said softly. "Wearing a symbol on your chest means nothing. Your fate is your own."

"Not here," Fidach said at last. "Here, blood…carries. Even you have blood that binds you here, through my father. I think only Catwin could ever be free in our lands." His eyes found mine and he smiled. "The only free woman in all Priteni. But you bound yourself to my cousin."

"I did." I tried to smile at Miriel, who sighed.

"Well, then," she said finally. "You will have to keep Morwen from watching me, cousin. For charm them, I must."

"You're sure you wish to do this?"

"Can you think of a better way? No? Then come along, both of you. We have Lugh and Morwen to distract, and Talyn to charm."

"Wait." Fidach sat up in his chair at last. "No. First you tell me your plan."

"We're going to get you out of here."

"Miriel, you may not have that option. Branwen gave it to you as a choice, but has she ever once pushed for my mother to step down? No, it always me she asks for. You have to face that we may not be able to win this."

"We're not just going to leave you here!" My voice rose and both of them looked at me, surprised.

"The trick lies in the breaking the court's will for war," Miriel said simply. "Break it now and Lugh will have no momentum. Give them farmland to feed themselves, pastures for sheep, and they will not so easily be stirred to battle again. We can show them that we can be trusted, but we must steal their desire for vengeance. No one *wants* war, Fidach."

"You truly think that, don't you?" Fidach asked her. "You think that everyone hates to fight, and you can soothe them and right their wrongs. You don't know what it is to have the world become a torment until the only way to keep yourself from going mad is to remember every slight, to unleash your rage so that it does not eat you up inside.

"Lugh knows it. It has overcome everything else inside of him. He was once not so different from me, you know. Talyn told me he was gentle when he was a boy. He worked in the fields with his tenants and he tried to shield them and he watched their children die of hunger and sickness, and he was forged into a blade. He wavered when he met us, but he has hardened himself against us. His heart is fire now. He has one will, and that

---

171

is to destroy us. Whether fate aids him...we have yet to know."

We stared at him, two women who had not seen our homes in near a decade, taken from our homes and forged into tools. I opened my mouth to ask how he knew, and closed it again, and Miriel cut me off.

"If we fail, those in Dun Druim will die, Fidach."

"Then you had best consider giving me up," he said shortly.

"And you had best consider what you told me," Miriel snapped back. "For if only destruction will do for Lugh, then we must destroy him whether or not you stay. I'm not going to let a madman remake Priteni."

Fidach looked over at her then, and he looked so bitter that even Miriel took a step back.

"You really don't know what you are, do you?" he asked. "You don't know what you have. If you could just let go of your damned morals for a moment and see the world as it is..."

"What then?" Miriel asked him, and he bit his lip, looked into the fire.

"You could build any peace you wanted. You think you're powerless, but you have more power now than anyone else, and you won't even use it."

"Fidach." He brushed past her and made for the door, and Miriel looked back at me, bewildered. "What did that mean?"

"I don't...I don't know."

"I'll stall for you," Miriel said urgently. "Go find him. Talk to him."

"You know Lugh won't tolerate us sneaking around."

"So talk some sense into Fidach," Miriel advised. "And anyway, you won't be sneaking. Make sure you're somewhere you can be seen. Say hello to the guards. But there's something there, Catwin, he let something slip—and it's the last piece. I know it is."

Chapter 26

And so, as Miriel danced and drank and spoke sweetly to Talyn once more, I crept out onto the battlements to find Fidach. The guards nodded to me as I passed, and I to them, remembering Miriel's advice to be visible. No sneaking. No ammunition for Lugh. I found Fidach waiting on the same tower roof, and I shielded my eyes against the moonlight to wait for him to see me.

"Do you want to be alone?" I called, and he beckoned me up.

"No. Join me."

Up I went, scaling the wall and listening to the rasp of air in my throat. It was pleasant to lose myself in the challenge, choosing footholds and handholds, knowing Fidach was leaning forward to watch my progress. I lay back on the thatching when I was up, and sighed contentedly.

"Did Miriel send you?" he asked, and I nodded.

"This time, yes. She said something about talking some sense into you so you'd be pleasant at the banquet." He laughed and lay back with me, and I rolled my head sideways to look at him. "She's afraid, Fidach."

"About me staying. Becoming their weapon." Fidach's voice was determined. "Well, I'm not going to be theirs. I'll still be me."

I tried to ignore the stab of pity when I thought about Miriel's words: *I know what it is to be traded like a commodity.* Something told me that Fidach knew exactly what he was doing, and it was heartbreaking. I could not afford heartbreak; I needed a clear head.

"I heard what she said to you last night," I admitted.

"You don't think she's wrong."

"I don't think you know what it is to have no one," I told him bluntly. "Branwen wants you to be here so that your mother doesn't have you, and your children *would* be a rival line to Connor's if you married Seiysell. If you married at all, really. And Lugh wants you for his own weapon. All of them count their loyalty here, even Morwen. Over time, you would sympathize. It wouldn't even be wrong, Fidach—d'you remember when you and Branwen talked about all of the massacres of the war? Maybe it would take months, or maybe years, but you'd learn their songs and listen to their stories, and you'd take their side someday. You'd begin to feel resentful that you were abandoned, that you were bargained away. You would think that your mother should never have agreed to it. It isn't you, it's just...being human."

"Did that happen to you and Miriel?"

I thought back to our years at court. We'd had friends, but only just. Donnett could never have shielded me, Temar had his own plans. Miriel and I had barely learned to trust one another before it was too late. If I had taken Roine's bargain when she first offered it out of pity, and I had run away, what would have become of Miriel? I did not need to wonder, and neither had she; it was why she had spoken to Fidach, even if he cold not see it.

"Miriel and I had each other," I told Fidach. "And it was only just enough."

He sighed and looked over at me.

"You told me not to stay, the last time we were up here. Was it because you thought I'd turn on all of you?"

"I don't think..." I propped myself up on my elbow. "I don't think *you'd* turn on us. I think anyone would. Me, Miriel. It's awful to be bargained like a thing. I know—I was even less than a playing piece. I was just Miriel's servant while her uncle..." My voice trailed off when I saw him bite his lip. "Anyway. It's not that I think you faithless. Miriel doesn't, either. Come home with us?"

"How?" he whispered. His eyes were closed. "There isn't any other way to get us all out of here without the army marching behind us. Lugh won't settle for less, Branwen won't settle for less."

"They said it's you or your mother's throne."

"And I told you on the ride to Glen Tuam—"

"I know what you told me!" I hissed at him. "I know what you said, but that was before we were bargaining *you* away."

"Does that change anything?"

"It does for me!" I cried, and sank my head into my hands as I saw the guards look up at us. "It changes things for me. Believe it or not, it changes things for Miriel, too."

"Miriel doesn't want a valuable weapon in the hands of the enemy," Fidach said, and there was a question in his voice. "Is it that, Catwin? Is that why you won't leave me here?"

"I..." I looked over at him, and could not think what to say. "No one wants to hand their enemy a weapon, it's true. But Fidach, we could have walked away and left you here, or even left before this all began. Miriel and I talked about running away. She's here because she couldn't walk away and let Priteni fall into war, and we're still here because we can't give you up. If you think she's cold, well, how much colder would it be simply to sign you away? And she hasn't, even though she knows it would be the solution. She put her life on the line for this, and she won't bargain you away—what she said to you last night was true. Call it stubborn, call it illogical, but she wouldn't...sell...someone. Not you, not anyone."

"Even if I offered to go freely?" he challenged, and I fought the urge to sink my head into my hands.

"What do *you* want?"

"Not to be a bargaining chip." I sighed, and he took a deep breath. "I apologize. That was...not helpful. All my life, I've just wanted to matter, not for what I was, but for what I could do. It was always about my blood, or my talent—the lords watching me, my mother watching me. No one seemed to care about *who* I was. I used to dream that I would take my father's fate someday. I thought he would be a conqueror, and in my dreams, I would be a mage king, and I would show all of them that I could be just and impartial. They would all see that they had been wrong about me. And my father. It was a childish dream, nothing more."

"You still want it," I guessed, and he met my eyes, looking for derision.

"Yes," he admitted after a moment. "I do. I kept hoping until my mother—well, I know now, anyway. My mother would never have allowed any of that to happen, and I should not betray her by taking this throne, instead. She's trying to do what's right for Priteni, I know that."

"And so is Branwen," I said softly. "But it's still you caught in the middle."

"So it is." He lay back on the straw and I looked down at him. His lashes gleamed in the moonlight, iron at his neck and the golden cloak pins strangely cold, dragons glittering at me. I wanted to brush a stray lock of hair behind his ear, and I blushed when he opened his eyes and saw me staring. He smiled. "What?"

"Just..." I shook my head. "It's nothing. Did you sit on the roofs at Dun Druim, too?"

He laughed.

"No. No, I did not."

"That's right," I said, remembering. "You snuck out to practice magic, didn't you? Was that what you were doing the day I saw the army?"

"Yes. Well remembered." He looked pleased, finally. "I didn't have any idea what I was doing, so I would make myself challenges."

"Challenges?"

"Like lifting rocks and placing them in trees. Trying to blow leaves into a pile. I learned some control that way."

"Some?" I had heard the note of pride in his voice, and saw a subtle loosening of his shoulders. He was yearning for something, happier to remember using magic than he had been in days.

"Morwen said I had done well," he said, almost shyly.

"I have no doubt of it. You know...you look happy when you speak about magic."

"It's like....singing. Or..." He gestured, looking for words. "Running. Swinging a sword perfectly, hitting a target with an arrow. It's everything inside you coming together into one moment, It uses focus and strength. I can feel it running through my body when I cast. When I use magic...then I am entirely free."

I sat up and crossed my arms over my knees, rested my chin on them, stared out into the night. He did sound free when he spoke of magic, that was the cruelest piece of this. Had it been an outer holding of the Morini, a partial exile, even a cave on the coasts, none of us would have hesitated to let him go. He was happy as a mage. It would be selfish of us to ask him to give it up.

But what else could we do?

"Catwin?" he asked, and I pressed my lips together. I could not speak; I was afraid I would tell him to stay, afraid I would tell him to come back. I did not want to ride back to Dun Druim without him, and I did not want to ride back with him grieving this.

At my side, Fidach sat up. He reached out as if he would put his arm around me, and then seemed to think better of it.

"I don't know what to tell you," I told him. "If you come back to Dun Druim with us, we'll have war sooner, and they won't trust your magic. But you'll be home, with people who...with your family. If you stay, you will be a mage, but you will give Lugh everything he needs to destroy the Morini."

"You're right." He looked out at the ocean. "Two mages could bring down Dun Druim. And they won't be pleased to have me back, you know. They never trusted me."

"It's too much to ask of you," I whispered, and he looked over at me, his eyes glittering in the darkness.

"No one else would say so."

"I'm not everyone else."

"Indeed you are not. Catwin, if I stayed—"

But I was not listening any longer. I put my hand, distractedly, over his mouth for silence and cocked my head. A low thrum sounded in the air. What was I hearing? Fidach, too, had his eyes shut in concentration as he listened. Then he shook my arm silently and pointed.

Torches flickered in the moonlight, down on the seashore, where troops were marching into camp. A camp that would be hidden from view to all in the castle. Marching songs that would be inaudible over the howl of the wind and the music in the hall.

Miriel had been right. Lugh was not willing to accept peace—he was preparing to march.

Chapter 27

"Catwin!" Fidach's hands missed me as I slid myself down over the edge of the roof and began climbing down.

"You have to warn Miriel."

"Catwin, wait!"

"He's going to march!" I hissed. "They're going to march on Dun Druim."

"Where are you *going*?" I heard the clatter as he began his downward climb, following me along the whole of the tower instead of sliding onto the walk at the top of the wall. I looked up and waited as he climbed; the wind was gusting, and I did not want it to carry the sound of my voice.

"We need information," I told him when he hit the ground with a thud. "You, go back to Miriel. I'll scout the camp."

"We should go back. Now. Tell them what we know, try to conclude negotiations."

"I don't think so. Not anymore." There was a cold pit in my stomach. "You don't look surprised at this."

"I argued when Miriel said this would happen, but...we all knew it would come to this." My habitual mistrust was met with raised eyebrows. "Catwin, we should go back."

"You go back. To Miriel. I'll go scout." He sighed and rubbed his forehead.

"Miriel will keep," he said finally. "She's got enough sense to stay put until we come back. *You* should have someone watching your back."

"Ideally, yes. But the point of that is in case I get caught, so that someone should not be a royal heir."

"Tough luck." He shrugged his shoulders. "You don't have anyone else."

"I can scout a camp on my own, your highness—Fidach. Sorry."

"Can you see into the past? Into their minds?" He had me,

and he knew it. "Let's go."

"Cover your hair." I took my overtunic and looped it over the pale brown shine of my own. "It'll show in the moonlight. Now: when I do this with my right hand, it means stop right where you are. When I do *this*, it means to get on the ground, and don't worry who sees. This, with my left, means to hide. Do you have those?"

He repeated them back to me, and I nodded.

"Good. Let's go."

The worst was crossing the scrub brush to the mountain path. We moved slowly, taking shelter behind the larger bushes as patrols went by on the walls with agonizing slowness.

"Shouldn't we speed up? What if they notice we're missing?" Fidach asked, and I pondered.

"Better than noticing we're crouched near their war camp."

"True."

The mountain path was treacherous in the dark. The wind seeming to carry sea foam up to lash against our faces. I scooped up some of the blackish soil and rubbed it over the paleness of my skin, and Fidach grimaced at me, pulling up his hood to shield his face instead.

We made our approach quickly, for the flickering fires of the camp did not cast their light far. It was the gleam of our eyes that we needed to worry about as we circled the camp, counting tents and marking horses. Three hundred horsemen, Lugh had brought when they marched the first time, but this was more than that: foot soldiers, chariots, archers.

"This must be every able-bodied warrior in the freeholds," Fidach murmured. "There can't *be* many more Cornovii than this."

We were crouched behind one of the jagged stone pillars, our backs to the sea and the mountain hiding Dun Beal from sight. The soldiers were drinking and laughing. I could smell roasting meat and guessed that these men would be eating well, the first fine meal they'd had in months. Lugh would want to entice them, give them a taste of the spoils of war.

"So..." I prompted him, and he shrugged his shoulders.

"This is all-or-nothing. If they fail, they'll have no farmers in the fields, no blacksmiths, no tanners. Every family will have lost someone, probably several someones. Lugh is playing for keeps. Like..."

"Like Miriel suggested." I looked over at him. "Would Nuall be planning to do the same?"

"He'd have suggested it," Fidach said. "But it wouldn't be hard to talk him out of that. We don't fight like this, not since we went up against the Gwyddu. Before that, and now, battles are skirmishes for territory, nothing more." He sighed and rubbed at his forehead. "They won't be prepared. They'll have sent a normal war force. This will cut through them easily—more so, if Lugh chooses the battlefield. And I'm sure he has that planned out."

I bit my lip and peered out from behind the boulder. There was little happening in the camp. Like the horsemen, these men would be traveling light, and there was little to pack, little to arrange. It was odd to me to see a war camp without the gleam of mail and plate armor, the ceaseless rasp of blades against sharpening stones. These men carried weapons or iron, not steel, and many carried bows tipped with stone or wood.

I wondered how the Duke had planned to outfit his army before taking Heddred, and shook my head slightly. It was the sort of challenge he would have enjoyed. And anyway, I knew without having to ask him—he would have swept through the poorly defended northern towns, occupying and raiding and forging weapons in their smithies before word ever reached Penekket. The north feared invasion from no one. The Duke had picked his target well, but he had not bargained on Temar.

I did not want to think of Temar. Not now.

"So we need to warn your mother," I said finally, and Fidach shook his head.

"Catwin, I don't think there's a way to warn her. We'd need to run, and we don't know the land. We can't outrun them in their own territory, not without supplies."

"We have to," I told him simply. "If we all go separately, there's a chance."

"No. Catwin, don't argue with me. You may know how to

sneak around a castle, but this is open land. This is fleeing from an enemy who knows exactly where you're going and knows the land better than you. And it's winter, Catwin. You could die out there, any of us could."

"And we're not going to die when he sets the army on us at Dun Druim? You think he'll kill all of them and let the three of us go?"

"He might. Have you thought of that? If we gave him Dun Druim, he might well let all three of us go. It's the best odds we have."

"What are you saying?"

"I'm *saying* that if you do this, you might die for it." His voice was passionate. "Catwin, this isn't your fight, but that won't matter to them if they catch you."

"I'm not going to let them massacre the Morini!"

"Catwin, listen to me—"

"Out of the question." My voice was flat, and then I felt a laugh well up in my throat. I stifled it on my hand. Miriel's sense of justice really was going to get us killed. Somewhere along the way, she'd gotten me to believe it all, too. Well, there was nothing for it. "I couldn't live with myself if I turned away now."

"I know," he said, and he sounded sad.

"Come on. I need to get to the stables."

"No. What we need is to stop them, right? That's the main goal: they can't overrun Dun Druim. But there's no time to get back to the army and get reinforcements before they come. They'll be waiting in the midlands." He sighed and sank his head into his hands.

"What is it?" I asked, when he did not speak.

"There is a way," he said finally. "They could do it, the Morini could break even this army. But they would need to know what they were up against, and we can't outrun Cornovii."

"We don't have any other—" I broke off when he clamped his hand over my mouth. We waited, absolutely still, and then I heard it, Lugh's voice on the wind.

"—came this way," I made out.

"We've seen nothing," another man muttered.

"Well, then look again!" Lugh snapped. "She's here. I'm

sure of it."

"You're determined to do this, aren't you?" Fidach asked me, so low I could barely hear it. "I can't talk you out of it."

"Fidach..."

He sighed, and closed his eyes, and I looked down at my hands.

"Do you trust me?" Fidach murmured, his breath stirring my hair. I looked up at him, startled by how close our faces were.

"What?"

"Do you trust me?" he asked again, low, as the voice drew closer.

"Of course I do."

"Remember that, Catwin." His eyes burned into mine, urgent. His hands were clenched. "When you hear me say, *maybe she went to the docks,* make for the mountain path. Don't look back." And he was gone before I could call him back, striding out into the moonlight and calling for Lugh.

"Your highness." Lugh's voice was cautious. "May I ask..."

"Why I am here? A very good question." Fidach managed to fill his voice with muted anger. "I'm looking for Catwin."

"You don't know where she is?" Lugh asked, and I could practically hear the wheels turning in his head. "The Lady Miriel would not say where her serving girl had gone, and we could not find you, either. I must admit we assumed—"

"To be honest with you...I am afraid of the same." Fidach paused, and I raised my eyebrows. I hoped he realized how difficult it was going to be to wipe away all the suspicion he was placing on me. "I will not lie to you, emissary. I hope you can forgive me. I came to find her myself—I thought perhaps if I could talk to her, explain that their ways across the sea are not ours..."

"Spying cannot be tolerated," Lugh said flatly.

"I accept that. You know that as part of her party, I *must* ask you formally for your mercy, but...."

"But?" Lugh's voice was like silk and I clenched my hands in frustration. I wanted to run. I was terrified. Fidach was winding his way through this conversation with all the knowledge of a native, and I had nothing but my wits and my

———
182

blades to keep me safe if he failed. I hated being helpless.

"Is there any other choice? I would kill her myself for bringing this on us. We needed no more mistrust between us, sir."

"I would like to think that one day there might be no cause at all for mistrust between the two of us." I sneaked a glance around the edge of the boulder and saw Lugh place his hand on Fidach's shoulder. "I should like to call you brother one day. You are a man of honor, wasted on the Morini. Don't let them claim you back like a bargaining chip. They care nothing for what you are."

"I wish you did not speak the truth." Fidach sighed. "But before anything, we need to find Catwin. I searched around the camp. There, there. Over there. She was trained by a spymaster, but I think I would have seen her."

My heart was pounding. I needed to run, and run fast. There was only one shot at this, a chance to get a horse and get away before Lugh found me. Could I get to Miriel in time? I did not think so. Fidach would have a plan for that. I was just wondering whether or not I could bear to leave her, knowing her safety would be in another's hands, when I heard Fidach say,

"She can't have gotten back up to Dun Beal yet. Maybe she went to the docks."

No time to think. I ran with everything in me. The cliff walk was before me, a tiny sliver of black, and I sprinted for it with the salt air burning in my lungs. No room for error, no second try, and for a few blessed moments, I thought it had worked. And then I heard,

"There! She's there!"

I ran out of desperation, but in truth there was no chance at all. Alerted, soldiers began to rise from their posts. The path was still a hundred yards from me and I could hear footsteps behind me, see shapes emerging from the dark at my sides. I put in a final burst of speed and then, knowing it for futility, skidded to a halt and planted myself to launch back at my pursuers. If I could take one or two of them out, perhaps, get a knife, take a hostage—

There were too many of them. It was Lugh himself who

reached me first, and although I dodged his first blow, there were hands reaching out for my wrists, an arm closing around my waist. My head snapped back with the second punch, and a third landed below my ribs. As I looked up, gasping for breath, I realized what I had heard.

Fidach was the one who had alerted them to my presence. He had not ever intended to create a diversion so that I might sneak away—he had ensured that I would be caught, and I had fallen for it all, fool that I was. Another blow caught me, and as I was dragged down to my knees I caught sight of his face, expressionless, his jaw set. I knew my eyes were wide with betrayal. I looked the fool, and the last thing I knew before another blow caught me to the side of the head and my world went dark, was complete, burning rage.

Chapter 28

Lugh took no chances. I knew from my nights of sneaking through the passageways that Dun Beal did not have dungeons, as such, but it had chains and rope. The guards bound me to a post in the great courtyard with a brazier just close enough that I would feel the hint of its warmth, making the cold air all the sharper, and my hands wrenched behind my back. Lugh spat questions at me all through, the same words echoed softly by Fidach when I didn't answer. The prince was the very picture of injured pride, hardly flickering at my glares.

"Was the lady working with you?" Lugh's hands jerked the ropes tight around my wrists and I gritted my teeth in pain.

"No." Little good it would do, but it was truthful.

"Tell me the truth." I felt steel at my throat.

"I am telling the truth!" I needed to calm myself. Lugh would not kill me, not yet, not now. The metal at my throat was only to spur instinct, to make me talk. I would not be taken in.

"She's lying," Fidach said with certainty. "She would never do something like this on her own. Miriel sent her."

"Bring the lady," Lugh said. When he turned, it was to hit me full across the face, and I felt myself sag against the ropes. My head was ringing, with warmth and pain spreading across my face.

"You see what happens when you lie?" Lugh asked me. "Don't do it again."

"Just throw her in the dungeon." Fidach leaned back against one of the wooden posts, arms crossed.

"Not before I see what she knows."

"You won't get anything out of her, you know. She was trained for this."

I said nothing. My eyes were fixed on the cobblestones. I could feel blood dripping from my nose, the rasp of pain at my wrists where the rope had broken skin, and beginnings of bruises at my eye and my jaw. I needed to go deep, down where the pain couldn't reach me and where the fear couldn't turn me. I had survived the Duke, the Lady, Roine...I could survive this.

"Oh, I'm certain she was trained to face her own pain. But another's?" Lugh's voice seemed to come from very far away, and a stab of fear lifted me partway out of my trance. I shoved it away and tried to sink back. *Don't think. Don't wonder.*

"What was the plan?" Lugh asked, his voice cold.

"There wasn't a plan," I heard myself say. My lips hurt.

"You may think you're brave." Lugh leaned down to put his face close to mine, his hands braced on the post. "But if you don't answer, I *will* get it out of the lady."

"There *was* no plan," I said, through gritted teeth, and he straightened up.

"Hit her again," he said, almost wearily.

"What?" Fidach stood up and I rolled my head to look at him. The prince looked panicked, and Lugh's eyes were narrowed. He wasn't ready to risk all of this on an untested turncoat. *Your own fault,* I wanted to say to Fidach. *You should have known he'd ask it. You wanted to do this without getting your hands dirty, but that's not how courts work.* The trance was beginning to set in; I wondered what Fidach would do, but the emotion was fading from me.

"You heard me," Lugh said. His own emotion was rising. He wanted so badly to believe that Fidach would join his cause, and yet he knew to doubt. As I had, I thought, and felt the twist of regret deep down. I felt almost sorry for Lugh. *Never trust a turncoat.* How long until Fidach had Lugh deposed? Or Branwen?

But Lugh needn't have worried in this case, for Fidach's hand cracked across my face without hesitation. When the prince bent close to me, I felt a twist of hope and hated myself for it. *You should have seen this coming,* I told myself brutally. He wanted to stay, and I knew it. He told me Lugh would need a turncoat to make his plans work. He asked me if I was willing to die for this. And then he betrayed me, and still, through all of it, I hoped this was a ruse.

"How could you, Catwin?" he asked me simply, and his face was as cold as I had ever seen it. Saving his own selfish hide after seeing the army, was he? I spat in his face and he jerked back, closing his eyes while he wiped the spit away. "I mean it, your grace. Get her in a dungeon. She was trained as a spy—she'll get out of anywhere else."

One of their tiny stone rooms. Locked away, and no chance of escape; the last vestiges of hope crumbled. I made a sound of protest and felt tears come to my eyes when Lugh laughed.

"She really thought you'd stay with the Morini, didn't she?" This last was directed at me, and he spared a glance for where Miriel was being hauled out of the castle. She had been cooperating until she saw me, and then I saw her lash out with her little fists. Lugh watched, a smile playing around his lips, and then leaned close to me. "You're going to get to see just how wrong you were. I'm going to bring you with the army. You'll get to watch him betray them all, you and the lady both."

"What?" Fidach's voice had risen. "You can't be serious. It's too much of a risk."

I looked up at him and smiled triumphantly. It was a pity that he was right about trying to outride the army. Between Lugh and his scouts, I would hardly last a day. But I was determined, now, to prove Fidach right in his fear of me—break out, ruin his plans. I might haul him back to the Morini to stand trial, if I could arrange it.

"Oh, I don't think she'll get away. You all seem to think she's some spymaster, but the truth is, any spy worth the gold would have known this would happen. If she was a real spy, you would never have fooled her—and she would have left the lady to die when she figured it out. So I think when we explain that the lovely Miriel is going to be a hostage for her good behavior, she'll stay put."

Miriel was hauled up beside me. Her hair had come loose in the struggle and her sleeve was torn where she had tried to break free of her attackers. They were hesitant to harm her, with her fine clothes and her regal bearing, but her arms were jerked tight behind her back and she was grimacing in pain.

"What's going on?"

Lugh's order to shut up wasn't enough to deter me.

"They're marching. Two hundred foot soldiers, a hundred spears, archers, cavalry. They have—" Miriel screamed when Lugh slapped me, but I could feel only relief. She might get away. She was noble, they would grant her indulgences. They might make a mistake with her, and she would remember. Fidach had said there was a way to beat this army—and his attempts to keep me here only proved it.

"Look well, my lady," Lugh instructed Miriel. "If either of you runs, the other dies. You'll be coming with us when we march and maybe, just maybe, I will be merciful. So while we march, you consider whether you would rather remain here, as a servant, or take your chances with the Morini against my army."

"And Fidach?" Miriel asked. I bent my head and heard Lugh laugh, delightedly.

"Your prince would rather keep you here, in our dungeons, to wait for our return."

"*Are* we returning?" Fidach said in a drawl. "When you have Dun Druim, we won't need this place. Leave them here to rot."

"Ah, but we promised the emissaries safe travel, did we not? And *we* are not oath breakers. Come, there is a feast to see us off." Lugh cast a glance at Miriel. "Put the lady in her rooms and bar the door. The spy can stay there."

"Catwin!" Miriel dug in her heels, but the guardsman only picked her up and slung her over his shoulder. She kicked and pounded at his back. "Catwin!"

I could not meet her eyes. I looked past her, to where Fidach was strolling away with Lugh's arm draped around his shoulders.

"Now that we have dispensed with this foolishness," I heard Lugh say, "perhaps we may discuss the other matter I mentioned..."

"Seiysell?" Fidach smiled. "Yes. Let us, indeed. Children for both thrones—you'll need to end my mother's line, though, or there would be rivals."

I felt my face twist. We had learned so much, come so far—and in the end it had been my trust that had undone us. Fidach had seen me waver, heard me tell Miriel that this was not our fight. He'd found a weak link in me, earned my trust while I wasn't watching. He might try to tell himself that he was fine and honorable for offering me a chance to join him but I had seen him steeling himself to it, knowing what he did was beyond betrayal. He would live with that for the rest of his days.

Which wasn't going to be long, because I had decided I was going to kill him.

Rage only warmed me for so long, however. The winters in Priteni may be warm when compared to Voltur, but it did not feel like long before I was shivering violently. I was not going to die, I was certain of that. Lugh was far too determined to twist the knife in the wound. Miriel and I might be killed in front of the Morini army, or we might be let go and then slaughtered with them, but either way Lugh would not let me die tonight. Still, it was one thing to know that and another to believe it when the shivers shook me against the ropes.

The soldiers assigned to guard me made no taunts and no threats, and I thought bitterly that Miriel would call it a sign of division in the court. I could nearly hear her voice, academic and dry: *the soldiers are uncomfortable with what they've been asked to do. You could turn them.* I tried to think clearly, no easy task with hunger and cold doing their slow work on my mind, and decided at last that pleas would only harden them to Lugh's cause. Tears might work. Silence was best; soldiers liked bravery. My best chance to get their sympathy would be to wait here in silence.

I must have drifted to sleep against the ropes, for I gradually realized that I could see robes of deep blue pooling against the flagstone of the courtyard. *Miriel,* I thought dreamily, but the figure did not speak and did not move to untie me. It took some doing, for my muscles were stiff with cold and sleep, but at last I lifted my head, wincing, to look at my companion.

Branwen.

My surprise must have shown in my face, for her jaw tightened. She looked around the courtyard and motioned the soldiers back.

"Lugh said she was a spy and an assassin," one of them protested, trying to keep the rod of his spear between the two of us.

"I'm well aware of that," Branwen said coolly. "And yet the knots seem quite secure to me." She waited as they shuffled away, and then her eyes found mine. "Is it true, then?"

"No," I said passionately. "There was no plan. We came to bargain, and *you* gathered an army to march while we did."

She jerked back.

"The army was gathered to march if peace talks failed."

"Oh? You should check their orders, your grace. They're speaking of marching on the morrow. They're being feasted and addressed by your consort."

"Well, now they shall." Branwen drew her cloak around herself as the wind gusted.

"You didn't know, did you?" I had seen the brief flash of her discomfort. "It was always Lugh's plan to do this."

"Lugh would not betray me."

"Then who else, my lady? The army is ready to march, and they were ready before Lugh caught me down by the seashore."

"And for good reason!" Branwen hissed back. "You knew I needed to keep my people fed and safe, and you gave me nothing for security. Aoife sent spies and liars to make some sham of peace, and in their wake she sent an army! She is false, your queen, and you are no better!"

"We promised you everything save bargaining away a man's life! I spied the army from the rooftops. If you had them in wait, then why are they massing now, your grace? Why were they already speaking of tomorrow's march?"

"Lugh," Branwen said icily, "is trying to keep us all safe."

I snapped.

"From what?" I yelled. I jerked against the bond and gave a cry of pain when the ropes slid across broken flesh. The guards started forward, and fell back reluctantly when Branwen held up a hand to keep them back. "We weren't coming for you. We weren't arming. Our army gathered because yours was riding down on us!" I wondered to myself when it had become *our* army, and decided that it did not matter. I was going to die for them whatever I considered myself.

"You didn't know, did you?" Branwen tilted her head to the side. The waves of her red-gold hair gleamed in the torchlight, lifted by the wind. She gleamed gold and iron and pale, a warrior queen. "What Morwen saw—you did not know. Did you know of Fidach?"

"None of us knew," I said sullenly. "We only knew that the army was coming and..."

My voice trailed off before I could say that Fidach saw we would not win. It was useless now, to try to keep secrets. Things surely could not get worse. And yet, I would not tell Branwen that we had seen our destruction coming in the form of her cavalry. I had been trained too well.

"Two years ago, Morwen dreamed of your prince. It is difficult to interpret the Call of Time, you understand, so she did not realize what it was she had seen—save that it was a mage with extraordinary powers, stalked by the fate of another. Whether he lived, or had lived, or was yet to be born, was not certain." The wind gusted and I gritted my teeth against the cold. Branwen did not notice; she was looking into the middle distance.

"The dreams became more urgent: a man with blood on his hands. A mage to rival the Gwyddu. Morwen became sure that this man would change Priteni forever, but she could tell us nothing more of who he might be. We scoured the Cornovii holdings for any young man with pale hair and blue eyes, and then a Morini farmer brought us an extraordinary story: in the fields outside his home, he had seen a young man with golden hair and blue eyes raise the very earth into a hill, and place it back." Branwen met my eyes, then, the grey-green of her own almost lost in the flicker of the torches. "It did not take long from there to discern who he was—the young man in the golden torc."

"And so you knew Aoife had broken the treaty." My lip had split at some point. It pulled now, and broke back open. I winced, and felt the soreness of my skin where the ropes were beginning to bruise.

"Yes!" Branwen's voice rose. "We were forced sign that treaty in *blood* to bind it, but we made an oath and we have held to it out of honor alone, even when our people starved! When

Talyn offered me a new land, away from the Morini, I took the chance. You think I *want* war, spy? But the ships did not return, and Morwen dreamed of Fidach at Aoife's side, and the ghost of his father, a man to remake the face of this land. The path branches, but one thing was clear: with him, she could have ended us all. And *that*, I will not allow. His fate is too twisted to leave him in Aoife's hands now. He comes to us. He will wed Seiysell and we will have a line for both thrones, to take back what your people stole."

"You're insane," I spat back. Anger was bubbling up in my chest. I could not believe this. Not again, not another woman facing me and telling me it was fate that led us all to death. "You all talk of prophecy and fate and maybe and branching paths, but you're bringing it all to pass yourselves, don't you see? *You* sent an army to us, and we saw a different future for that act. Fidach—" I broke off. My throat closed with an ache. Fidach, who I had trusted so foolishly....

"It hurts you that he has come to us." Branwen watched me impassively. "I did not think he would choose to stay. I came to see you because I thought it was no more than another plot. And yet you are proof of it."

"Are you finished?" I wanted her to go. I wanted to be alone with my hatred.

"You are a woman of honor, Catwin. You see what he did as betrayal. But he is paying a blood debt to us, he is avenging the lives that were lost and clearing the lives that would be given for this war. And you, soldier-spy, assassin, are on the dishonorable side."

"What do you know of dishonor?" I thought my chest would burst for the surge of rage. "You know nothing of me. You do not know how I was trained, or why. You do not know the man who turned me into this, and you have no right to accuse me of dishonor."

"It is not you who are dishonorable, it is your choice of allies."

"Don't you see? That's all this is! You're measuring us by Aoife, and we're measuring you by Lugh, but we're all only people, Branwen. That's why Miriel came, because war only ever claims innocent lives. Because your farmers in the fields, and ours, don't care about these blood debts anymore, they only want to be safe."

"Do not try to soften my heart." She had stepped back. I saw her throat move where she swallowed convulsively.

"Branwen, listen to me." I was desperate, pressed against the bonds. She was weakening, I could tell. "You don't have to do this. Hold us captive, make Aoife come to us—we will give you peace, we will give you fields and woodlands, we will swear blood oaths that we will never come after you. Please—"

She whirled away, and made to run, then shrugged her own cloak off her shoulders and handed it to a guard.

"For the captive," I heard. "I'll not have her die."

And she strode away into the castle while I called after her to stay, to listen to me. While I pleaded with her not to march, and my words fell into the silence of the courtyard.

Chapter 29

The army moved before dawn. Their line of torches lit the road and the earth shook with their feet. I could hear snatches of marching songs carried on the wind, oddly hopeful. Of course they were hopeful; they were hungry and scared and cold, hearing stories of a land ripe for the taking. Light glinted over ragged rows of spears. It was a poor army, badly trained and ill equipped, but it could still cut through the Morini with the element of surprise, with the sheer numbers they commanded.

Lugh came to oversee my transfer to a horse, my hands lashed to the pommel while I bit my lips against the pain. Blood glistened where the skin was rubbed raw once more. The queen's consort did not bother to hide his satisfied smile when I shuddered with pain.

"Have you decided?" he asked me, and I looked over at him dully. Branwen's cloak had been warm enough, but I spent the night shivering nonetheless, trying to wiggle my fingers as they stiffened and reminding myself that pain was what I must have. Warmth was bad. Drowsiness was bad. I was so exhausted now that I feared I would slip from the saddle, and I could not think what Lugh might be asking me.

"Decided?" I asked him, when it became apparent that he would not leave with an answer. My right eye was swollen, and it was difficult to focus on his face. Behind him, I saw Miriel being dragged from the castle, and I turned my face away. I could not bear to see what I had brought down on her.

"Whether you would prefer a life of servitude, or a quick death." He leaned back against the post where I had been held and crossed his arms. I did not answer.

"What will you do when this is over?" I asked him instead. "When there is no one to crush and no battle to give you glory? What will you do then?"

"Then I can rule the land I was made to rule: fields and

farmers, not rocks and sand at the end of nowhere. Victory will be sweet, don't you think?"

"Not for you," I predicted. "You'll never be happy. You let your desire for vengeance burn the rest of you up."

"Shut up," he said, trying to be bored, trying to conceal the dawning doubt in his eyes.

"You'll sit on Aoife's throne and wonder why you are not happy," I told him, almost longing to drive him to violence once again. Then I would know I had broken his contented smugness.

"I said shut up."

"You'll think of the battle every day, and how you felt when you saw Aoife fall. You'll think of walking into Dun Druim and taking the throne beside Branwen, and you'll wonder why it isn't enough to make you happy."

"Trying to make me angry, spy?" His fist tangled in my tunic and pulled me down for him to hiss at me. "Say whatever you want. Nothing you do can change what's coming. Think on your prince. Think of the man who condemned your army to death. Your betrayal has a certain...savor."

He thrust me back from him before I could lunge forward, strike his head with my own, spit in his face, snarl at him that I would see them both dead for this.

"Put her close enough to the front to see the prince," he told his men with a smile, and then he turned to go to where Branwen waited, white-faced at our fight. She clenched the reins of her horse with white-knuckled hands. "And keep her away from the lady. No matter what they tell you."

"Catwin!" Miriel called. Her voice carried on the wind. I did not even think, only tried to urge my horse towards her. Miriel needed me. She was scared. I must go to her. The guards yanked on the reins me back and I gasped in pain.

"No matter what you tell us," one of them said roughly, and as promised they bound my horse to one of theirs near the front of the column—in perfect sight to see Fidach, talking and laughing with Lugh as the army set out to kill his kin.

They came to see me that night, the lot of them, Fidach ducking into the tent first, and then Morwen, Lugh. Branwen had ridden some ways with the army to see us off, but remained behind, too precious to trust to Morini treachery. The twins, Branwen's eldest children, hovered near the back of the tent with their eyes wide. Seiysell tried to keep her face impassive, but she was wavering; there was compassion there. Aeden kept his hand on the pommel of his dagger, clearly ill at ease. I looked at them all, staring me down, walking free while I was chained, and wished that hatred was not burning so deep in my blood. I could not think clearly.

"Where will Aoife wait in the midlands?" Lugh asked, crouching down to be on a level with me.

"Why not ask *him*?" I asked, my eyes narrowing at Fidach. "Hasn't he told you everything?"

"She doesn't know," Morwen said softly as Lugh leaned forward. He shot her an annoyed look over his shoulder and I saw her swallow. But she held her ground. "We know what we need to from Catwin. This is unnecessary, and—"

"What did the lady have you seek out?" Lugh asked, cutting his sister off. "What did she tell you to find?"

"I told you, *we* didn't plan this." I looked desperately up at Morwen, at Seiysell. "This war wasn't our doing, not from the start. Seiysell—"

"Don't talk to her," Lugh said flatly, and Seiysell sank back, biting her lip. She did not know what to do, so far from her mother's steadying influence. I looked to her brother, who backed away.

"You can still stop this," I said desperately him, and Lugh shoved me back. My hands bound, my muscles aching from a day in the saddle with no way to adjust my posture, I fell. I managed to bite back my cry of pain, but could not get to my feet again.

When I looked back, I could see them wavering: Morwen, her lips pressed together and Aeden back as far as he could get, as if he would melt into the shadows at the edge of the tent. Seiysell had lifted her jaw and her teeth were clenched; she was determined not to be soft. Lugh was unmoved, and Fidach was staring down as if he had never known me at all, as if I was some sort of curiosity and nothing more.

"Catwin, what is the point of drawing out the battle?" he asked reasonably. He ushered Lugh back and came to crouch at my side, and I moved as far from him as my chains would go. "Fewer will die if the battle is over quickly, you know that. You know we will win in any case."

I wanted to cry. I was cold, I was tired, every part of me hurt. I was going to die when we reached the battlefield, I knew it in my bones. I did not want my last days to be spent alone, knowing that Miriel was close, and scared, but with no way to comfort her. And I did not want to see Fidach, listen to that reasonable voice that made me think of the Duke, reminded me to Temar warning me to stay out of matters that didn't concern me. I did not even want to see Fidach, who had smiled at me so kindly, whose blue eyes had been so warm. I hung my head. Pain could be made into anger, I reminded myself, and anger was better than fear.

"Catwin, you care about these people. You know we don't want to kill any more than we have to."

"No," I snapped. *That* had sparked fury. "If you didn't want people to die, you would have turned to Branwen, not Lugh. If you weren't in this for revenge, you would have worked for peace, not allied yourself with a madman. You think he's going to stop when there's a surrender? He's going to kill them all."

"Not *all* of them," Lugh said idly, and his tone made the hair on the back of my neck stand up.

"They would be given the option to stay on their land," Fidach explained, "as servants to the Cornovii."

"How do you *live* with yourself?" I spat the question and he jerked back. There was a flash of genuine pain in his eyes and I had no opportunity to wonder at it, for he leaned back to me at once and I shrank away.

"You had to know this would happen, Catwin, with or without me. Miriel said herself that to condemn them to this life was to invite retribution."

"So you decided to *help*?" I lunged forward and felt the ropes jerk me back. "She was speaking to your mother, Fidach, her alone! But that didn't mean anything to you, did it, and so instead of trying to right any of this, you decided to cut half your people down like animals and turn the others into slaves?"

"Enough! Fidach." Lugh summoned him with a word and I stared up at him as he left. He was the last one out of the tent and I saw him turn, consider speaking.

"If you hurt Miriel," I told him, "there you will be nothing you can do, and nowhere you can run. I will get free, and I will find you, and I will make you wish you had never been born." He stared at me, shaking, opened his mouth to speak—and then I heard Lugh call his name. Fidach dropped the tent flap and left me in darkness, and I was alone.

Chapter 30

This time, with soldiers marching and supplies to be hauled, it took us nine days to reach the battlefield, a little over halfway to Dun Druim. The march was a misery, and my only comfort was Lugh's promise that we should be given safe passage back to the Morini. That he would launch an attack the moment we were returned, I had no doubt. That he intended us to die, or be captured and forced into servitude, was a certainty. And yet...safe passage meant that Miriel would not be harmed. Safe passage meant that we might have a chance to say goodbye. Safe passage meant we could die together, at least.

Knowing I might see Miriel again was all that kept me sane. We had never been apart for so long, and I feared for her. No logic could help me believe that she was safe if I was not at her side. Was she scared? Was she hurt? It was agony to think of it.

But we were kept far from one another, a move that was as admirably practical on Lugh's part as it was distressing for me. Miriel, it seemed, was kept in a royal tent, while I was kept in one of the supply tents, little more than canvas lashed over barrels if truth be told, meant to keep any snow away from the supplies. With no fire and the canvas loosely anchored, it was a poor excuse for shelter in the cold. The first night, I gazed around myself and wished for lock picks and poison. There were no great barrels of water to pour out or flour to scatter, but if I could only get my hands free, I could strike their army in the belly and stop them dead.

For the first three days, when Lugh came to me with Fidach and Morwen, I would look down at the floor of my tent. I told myself to wait it out. I need have no fear of spilling secrets, for I knew none—and so I cloaked myself in savage satisfaction. *Do what you will*, I wanted to tell him. *None of it will give you the answers you seek.*

On the fourth day, slumped on the back of my horse as it plodded along, I realized that Lugh did not believe for a moment I had any answers. He came to see my rage at Fidach. Why, I could not understand, but I had seen that he asked me a question, slapped me sometimes when I refused, and then, when I was struggling to calm myself, he would push Fidach forward. Fidach, who asked me questions he knew I could not answer, using my sullenness to highlight his own reasonable acquiescence to Cornovii victory. Consumed with anger, I had not noticed. Lugh did not think I had information. This was a different game.

Well, he would not win it.

I spent the day in careful thought. The soldiers who guarded me did not speak of strategy, but did talk of the battlefield itself. It might be considered an advantageous site from the Morini camp, for the land beyond was thick with forest and valleys scattered throughout. If they must fall back, the Morini would have an easy retreat—and if the Cornovii fell back, there would be only plains, and their soldiers would be easy prey for enemy archers. And yet, the Cornovii camp sat at the break of an incline. The cavalry would be prominently on display, foot soldiers hidden. The ground rose to the north and south, the men said, and I wondered at Lugh's strategy. Now I had a chance to pry some of the information out of him.

There is a way... Fidach's words echoed in my head. There was a way to defeat the Cornovii, and he had betrayed me to keep the information from the Morini. If I could only discover the key to all of it, I could have a purpose to escape once more. If it had been Fidach alone, I might have gotten the answer out of him, but with Lugh here, he was watching himself too carefully. It would have to be Lugh to let it slip.

That night, I did not even look at Fidach. My eye was beginning to swell from where Lugh's fist had caught me but I fixed my gaze back on the consort.

"So, tell me." I smiled and felt my lip crack. "Are you planning to watch the massacre from a hillside? Or will you actually have the courage to lead the charge?"

"Catwin..." Fidach's voice was a warning, but Lugh

actually smiled.

"It's a pity your prince is more useful as a mage. It would be only right to let *him* strike the killing blow, wouldn't it? As it is, I'll have to do it."

I had prepared for this. Lugh courted the favor of the warriors, liking to show himself as one of them. It made sense that he would be out on the field with his men, and the readiness of his answer suggested it was no subterfuge. His surety was the key to him, his weakest point. I laughed in his face, as I had practiced in the darkness while I waited for them to arrive.

"Oh, you think Aoife will walk out to meet you, and lay down her life? Maybe Fidach told you the size of the army she's bringing, but even matching it won't help you."

"What?" Fidach's voice rang out, panicked, as Lugh rounded on him. "Catwin, what are you talking about?"

"Isn't that why you had the Cornovii bring so many?" I gave a little frown, trying not to wince at the pain in my eye. Even if Lugh would not betray their strategy, I could sow doubt between them.

"Is this true?" Lugh asked Fidach dangerously. "You said they would bring a smaller war force."

"I thought..." Fidach narrowed his eyes at me. He remembered my questions while we had scouted the Cornovii army; he knew that I did not know. And still he knew that at his side, Lugh was wondering what was truth and what was a lie. As I watched, the prince drew himself up. "They haven't brought anything to match us. She's lying. I was in the council when the decision was made."

"You think your mother would trust you with that?" I challenged him. "She planned for this." He went very still, and Lugh grabbed my chin, forcing my face towards Morwen.

"Is she telling the truth?"

"Yes." Did I see a lie in her face as she nodded? A flash of understanding, the fact that she had seen my own misdirection? "If you wish to win, you must know you face bad odds."

"I see." Fidach's lips hardly moved. He was gone in a swirl of his cloak, and Lugh after him. Morwen lingered in the doorway, her eyes resting on mine, and then she gave a tiny nod and left me alone, to wonder what it all meant.

I had intended to twist the knife farther, but Lugh did not return that night, or the next. I was left alone with my rations and my chains, helpless to turn the army. I could find no reason that Morwen would have failed to see the truth, and if she lied on my account, I could not think why. Still, if she had told, I was sure I would have been beaten for it. I lay in silence, and I wondered, flexing and clenching my hands from habit to keep the blood flowing.

The silence was the cruelest of any punishment Lugh could have inflicted. With his anger, even with his blows, I could measure my existence. Without, I had only my own pain to show me that I was real. The soldiers did not speak to me, even to bring me food. Fidach did not come any longer to taunt me. No one said my name, no one even said hello. I was hauled down from the saddle like a bag of grain at the end of each day. I found myself whispering aloud as I rode, unable to keep from giving form to myself—I was fading into a ghost, a shadow. I recited poems, histories, dates of the battles that had shaped Heddred, and the guards did not even speak to tell me to be quiet.

I tried to believe that I had created a seed of doubt in Lugh's heart, but with no proof of it I began to doubt. Even if I managed to escape, an unlikely proposition, and save Miriel with me, even more unlikely, what could we tell Aoife beyond the numbers? The cold, the pain, the silence, all were wearing on me now.

We reached the battlefield at twilight and I was shoved into a tent.

"Get ready," one of the soldiers said with a grin. "You're to be presented back to your queen tomorrow."

I looked up at him blearily as he left, and felt my heart sink. Presented, yes, and shot as soon as we were back amongst the Morini lines. If not shot, flanked—would the army sweep up the hills, perhaps? They would keep Fidach at the back, I thought, well away from the archers. Unless his powers required him to be closer.

I turned away from my rations without eating and curled into a ball on the ground. Dawn would be when I died. It was going to be a long night, and I had only anger to warm me.

Chapter 31

Night. I lay in the darkness and twisted my hands against the shackles. It didn't matter how many times I tried to slip free and failed. There was always one more try, and the struggle kept my blood moving in the chill air. Pain warmed me.

I had no way to track the passage of time, but seemed near to midnight when the tent flap was pushed aside and a dark-hooded figure entered. He stood still for a moment, looking down at me, and I watched him through slitted eyes so that he might not see the gleam. I did not need to see him clearly, for I had learned the flow of his movements in my many moments watching him. For now, I would let him think I was asleep, and see what he would do.

He surprised me by dropping to his knees at my side. A felt-wrapped package was laid on the ground and he leaned close to me, casting a glance over his shoulder.

"Catwin?" Fidach asked, and I did not move. I was unprepared for the surge of rage at the sound of his voice. It was helplessness transmuted. How dare he trap me here, at the mercy of a madman? How dare he make me suffer for a war that was not mine? How dare he?

"Please wake up," Fidach said urgently.

"Are you here to gloat?" I asked, after thinking it over. My voice was pleasantly steady, but I was terrified. I had faced death before, but it had never hit me like this. I was far from home. I was alone. If I was going to die for this, I wanted it to be with Miriel at my side. My other half.

"I'm here to free you. I swear it."

"Yes. I can tell from the way I was beaten and hauled all this way in chains."

He said nothing, only unwrapped the felt packet hurriedly, and held the lock picks out to me. I looked at him, his face shining sincerity, the lock picks held forward, and after a

---

204

moment of considered thought, I took the opportunity to spit in his face again. He jerked back, but wiped his face and looked back at me pleadingly.

"Catwin, listen to me. I'm sorry." His face was miserable. "I didn't think he would beat you. Emissaries aren't treated like that, it's not done."

"You seemed to have no trouble hitting me," I observed.

"What was I supposed to do? Listen to me, just listen. I had to gain Lugh's trust. He wanted me to turn on the Morini, but he's no fool. He'd never believe it without proof, and all I had was you. You looked so betrayed when I let them catch you—*that* was what Lugh needed to see, to believe me."

"And now you expect *me* to believe you just like that! After you—"

"After I hurt you and lied to you—yes, and I'm sorry, but there wasn't any other way! My gift shields me from Morwen, but she can see into your head, yours and Miriel's both. She needed to believe. They all needed to believe." His voice dropped. "I would have fought to the death if he'd tried to kill you, but he wasn't going to let you die. *Please.* Let me get you out of here."

"So Miriel didn't know, either?" *Please tell me she's still alive, Fidach.* Even if he was a liar, I needed to hear it.

"I didn't tell her." His lip quirked. "She threatened to disembowel me the last time we talked."

That did sound like Miriel. I chewed my lip and looked at him mistrustfully.

"So you had some grand plan, then?"

"I had thought—well, never mind, it didn't happen that way. I'd hoped Branwen would come with us, for me to persuade her, but it's battle now. You have to warn my mother. I've written down Lugh's battle plans, and what I plan to do. That will be enough to turn the tide, gods willing."

"You're not coming back with us?"

"I need to stay here."

"Need? Or want? And what the hell are you doing?" He had climbed around me and I, still mistrustful, tried to escape his grasp. I felt his hands as they set to work on the mess of shackles and rope.

"I'm getting you out of here. Catwin, say what you like, but think about this. I promised you that if you ran, they would catch you and they would kill you. Now, instead, we're all here, and I know what they're planning to do. And I can distract Morwen." The handcuffs came free with a click and he unhinged them. "Let me see your wrists."

I curled my arms into my chest protectively, examining the broken skin myself. Red stretched away from the wound itself, offering a stab of pain when I pressed on it. It would start to fester soon, and it was no comfort that this was hardly my most pressing concern.

"So why do you need to stay?" I reached to take the lock picks away from him and set to work on the shackles at my ankles. "I'm not saying I believe you."

"*Can't* you believe me?" I could hear pain in his voice. "D'you remember sitting up on the roof together, and you told me—"

"I remember," I said flatly. "And I remember that you kept telling me how you needed to stay, and if the army wasn't stopped, it would destroy the Morini. I remember you saying that Lugh couldn't win without an insider. And then you betrayed me when I could have gotten away."

"I saved your damned life," he hissed back. "The old customs are all that kept you alive. If they caught you riding for Dun Druim, they could kill you, do you know that?"

"Well, what's it to you?" He looked away and rubbed at his eyes with the palms of his hands.

"Oh, for—Catwin, I couldn't let you ride out to your death. Let me help you escape. Please."

I sighed, and the thoughts turned over in my head, rolling again and again. Hardly knowing what I was doing, I reached out to the iron collar, steadying it with one hand and holding the lock picks in the other.

"Lugh will know..."

"And how were you planning to do any magic with it on? What if he decided you were too much of a liability after all, did you think of that?"

"No."

"Then sit still." He craned his head away and I let go of his hand to pick up the lock picks. I set to work on the first, a stylized bull. Lugh, I thought, was not very subtle.

"So you trust me now?" I caught the hint of a smile.

"If you're lying, I won't be any less dead if I stay put," I said testily. "Tell me what you're planning." The longer he talked, the more time I had to catch him in a lie. So far, he seemed to be telling the truth, and I wasn't sure how I felt about that.

"I'll stay here to deal with Morwen," Fidach said impatiently. I broke off my work to stare at him, and he shrugged his shoulders. "Who else could stop you now? Their army is large, but my mother will know what to do to break it when she hears my message. It's Morwen she can't beat, not if Lugh has her covered adequately."

"Morwen went along with it when I lied about the Morini army. Might she defect?"

He considered.

"No," he said finally. "And it was hell trying to talk my way out of that particular lie, I'll have you know."

"Yes, well." I wasn't particularly sorry about it. Fidach sighed.

"Morwen was the one who spoke against bringing Branwen. If I had to guess, I'd say she thinks it's all too risky. Maybe she was hoping that if Lugh thought my mother had an army beyond his, he would turn back. But he hasn't and now she can't refuse. It's her brother and her queen asking it of her."

"If only we could have convinced Branwen…"

"Catwin." He caught my eyes. "Branwen made up her mind. I'm not sure in her place, I'd do any differently."

"But you know your mother can be trusted."

"Do I?" he asked me bitterly. He jumped when the first lock sprang open, and I caught it against his chest, held it out to him. He turned it over in his hands as I set to work on the second lock, a carved dragon. "I'm half-sure my mother thought we would all be killed and then she'd have a blood debt and no reason to give up the throne."

"Fidach." I sat back on my heels. "Your mother loves you."

"That doesn't change the fact that I've been an inconvenience."

"Children do that, I hear." He didn't laugh, and I sighed. "She wouldn't have sent you if she thought you would die."

"No? Then why? Why send me? It had to be as a hostage for her good behavior, for all Miriel objected to that plan—or to stop their mage. And she knew that would cost my life. I've had no training."

"*Now* you have."

"Four weeks of it! And that's from Morwen."

"Have you thought maybe *that's* why your mother sent you?"

The question stopped him dead.

"What?"

The second lock sprang free and I caught it, set it next to the first. I wanted to reach out and brush his hair away from his eyes. I wanted to comfort him. It was a strange feeling—Miriel and I had made a shelter of our shared suffering, for certain, but we had not offered comfort so much as resolve. Of course, I thought, we had disliked each other too much to know how. Still, now what I wanted more than anything was to make the look of pain on Fidach's face go away.

I just didn't know how. I swallowed and looked down at my hands.

"Fidach."

"What?" His voice was quiet, warm.

"Your mother is afraid to leave the Morini in anyone else's hands, but she would never see you dead to keep her throne, just for the sake of it." He drew breath to speak and I cut him off. "There was no one at Dun Druim who could teach you, haven't you thought of that? She would have known it. What if she sent you to show you this world, where mages were celebrated— what if she knew she couldn't give you that in her court, and so she let you come to study with Morwen?"

He looked down at his hands and swallowed, and I was glad for the moment that I could not see his father's pale eyes.

"Do you think that's why?" He asked finally.

"I do. She doesn't trust magic, but she trusts you." I

reached out to take his hand again. They were not the Duke's eyes, I realized. The Duke had never been so unsure, so unwilling to take power that lay at his fingertips. He would have changed his allegiance in a moment, and gods help me, I was more sure every moment that Fidach had not betrayed us. "Come with us," I said softly, and he shook his head.

"Morwen can stop you from reaching my mother. I can stop her—and you two can escape. That much, I can promise you."

"You can stop her from the other side of the battlefield," I said instantly.

"Catwin..."

"I am not leaving this tent until you agree to come back with us." I met his eyes stubbornly, and realized that it was true. When I heard Fidach betray me to the soldiers, there had been a moment before anger, when all I had felt was disbelief. After so much doubt, and the long days of the march wondering how I had not seen his treachery, I had come to the answer now, in this dark tent, looking at the fear in his eyes: he was no traitor.

We measured our will against each other.

"I am your prince," he said softly. "I could order you to go. It would be wise to save our emissary."

"It would be *wise* to save the prince and the only known mage of the Morini," I countered. "It's not you or Miriel, Fidach. Come with us."

He looked at my face for a very long time, as if memorizing it. His hands squeezed mine.

"All right. I'll be right behind you. Go quickly and get the horses. It's at the northern edge of the camp."

No one else would have seen it. Not Miriel, with her quick mind, not Lugh with his distrust, perhaps not even Aoife. But none of them had heard the same lie before, given on the eve of battle. I had, and it hit me in the gut.

"No," I told him. My voice was shaking. "Don't lie to me. You're not going to fool me with that."

It was like a nightmare, it was unfolding and I could not stop it. I was desperate for him to tell me the truth, and yet I could not bear to hear the words. We were gripping each other's hands and I wanted to cry out that this could not happen again. Not again.

"My mother must be warned. So you must go, and Miriel. And Morwen cannot let that happen. You know all this, Catwin. You know someone has to stop her." I thought I saw the sheen of tears before he blinked them away. "And so it *is* me or you."

"Do you really think there's so little to live for that you'll give yourself up like this?" I cried. I wrenched my hands out of his and made for the entrance to the tent. I could hardly see. I threw the accusation back over my shoulder: "You keep saying it will mean your death if you stay, but you're hell-bent on doing it. You always have been."

"There isn't anyone else who can do this, Catwin! There isn't any other way."

"There's always another way. You won't even consider—" I broke off. I couldn't have put words to it. Part fury, part grief. "You're throwing your life away, and for nothing. If you're doing this for some stupid, misguided attempt at honor—"

"I'm doing it for you!" Fidach finally yelled. We had kept our voices to a whisper and his burst into the stillness of the tent like shattering glass. "For *you*, Catwin!"

I didn't even have time to react before his lips met mine. I registered a moment of surprise, but not a second of hesitation. His hands were at my face, and my fingers clenched around the fabric of his shirt, drawing him closer. The kiss stretched until we stumbled and caught each other; a moment of laughter, hastily cut off with the reminder that many ears waited outside.

And then the moment faded and it was only two of us, drawn together in the cold of the tent, my arms wrapped around him and his around me, and our foreheads leaned together, our breath mingling. I must have closed my eyes, for when I opened them he drew away and then rested his forehead against mine. I curled into the warmth of his arms and felt, for the first time in years, as if I had found a home.

"Catwin," he said softly.

"Fidach?" His name felt strange on my tongue now.

"Do you see now?" I couldn't help myself, I gave an undignified snort of laughter. He grinned. "What?"

"You could have tried poetry." He laughed and tightened his arms around me, but his smile faded.

"I can't just let you die," he said softly.

"And I can't let you throw your life away," I whispered back. I was shaking now. "Please, Fidach."

He looked away from me, and I saw him calculating.

"I'll come with you," he said finally. "But I have one condition: if Morwen tries to stop us, you must promise me now that you will keep riding. You will not stop. You will not look back. You will go, and save yourself. Promise me, Catwin."

I looked up into his familiar, stubborn face, and knew there would be no arguing with him.

"I promise," I said, and he tried to smile.

"Then we should go."

Chapter 32

My makeshift prison was near the back of the camp, and the few soldiers left to guard me had gone to cluster around a nearby campfire. They did not like to see me, for my silence unnerved them. An emissary should not have blood at her wrists and bruises on her face. They should not keep her imprisoned, knowing that she would be killed as an example to her people. This, they knew. Perhaps they wished I would plead with them to let me go, so that they could harden their hearts and speak amongst each other of Morini treachery, and I refused to give them that. I had known the whole journey that they would not break, but I was damned if I would let them absolve themselves for this.

We slipped from my tent to the shadows across the road, two hooded figures trying to walk purposefully. I winced as I moved. Long days in the saddle, and nights bound and cold had left me stiff. I must walk normally, for the Cornovii were watching each other for signs of weakness. I must keep my head down, so that they would not see my bruises and split lip. Fidach and I were Heddrian; no one could look too closely, or all was lost.

The tents lay in close rows, no good outlet to the edge of the camp, and so we must move forwards before detouring out again. In the blaze of each campfire, I scanned quickly for familiar faces: Seiysell, Lugh, Morwen, Branwen—even Miriel, perhaps. The figures were black silhouettes against the blaze of the flames, and yet my breath caught at each movement, the turn of heads. My training was strong, and yet I fought the urge to drop my head, increase my pace, any of the things that would mark me instantly as a guilty party, alert these soldiers to my presence.

You are only a woman in a cloak, I told myself sternly. *You are in darkness, they cannot see you well. Do not disgrace your training for fear alone.*

It was near the center of the camp that the commotion started: a fight between drunken soldiers, the sort that starts for nothing more than a nudge or a mutter and grows to a matter of consuming rage in a few moments. It is a difficult business, waiting for battle, helplessness and fear and anger at one's enemies, and I had seen enough spats in the Heddrian camps to be familiar. But these soldiers were no standing army, and they were unaccustomed to it. The scuffle drew attention where it should not, and someone must have gone running for the commander, for the next thing we heard was Lugh's bellow.

I froze, and Fidach with me. Soldiers were pouring out of the tents to watch, and the way was too crowded to move back. The crowd pushed us inexorably forward into the ring of light, and though we ducked our faces away, who could say that Lugh would not notice two blond heads, would not see Fidach without his collar? Caught with no escape behind me, and Lugh ahead, I was glad enough when a hand snaked out of one of the tents to grab my wrist. If this was a trap, I thought, it could hardly be worse for me than Lugh's wrath. I managed to snag Fidach's cloak, and the two of us tumbled together into darkness.

"This way," a voice hissed.

"What?" Fidach demanded.

"To the horses! To escape." Dim light filtered in as our companion lifted the back wall of the tent and slipped underneath. After a moment we heard, "It's safe. Come on!"

"Who are you?" I asked, when we emerged into a narrow gap between rows of tents. I took stock: a skinny boy with a shock of brown hair. His clothes were patched and dirty, and he wore no weapons. I struggled to place him, for I knew I had seen him before, and he shrugged his thin shoulders.

"I'm Amon. The baker's boy."

"What are you doing here?" I demanded, horrified. He would be killed tomorrow, he would be cut down in a moment. This boy was no warrior.

"I came for you," he said shyly, pride showing in the way he ducked his head against my stare. "You, and the lady. She's nice to us all, you know. An' I heard your story about Dukes and lords, and we all talked about it, later—and yer right about her.

Jemmis, he's one of the servants in the Queen's halls, he said the lady wanted to give us farmland, but the Consort wouldn't allow it. We thought if we came along, we could set you free—get you back, to bargain."

"Amon..." My throat closed. I did not know what to say. At my side, Fidach stood in anguished silence. "Amon, what's coming is battle."

"Maybe." He grinned, a secret little smile. "Maybe not."

"You must get to the back of the camp. Take a horse and some supplies, and ride for Dun Beal." I took him by the shoulders, but he only shook his head and smiled at me.

"We have to get you out first."

"Then you'll go?" I asked him sternly, and he nodded. "And all your friends."

"Yes, ma'am."

"Then let's be quick."

Amon led us through the back alleys of the makeshift town, weaving and ducking with Fidach and I following in a half-crouch, afraid to let anyone catch even a glimpse of us. We could still hear the commotion rising behind us as the fight spread, and shouting as others tried desperately to contain it. I could only hope that the distraction would last a little bit longer.

Miriel waited for us at the edge of the camp, a little hooded shape crouched near a barrel—almost indistinguishable from the sacks of grain that leaned nearby. Despite everything, I smiled. Miriel had listened when I spoke of my training all those years ago. Even alone and scared, she was holding onto her discipline. She was as still as any human could be, and at her side I saw Talyn, with two followers, armed, in heavy hoods. He nodded at me.

"Miriel," I said, when I had checked for followers. Her head came up, and I saw her take in the blood at my wrists, the bruises on my face—and Fidach at my side. Her lips parted in shock, and anger sparked deep behind her blue eyes.

"Catwin, what have they *done* to you?"

For a moment, I could say nothing. My breath came short. She was safe, at last I could see it and know it for truth. I ran to her and caught her up in my arms, and she wrapped hers around me as well, burying her head against my shoulder. I thought I felt a sob shake her, and I squeezed my eyes shut. She was alive and well, and I could hardly keep from crying in relief. I had not believed it until now.

"Are you all right?" she asked me softly, holding me close. Her head was turned down as if she was afraid to look up. "I swear to you, if I had known—I never would have stayed in that tent. I didn't think they would ever dare hurt you. What did they—"

"Not important." I let go of her at last. "We have to go."

"Why is he here?" she asked, and I heard mistrust in her voice. Talyn, standing at her side, stirred and made to speak, but Miriel cut him off with a glare. "I know what *you* say. I also know what I saw with my own eyes."

"He came to free me himself," I said, before Fidach could speak. "I'll explain later. Please, Miriel."

They wavered, staring at one another in mutual dislike, and Miriel broke first, lifting her shoulder in one of her elegant shrugs. She turned away with a toss of her black curls, and the Cornovii led five horses from the shadows.

"I will do what I can here to keep Lugh from noticing that you are gone," Talyn said urgently, "but I do not know how long I can hold him. You should go now. These two will accompany you."

"We cannot bring—"

"They are unarmed. And you will need them. Trust me." Talyn himself helped Miriel into the saddle, and to my surprise, he reached out to touch her hand. "You ride with all our hopes, my lady. Go quickly, and bring us peace."

"How?" I whispered, and Miriel shook her head. I saw despair in her eyes. We might save the Morini, but no more. She only nodded to Talyn, mute in the face of her own helplessness, and the truth of it hit me then: that this was giving up. This was our failure. We were sent to bring peace and the best we could do anymore was to limit the bloodshed. Dawn would bring battle, and we would be firing on all who had helped us escape. Horror was dawning in my chest. I was shaking my head, and it was only Fidach, leaning to hold his hand over my mine, who kept me sane enough to seek out Amon from amongst the group of servants.

"Run," I told him. "All of you, get out. Quickly. Go now, while they're distracted by the fight."

He nodded, and we spurred our horses out into the night, one hooded rider leading the way and one bringing up the rear. We spread out as we thundered across the plain, with the silent spread of the stars above us and frost on the moss below. We kept our silence, hearts pounding; we were all waiting for the shout that could bring the archers after us.

The armies lay close together, waiting for the hour before dawn when they would mass, and begin the slow advance to shooting distance. As we grew closer, I could see the campfires of the Morini camp and I despaired. This force was as Fidach had described, little more than a raiding party, meant to defend against the horsemen that had come for us in the first advance. There was no way this army could beat back to the Cornovii, surely...

The shouts began as we approached the camp, and we raised our hands into the air to show our intent, letting the horses slow to a trot.

"Hail," Fidach called, spurring his horse ahead of the others.

"Hail," one of the guards said cautiously. "Who rides with you?"

"We will explain when we see Aoife," Miriel said impatiently. "Is she here?"

"Why have you come now, instead of at dawn?" asked another.

"We don't have time for this," I snapped. "Unless you want to be run down like dogs by an army four times the size of your own, you will take us to Aoife."

"Yes. At once." The guard pointed to the two riders who had come with us. "The two must stay. We cannot let them into the presence of the queen."

"Of course," Miriel said impatiently. "But if you hurt them—"

When the two figures at our sides dropped back their

hoods, she broke off with a strangled exclamation.

"I am Queen Branwen of the Cornovii," said Branwen. "And this is my heir, Seiysell. I come unarmed and demand safe transport to your queen to bargain, as is assured to me under the treaty signed three generations back."

The guards wavered, and then a voice spoke from the darkness behind them.

"Well met, your grace," said Aoife. "Come, and let us see what we can agree upon."

Chapter 33

Aoife's tent was well-lit, filled with makeshift tables of supply crates, on which were spread maps and scrolls held in place with heavy iron counters and rocks. The Morini army had traveled more slowly, well equipped and well fed, and the camp was at ease, unaware of the odds they faced on the morrow.

"My lords," Aoife said coolly, just the hint of amusement in her voice, "may I present Queen Branwen of the Cornovii, and Seiysell, heir to the Cornovii throne."

"You can't be serious," Nuall said, rising. His hand was on his dagger. "You bring her into our camp and expect—"

"My lords." Miriel had been well trained in the art of oration, and her voice resounded through the tent with the force of a blow. All faces turned towards her. "This is not how we begin negotiations. Branwen has come to bargain."

"Why we are bargaining, I still do not know!" Nuall slammed his hands down on the table, glaring at Branwen and Aoife alike. "They are poorly armed. They bring ill-fed horsemen and expect us to quake in our boots—and we do. It does not make sense."

"That is because there is more to it than your queen is telling," Branwen said shortly. She withdrew a scroll from a pouch at her waist, pretending not to notice Aoife's sudden stillness. "Your grace, this is the document that was drawn up in preliminary negotiations between your emissaries and mine. A good starting point, I think."

"Your emissaries do not come to bargain for you?" Branwen might be made of stone, but Aoife seemed coolly amused. Relief, I thought, disguised in hauteur—Aoife's eyes went to Fidach every few moments, as if checking that he was still well. I read worry in the slight flare of her nostrils. Branwen noticed her concern.

"Your son," she said to Aoife, and grudging amusement

showed in her tone, "is quite an actor, your grace. He has my consort quite convinced that he is a turncoat—or did. I rather think this escape will put that to rest. Fidach freed the other two emissaries, so that they might warn you."

"My emissaries were imprisoned?" Aoife asked dangerously. The lanterns were guttering, and the tent was silent but for the snap of the wind in canvas and the faint footsteps of the patrols.

"They attempted to spy upon us, and then flee."

"Catwin, is this true?" Aoife had seen the flare of anger in my eyes.

"No," I said shortly. "I was on the battlements, where I had every right to be, when I saw their army massing."

"Massing, because every day we received reports that the Morini army was being reinforced."

"And waiting! They had not marched on Dun Beal."

"Enough," Miriel snapped. "Their camp seems set on war. Why Branwen is here now is what we must know."

"Because I, too, wish for peace," Branwen said coldly. We stared at her, and at Seiysell behind her. The younger woman lifted her chin against the glares of the Morini, and Branwen drew her cloak around herself and stared them all down.

"Then why not hold your army at Dun Beal and conclude negotiations?" Miriel asked. She was in her element once more, grave and lovely, shining with confidence. Her eyes were narrowed slightly, and I saw her fingertips press together; she was holding herself still and grave by force of will alone.

"I may wish for peace, but I am not certain it can be accomplished. When your enemy masses a great army to cut you down if negotiations should fail, do you not arm yourself?"

"That is precisely why we are here," Aoife said drily. "Why attack us in the first place?"

"To make you take notice," Branwen snapped back. "For three generations you've lived well off our fields, tended our herds. You watched us starve without a moment of compassion—"

"If I could have helped," Aoife began, and Branwen's shout cut her off:

"You could have! You know you could have! What would it have cost you to come to us, to say the battle was between our ancestors and nothing to do with us now? Nothing! You could have mended matters between our tribes within days if you wanted. Your grandfather sent us from Dun Druim for greed alone, and your father did nothing to right matters. And then there was you."

"Please," Aoife said, and nothing more. She was pale as death. We were coming to the heart of the matter, and she knew it. I began to move, quietly, threading my away around the war party until I stood between Fidach and the lords, and Miriel cast me a quick look. "You are a mother. Please."

"Will someone tell me what is going on?" Nuall asked, and Miriel cut over Aoife's prevarication, her voice light and clear.

"We are here to rewrite the treaty between the tribes."

"The treaty stands," Nuall said heatedly.

"Then who will rule?" Branwen asked. "Aoife? Or will you cede your son to us, your grace? The choice is yours."

"The treaty will not stand," Miriel snapped. I saw her cast a quick look to where Aoife was still shaking, refusing to look at Fidach. "A new land is no answer for the Cornovii, and selling sons is no answer for the Morini. The treaty was drawn in bad faith, it has caused only pain. You will all be at war until you end it."

"Priteni has always been at war." Aoife looked up bitterly. "Would you change our ways, outsider?"

"Your ways were raiding parties and squabbles between tribes, not one alliance forcing another into starvation!"

"They would have the mage kings back in a heartbeat," Nuall hissed.

"Would they? For there is a mage in the Cornovii court, and Branwen has not yet become a tyrant."

"It is only a matter of time," Nuall said confidently. "No one can resist such power."

"What would you do, then, cast out all mages? For a mage may be rewarded with endless riches for supporting a king. A mage may indeed be more powerful than a king. It is not family that gives a mage power, but the weakness of the monarch. Your treaty was flawed from the start."

"Perhaps we should cast out the mages," Nuall said coldly. "Kill them in their youth. If no ruler can be trusted with such power—"

He broke off when Aoife made a strangled sound.

"No," she said. "No."

"Every time we speak of this—"

"Every time we speak of it, I tell you no! And I am your queen." Aoife stared Nuall down, and at my side, Fidach clenched his hands.

What if that was why your mother sent you away? Idle words in the dark, bitter speculation on a rooftop. To give him freedom, I thought. A chance at a better life. Never had it occurred to me that Aoife was afraid for her son's very life. I had not dreamed the depth of Nuall's hatred—nor, from his white face, had Fidach.

Please. Aoife's words rang in my head, and I understood now. *Please, you are a mother.*

"And by what right are you his queen?" Branwen asked coldly. Either she did not see it, or in her anger she did not care. "Let us speak of how you treat mages, your grace."

"We will not speak of mages," Miriel said. She moved her hand sharply, cutting off the Branwen's words. Her other fingers gestured to me, warning me to be on my guard. I could see worry in her now. She seized upon the chance to bargain, confident and serene, and now we knew the final piece—not lust for power, as we had thought, but fear.

"Mages are why we are here," Branwen said, and Miriel slammed her fist down on the desk.

"No! This treaty was never *about* mages, you said it yourself. It was about land and riches and greed, like any war, and I will not watch you cling to it out of spite. This treaty has done nothing for your people. Food and safety were what you said you needed—*that* will be your concern. Aoife, no less will it be yours. Your borders will never be safe while kin to the Morini starve on the western coast. Your blood debts will never be put to rest while the treaty is upheld. And your throne may well be

---

221

something you must cede."

"To whom?" Nuall demanded. "The Cornovii queen and her brats? The line of Morin has ruled well. Our people are well-fed, well-housed."

Beside him, Aoife looked down at her hands, and I saw her eyes squeeze shut for a moment. Fear was radiating from her in waves. *I could end it now,* I thought to myself suddenly. Tell them what Fidach was, kill Nuall when he made his move. I could end it. Temar might have told me to do so: lie in wait in a dark corridor, add a pinch of powder to the man's wine, bribe a servant.

Temar was not here anymore. I was, and I kept my silence even as I kept my hand near my dagger.

"Your people are well-fed by a treaty that gives them more land than they need," Seiysell said bravely, and Miriel nodded at her.

"I have seen the surplus stocks of grain. Aoife—"

"I told you when I sent you to bargain for me that you were bidden to keep me on the throne, and Connor after me," Aoife said dangerously.

"You asked an impossible thing," Miriel said. "For that, I count my debt to you unfulfilled, and bid you ask me any other thing that is in my power to give you. For that is your right."

The air in the tent changed in a moment, and it was all I could do not to draw my dagger. I could not understand the danger, but I could sense it. Power was massing her, raising the hair along my arms and at the back of my neck. Aoife and Fidach had gone very still, and I saw Miriel's secret little smile, a look of satisfaction and bitterness all rolled up into one. Branwen looked between them all, wary, and Nuall seemed utterly bewildered. Miriel stared them all down with a look of absolute triumph.

"You have hidden something from me," she told Aoife. "All these long months. There is a debt between us." Aoife had been watching her steadily, but at the last words, she flinched.

"I did not hide it," she said carefully.

"But you did not tell me, either." Miriel's face was like stone, and Aoife bowed her head.

"Miriel..." My own voice was tentative. *What is this?* She looked at me and smiled, but her words were for the queen.

"One thing. One request." The words meant nothing to me at first, and it was only when Aoife bit her lip that I knew. There were only two things that unsettled Aoife: her son's powers, and...

...the Duke.

"No," I said softly. "Oh, no."

But I knew. *Blood calls to blood,* Miriel told me. *Temar turned the Duke's fate.* And when the Duke left these shores with their prince, he had left a bargain unfulfilled, a bargain Aoife had called on so ambiguously when she sent us away. The fate, the violent fate for which so many had mistrusted Fidach, had never been meant for him at all.

"Yes," Aoife said. "Say what you will, call me an oath breaker, but I would never let my son become as the Gwyddu. I could have given him that fate, it was in my power, and I never did. Have I not shown my mettle?"

"Your son..." Nuall said in dawning horror.

"Fidach is a mage," Aoife admitted at last, and I saw her hand go to her side, to clasp at something underneath her cloak. A knife. If Fidach saw it, too, I did not know, for I could not look away.

"A mage bound in iron and forbidden from practicing the gifts of the Nine," Branwen added, fury in her voice. "A cruel fate for any man, more so when given by his own mother."

"A mage in this court would have faced suspicion, whether or not I was queen!" Aoife cried. "You have heard only merest part of the things they say. He would never have been safe, he would never have been trusted."

"He *cannot* be trusted!" Nuall's hands slammed down on the tables once more. "No mortal should have that power. It is unnatural."

"Unnatural? There have been mages since before the clans." Branwen's chin jutted forward, and she shot a glare at Miriel. "You called it barbaric to bargain him away, but we, at least, would have offered him a home."

"Save your moralizing," Miriel said wearily. "You're moral

when it suits you. You say you want no war, but you brought an army to cut down your enemies if the peace talks fail—an army that was a betrayal of the peace talks to start with. You say you would offer Fidach a home, you spit curses on Aoife, but you only fear to have a weapon in your enemy's hand. You wanted an heir to take Connor's throne."

"I would protect my people. If the talks succeed, we shall go home on the morrow. If they fail, if I do not return...."

"Then we, knowing what we face, will end your tribe." Miriel stared her down, unimpressed.

"You cannot know that for certain."

"I know enough!" Miriel shouted back.

I pressed my fingers to my temples, trying to drown out the noise that was pounding in my ears. No one would listen, no one cared. Nuall was seething, Aoife in a passion of fear and anger, and Branwen wanted—oh, how I could see her desire—to let Lugh crush them all.

It was then that I realized Fidach was no longer beside me. Cold air swirled at my feet and the tent flap was pushed aside. A glance showed Nuall still shouting, in amongst the fray. I glanced around. Shouting, yes, but no weapons drawn. Miriel's hand stayed close to her own knife, as I had taught her, and as I bit my lip, I felt the ground give a slight tremor beneath my feet. An earthquake.

Fidach.

I pushed my way out of the tent and ran.

Chapter 34

They stood at the edge of the camp: my prince, in his
golden torc, hair shining in the moonlight; and alone, garbed in
white, Morwen. A rising wind whistled across the midlands, and
the ground shook once more, but neither of the mages moved.
They might have been carved from stone, if their cloaks did not
flare in the gusts of wind.

Morwen saw me first, and her calm eyes appraised me.

"This is not your fight, child. This is between Gwydion's
children."

"You don't have to do this," Fidach told her. I looked to
him and was surprised by the depth of anguish I saw in his eyes.
"We would find you a safe haven. Perhaps even your own queen
would not reproach you. You know this battle is dishonor
against us all."

"And you know very well that I cannot betray blood and
clan. My queen would bargain away everything I hold dear, and I
cannot let that happen. I did not allow it at Glen Tuam, when I
saw my brother charmed by a pretty face and I knew my queen
would fall for the same tricks, and I will not allow it now. I would
tell you to step aside, but I know you will not." She held out one
clenched hand, opened it to show three iron keys. "To your
collar, although I see it is now undone."

"Why?" Fidach asked the only important question, and
her mouth twisted.

"Why train you? You have the sight, younger brother. You
knew it would come to this."

"I hoped..."

"And I am old, and know when hope is no more than
foolishness. I knew what would happen. And I would not have it
be a slaughter."

I saw Fidach consider. Dragons glittered at his throat.

"I would not fight you."

"You do not get to choose."

"No?" Fidach challenged her. "Can you compel me?"

"I can." It happened in an eyeblink: the air was sucked from my lungs and I doubled over, clawing at my throat. "This is no idle threat, princeling. You know the power I can call. If you do not fight, all of them will die."

I had to get to her. I stumbled forward, but waves of air buffeted me back. I could not breathe, there was no air in my lungs at all, and where I should have driven my shoulder forward to drive it against her legs, there was a wall of air blocking me. I slid down it, pounding my fists weakly. *Fight, Catwin. You have to fight.* Whose voice?

The gale ripped tents from their mooring nearby and knocked me from my feet. I thought I saw the earth lift and roll, or perhaps that was only the spots dancing in front of my eyes. I was losing consciousness and all I could see was Fidach's face, desperate. Above my head, clouds were swirling against the stars. *The call of storm,* I thought dreamily. I hardly heard Fidach's yell over the sudden clamor of the camp.

"Catwin, go!"

Air. I sucked it into my lungs and scrambled for cover. People were screaming. A patter of rain began, thunder boomed over our heads. The ground rolled, and I saw Morwen fall. A gust of wind caught me and blew me sideways; her wind, I thought, though it might have been Fidach trying to push me away from the fight.

"Why come now, when you doubted this war from the start?"

"I doubted a war that would end in any peace with the line of Morin." Her voice was ugly. "My people are dying slowly. I have watched it all my life and now you would stand in my way and tell me to forget my anger. You call Lugh a madman, and set you against you, but you do not know how weak he is, how weak Branwen is. They would have taken pity on you all."

"I would tell you to forge a peace of your own making!" The wind was a shriek now, and I longed to cover my ears against the sound. I knew that Fidach would tell me to run, but I could not leave him. Not against this. Not alone

———

226

"The peace talks meant nothing," Morwen cried against the wind. Her white hair was escaping from its braid and she battered Fidach with wind, sending him staggering sideways. "I know what you planned, I saw it in your thoughts every day. You would have twisted the truth and blackmailed us and played us against one another until you kept Aoife on the throne. All we needed was food and warmth, did you not say so amongst yourselves? Did you not?"

She stared until he nodded, gritting his teeth as he built himself a shield of swirling winds, and her face twisted.

"What we needed was vengeance," she whispered. "Not blood money. We needed justice, for what came before, for what you wrought on our ancestors."

"And what would that be?" Fidach demanded. "What is justice enough for you, if not an end to this?"

"Not this! Not a new treaty and more false promises! You would offer us scraps, deign to let us crawl back to our old lands while you spoke hollow words of welcome and watched us with suspicious eyes. And when mages dared show their power, you would chain them in iron and call yourselves merciful for not killing them outright, call yourselves great kings for not becoming the Gwyddu reborn."

"We are not our ancestors," Fidach said desperately. "We could make a new peace."

"A new peace where the Morini still rule at Dun Druim?" Morwen spat on the ground. "No. It should go to us! The Cornovii were forged in hunger and cold. It is *our* people who should hold Dun Druim. It is *our* people who should take Innis Tearmen."

"And what, would you spill our blood? Or would you leave the Morini to starve on the coasts as you did?" The clouds above were beginning to descend, still circling, the very heavens lowering to meet us. From the strain on Fidach's face, and the wariness on Morwen's, I knew it was his storm—crackling with energy and crashing cloud against cloud, towers of black rising into the night. "Have you learned nothing from your own exile?"

"Our blood?" Morwen cried. "You are not one of them, brother. You are a *mage*, and they would kill you as soon as look at you. Even now they ready your bows to destroy you. Turn your back on them if you dare. Take Dun Druim in blood and fire, and cast out the Morini. Why should they rule?"

"Then find a new ruling line!" Fidach cried desperately. "It is nothing to me. Just let it be finished, let it end without bloodshed."

"And the blood spilled since the treaty was signed, what of that?" Morwen's face was a mask. "You thought my brother a madman. Reckless, to march on Dun Druim. Bloodthirsty."

"Yes!" Fidach shouted back.

"He is not the man he should have been!" Morwen cried, and I heard anguish in her voice. "He was a child of honor and joy. He would have saved our people in any way he could, but every winter he must endure without enough fuel to burn, every harvest with not enough to put in the storerooms, every ship lost on the North Sea, he was twisted—more and more! I lost my brother to your treachery. It was your queen's oath-breaking that turned his mind to war, nothing of us!"

"No." Fidach was shaking his head, horror dawning on his face. "It wasn't me you lost him to. It was you. You were the one who twisted him. It was you all along, wasn't it, Morwen?"

I stared back and forth between them, and saw her draw herself up.

"I did not twist him. I reminded him of what he had seen. What he had endured."

"Leaning in to whisper in his ear—we thought you were calming him, but you were always stoking his anger, weren't you?"

I looked over at her so sharply that my neck twisted. Foolish, I had called Morwen. Always saying the wrong thing, always catching Lugh's suspicion. And yet it had all been on purpose, every last word of it, no matter how reasonable it sounded. When Branwen demanded of Lugh what had happened, what had been changed—it had been Morwen.

And when Morwen suggested that Branwen stay back at Dun Beal...

"And what now, Morwen?" Fidach asked. Tears were streaming down his face, from the power in his veins or his own grief, I could not say. "Your brother is gone, and what of us? We face down his shadow and his army, and you tell us not to fight for our lives."

"I tell you that I will not let my queen wipe away every injustice that stole my brother away. Stand aside, Gwydion!"

I could see the blast she sent for Branwen, a ripple in the air that came with a crack so loud my ears rang. I clapped my hands against the side of my head with a cry of pain, and saw Morwen's wave of air hit an invisible wall. Fidach threw his arms down and pulled them up once more, strain showing in his neck, and this time the ground bucked and rolled so strongly that I was thrown into the air. Horses were screaming, and I could smell fire.

Then my head slammed onto the hard ground and the world dimmed. There was a shadow in my vision, a dark figure racing across the unstable ground. I could hear sounds but could make no sense of them. Nuall. I saw the flashing of a knife as he lunged for his prince, and though I tried to roll and push myself to my feet, I was too clumsy. I staggered and wove as I tried to run for them.

Fidach.

The blaze of flames in the camp was growing brighter and the heat seared across my face. Another figure struggled with Nuall now, silver and gold flashed too-bright-too-clear against the black shapes, and beyond them, the battle raged on. The clouds near enough touched the earth now, enveloping Fidach and Morwen in a fury of rain and ice as the earth roared.

It was only when Nuall's blade tore into his opponent that I recognized her: Aoife, her dark hair whipped sideways in the wind, fighting desperately to keep Nuall from her son. She staggered to her knees, blood soaking the front of her gown, and Nuall shouted in triumph.

He discounted her too easily. As he made for Fidach, Aoife's knife flashed in the light. Even I, my ears ringing, heard his scream. The back of his leg was pouring blood, near black in the dim light. Aoife staggered to her feet, one hand still clutched over the wound in her stomach. Her final strike took Nuall in the back, and the two of them sank down together.

And then the clouds slammed to earth and the earth leapt

for the sky. I felt my knees buckle and the roll of thunder resounded in my bones. The world went dark.

Chapter 35

When I came to, there was shouting in my ears, and the biting cold of winter air. My wrists were throbbing. Words were reaching my ears in fragments, sounds jumbled together. Pictish, I realized, Of course. I was in Priteni. Such were my first exhausted thoughts. Hands were touching my wrists—pain, such pain—and my head. I thought I could hear my name, but it was distant.

Priteni. Pain. The storm. A battle. I opened my eyes once more to take in the feel of frozen ground under my cheek and the first rays of dawn rising behind me; my shadow slanted away across the ground. The hands shook me desperately, then fell away as I rolled over, giving a little cry of pain.

Pressing myself up was an exercise in willpower alone, but I knew I must stand. Something had been very wrong before I slept, and I must try to remember what it was. Something nearby, I thought, and I turned, limping, to look around me.

The camp was in an uproar, human chaos against eerie beauty. Flames danced still over the ruins and ice glistened in the sunlight. Snow was still drifting gently down as clouds rolled back overhead, a storm dissipating into nothing.

The soldiers flickered dark among the falling flakes, helping figures from the tumbled tents and smothering flames. People moved about me in a constant flow of motion that made me want to throw up. The whole world seemed to be spinning.

Beyond the camp, two figures walked in the swirling snow towards the Cornovii camp. Branwen's red gold hair shone like a beacon in the dawn light, and her daughter's dark hair seemed a shadow of it. Beyond them, I could see dimly that the Cornovii waited in ranks, their numbers set back as Lugh had planned. It looked like a raiding party.

But they did not move. Lugh would have noticed Fidach missing, and me, and Miriel. Had anyone told him that Seiysell left as well, or that another figure rode to the Morini camp with her red hair streaming down her back? And had he sent Morwen to end it, or had she come herself, fearing that he would be moved to honor his wife's peace treaty?

Now he was watching his wife come to him from the Morini camp, knowing that she had not trusted him. Still, he did not move to strike her down. He waited, the gentle brother Talyn remembered, the kind man Morwen had spoken of. He did not order his soldiers forward, even though he knew not what news his wife brought him.

It occurred to me that I did not know, either. I had left them, I remembered that now. I left them in the tent to make their peace, sure that Miriel would find some way to bind them to an agreement. Was she not her uncle's heir, named so by him and by Temar and, now, by Aoife? Did she not have the fate of a conqueror clinging to her?

It was then, having turned in a full circle, that I saw Miriel. Her hands held out a blanket. Ointment and bandages lay on the ground nearby. She had been trying to bandage my wrists, I realized now. Her lips were moving but I still could not understand the words. I was shivering violently as she wrapped the blanket around my shoulders and bade me sit on the hard ground, and I leaned my head on her shoulder while she brushed dirt gently from the broken skin at my wrists. She wiped the ointment on with a muttered apology and I hissed through my teeth at the burning, but had the good sense to stay still. She wrapped the bandages quickly, lest I try to scrape the herbs off, and then took my hands in hers.

"Catwin?" I knew that word. I looked up at her face and nodded to her, and her eyes filled with tears. She leaned forward to wrap her arms around me and I cradled my hands close to myself, leaning in and feeling the warmth of her. She was real, solid; I remembered that it was not so long since I had been terribly afraid for her.

"Are you all right?" It took a few moments to compose the words in my mind, but they seemed to come out well. She drew back and wiped at her eyes.

"Yes. It's done. It's finally done." Her face was pale. "I

persuaded them to join tribes once more. Seiysell will wed Connor. Dun Beal will be abandoned."

"You did it. You made peace when..." *When no one thought you could do it.* It seemed ridiculous now. I had doubted that it was possible, and somehow I had still never doubted her. I smiled as the memories began to filter back, and she smiled back at me, ducking her head against a blush.

"It was the storm that frightened them enough to agree, I think."

The storm. Fidach. It came back to me in a rush and I looked around myself frantically. Nuall's body lay twisted on the ground, blood glistening bright in the sun, and Morwen's beyond it, and Miriel bit her lip as she looked at them.

The lord lay where he had fallen, desperate to save his kingdom from a threat long since dead at Glen Tuam. For a moment, I could think of nothing so much as Lugh: *I am trying to save you from making a terrible mistake. I am the only one who sees the truth!*

Where Nuall had been bloodied and ruined, Morwen lay calm and composed even in death, her greying hair spread out on the cold ground, her white dress arranged neatly. Seeing her so still, I realized what I had not seen before: fury in every controlled movement, in every calm statement.

The sight of them, lying prone, sent a chill down my spine. Two of them, assured entirely of wrongs against their people. Only two people, and yet we found ourselves here with two armies, thousands preparing to lose their lives for blood debts. It was Nuall and Morwen who had failed, but only by a hair's breadth, only by chance. I shuddered and clenched my hands, wincing as pain shot through my wrists.

Beyond Nuall, a crowd had gathered, and a muffled sob caught my ear. Miriel and I exchanged one anguished glance, and I pushed myself up again and through the crowd of people assembled.

I felt my throat close instantly with the pain when I saw Fidach. He cradled his mother's body in his arms, his head bent against the gaze of her lords. Her torc glinted at her neck, and her face, at last, was peaceful. Blood and dirt streaked her pale skin, and her dark hair tumbled in waves, glints of grey shining in the dawn light. With Fidach's cloak draped over the wound that killed her, she might be sleeping but for how still she lay in his arms.

I did not go to him. His grief was too private and too raw for me to intrude. I stood with Miriel and she slipped her hand into mine. Her eyes were fixed on the horizon, on the last wavering glimpse of Branwen's bright hair. Pikes glinted and I could see the warm color of horses where they stood, rows upon rows. Shouting drifted on the wind from the Cornovii camp, and those gathered around Fidach watched them, knowing it was only mercy that could stay their hand now, for our camp lay in disarray and our queen was slain.

And then, like fog, they began to disperse. I could yet see the blaze of Branwen's hair, and thought she was looking back over her shoulder at us. Though I was too far away to tell, I almost thought I saw her nod, once, to Miriel, and Fidach's voice echoed in my head, a despairing question: *It was you the whole time, wasn't it?* And so it had been.

I knelt at his side, awkwardly, and he leaned against me.

"It's over," I whispered to Fidach. "Let's go home."

Epilogue

"Just a little ways farther," Miriel said. Gulls cried overhead, and the smell of the salt air was heavy in the wind. I thought I could hear Miriel laughing as I fumbled my way down the stone steps.

"You know I never really wanted to come back here."

"Yes, yes," she said impatiently. "But it's worth it. It will be worth it. I promise."

"It had better be." But I was smiling.

We walked slowly over sandy ground, Miriel leading me dutifully around tufts of sea grass that brushed against my outstretched hands. The low whistle of the wind gave way to creaking, and a few thuds.

"We're at the ship yards?"

"Shh. No guessing."

"I don't have to guess," I said, sighing, and she laughed.

"Well, anyway, we're almost there." I could hear excitement bubbling up in her voice. I smiled—Miriel's joy was contagious. "And...look!"

The blindfold was yanked off and I found myself face to face with the prow of a ship, new-built, bobbing gently in the tide. Miriel took my hand and pulled me around to the side, standing on tiptoe to put her hands on either side of my face and turn my head.

"The Rebel Star," I said, and I looked back to the figurehead on the prow, an elaborate scroll.

"For Norstrung. See, the figurehead is the treaty!" Miriel very nearly clapped her hands with glee before regaining her composure, and I smiled. I could not help myself. She had been writing her own treatise in these past few months, setting down the theories she had so loved in her own words, honing the concepts, readying them to present to Connor. Often I found her muttering to herself, lost in thought with the ink long-since dried on her pen and her eyes fixed on something faraway.

But better, by far, was her joy. It was two years since Miriel had lost her love—and with it, the love of the rebel cause. She hid grief behind composure, loss behind smiles and curtsies, but she had been without a heart. Now, at last, she was regaining herself.

"She's beautiful," I said, casting a smiling glance up at the ship. "But did we really need to come all this way?"

"Mmm." Miriel bit her lip and swayed from one foot to the other nervously. "Well, you see. You said...a while ago...you said when it was all over, you would want..." Her voice trailed off and she watched me, wide-eyed, until I remembered.

"I said I wanted to sail away on one of Talyn's ships." I said slowly. "You remembered that?"

"Of course I did." She sounded indignant.

"So you just had a ship built?"

"Well, you remember he said he was sending another expedition," Miriel said. "And I thought—well, they don't really need us here anymore. I finished my treatise. Seiysell and Connor seem to like one another, and Lugh's being...reasonable. Why shouldn't we sail?"

"We're going to Innis Tearmen." I blinked at her, shook my head. I could not believe the words.

"If you want. I mean..." Her voice trailed off and she hunched her shoulders, gave an uncertain smile. "If you still want to."

"You did this for me?" I felt a smile spreading on my face, and she grinned back.

"Yes. But there's more. I knew you might not want to go without, well..." A smile, and she pointed up to the ship again, where a familiar blond head peered down at me.

"I heard there might be an adventure," Fidach said, and I laughed incredulously.

"You were on the south shores!" It had been weeks since I had seen him, riding away into the mist. There were shadows, still, behind his eyes. He did not laugh so readily any longer, my prince. He was more serious now. He was quieter. But he was learning to smile again.

"We wanted to surprise you," he said, and he vaulted over the rail to embrace me. "I've missed you."

"And I you." I leaned my head against his shoulder and felt the comfort of his arms around me, and I smiled over at Miriel.

"An adventure," I said. "That sounds like a good idea."

Thank you for reading Shadow's Oath! I encourage you to take a few moments to leave a review for other readers. For news about $0.99 preorders, sales, and never (ever) spam, you can join my mailing list from my website, moirakatson.com (the link is on the right-hand side).

If you enjoyed Shadow's Oath, I recommend that you try out Saira & the Dragon's Egg, an epic fantasy serial with a steampunk twist! Episode 1 is Saira & the Magic Sword.

If your tastes run more to Science Fiction, start the Novum trilogy with Crucible!

-M